MW01133334

Masters of Time

Books in the *After Cilmeri* Series:
Daughter of Time (prequel)
Footsteps in Time (Book One)
Winds of Time
Prince of Time (Book Two)
Crossroads in Time (Book Three)
Children of Time (Book Four)
Exiles in Time
Castaways in Time
Ashes of Time
Warden of Time
Guardians of Time
Masters of Time

The Gareth and Gwen Medieval Mysteries:
The Bard's Daughter
The Good Knight
The Uninvited Guest
The Fourth Horseman
The Fallen Princess
The Unlikely Spy
The Lost Brother
The Renegade Merchant
The Unexpected Ally

The Lion of Wales Series:
Cold My Heart
The Oaken Door
Of Men and Dragons
A Long Cloud
Frost Against the Hilt

The Last Pendragon Saga:
The Last Pendragon
The Pendragon's Blade
Song of the Pendragon
The Pendragon's Quest
The Pendragon's Champions
Rise of the Pendragon

A Novel from the *After Cilmeri* Series

MASTERS OF TIME

by

SARAH WOODBURY

Masters of Time
Copyright © 2016 by Sarah Woodbury

This is a work of fiction.
All rights reserved. No part of this publication may be
reproduced, stored in a retrieval system, or transmitted in
any form or by any means without the prior written
permission of the author, nor be otherwise circulated in any
form of binding or cover other than that in which it is
published.

Cover image by Flip City Books

www.sarahwoodbury.com

To Gareth
In thanks for the loan
of his car

Cast of Characters

David (Dafydd)—Time-traveler, King of England
Lili—Queen of England, David's wife, Ieuan's sister
Llywelyn—David's father, King of Wales
Meg—Time-traveler, David's mother
Anna— Time-traveler, David's sister
Math—Anna's husband, Lord of Dinas Bran
Callum—Time-traveler, Earl of Shrewsbury
Cassie—Time-traveler, Callum's wife
Ieuan—Welsh knight, one of David's men
Bronwen—Time-traveler, married to Ieuan
Arthur—son of David and Lili (born June 1289)
Alexander—son of David and Lili (born December 1292)
Gwenllian—daughter of Llywelyn (born June 1282)
Cadell—son of Math and Anna (born July 1285)

Geoffrey de Geneville—Norman/English lord
Justin—David's captain
Samuel—Sheriff of Shrewsbury
Rachel Wolff—Time-traveler, physician
Abraham Wolff—Time-traveler, physician
Darren Jeffries—Time-traveler, MI-5 agent
Mark Jones—Time traveler, MI-5 agent
Bridget Donaldson—Time traveler, Peter's wife
Peter Cobb—Time traveler, Bridget's husband

Elisa Shepherd – Meg's sister
Ted Shepherd – Meg's brother-in-law
Elen Shepherd – Meg's niece
Christopher Shepherd – Meg's nephew

1

Aquitaine

Near Midnight

12 June 1293

David

"Couldn't sleep?" David straightened and turned to look at the French king, who'd just appeared on the top step of the stairs leading to the battlement. When David had been up here earlier in the day, he'd watched the river run past the walls and found it soothing and mesmerizing. A bridge spanned the river slightly upstream from his position, and if any of David's twenty-first century companions had traveled to Aquitaine with him, he might have proposed a game of Poohsticks. He'd also taken a look at the castle accounts, which documented the money spent shoring up the wall.

"I was hoping the open air would provide a better atmosphere for thinking than my chamber." Philip rested a hand on a nearby merlon and peered through the crenel into the darkness of the river below them. The crenels at Chateau Niort were lower than normal, well below waist height, and could be uncomfortable to get too close to. "It seems you thought the same."

They were speaking in French—in Philip's case with an austere aristocratic accent. David was fluent in the language, but even he could hear the lilt of Welsh in his voice, a holdover from his first teachers. David was dressed like a Welshman too, in simple shirt and tunic, belted at the waist, breeches, and boots, albeit all of fine quality. Philip, on the other hand, was dressed like a European aristocrat in a light green linen shirt, a gold-embroidered deep green kirtle to match, those tight-fitting stocking-like pants the French liked to wear, these in brown, and matching brown knee-high boots. It was a warm night so he, like David, had left off his cloak.

Neither man was wearing his sword or customary knives either. Gilbert de Clare, one of David's foremost advisers and the man who'd done most of the work to arrange this meeting, had suggested that both men go weaponless this week as a gesture of good will. It was purely symbolic. Although David had climbed to the battlement alone, he'd left a fully armed Justin at the foot of the stairs. A half-dozen more of his men lounged around the bailey below him, keeping him safe while the rest of his guard slept.

David cleared his throat, searching for something to say to continue the conversation. Since he was technically host—Chateau Niort was David's through his title as the Duke of Aquitaine—it was his duty more than Philip's. "I hope your accommodations are to your liking?"

"I have no complaints." Philip frowned. "I was sorry to hear that Lord Clare has not yet arrived. Throughout our negotiations, he has been a voice of reason, and I was pleased to learn that he would be accompanying you here. I hope the delay isn't due to something untoward?"

"Not that I know of." David had also been surprised at Clare's absence. He'd expected to see Clare on the dock at Bordeaux, where the royal party had disembarked. Although Clare's wife had died in childbirth in January, he retained her lands in Aquitaine, as was his right. These lands were not so far from either Bordeaux or Chateau Niort that he couldn't have ridden the distance in a few days. "I do not know what has prevented his immediate presence, but Clare's men are here, and they assure me that the man himself should arrive tomorrow."

"That is good. Otherwise we'd be forced to speak without a mediator." Philip spoke in a tone so completely flat that it took David a moment to realize that he'd made a joke.

David laughed. "It is good to finally meet you, Philip. It is my hope that we can put aside our recent differences and come to an understanding over the next few days."

Although David had been proclaimed Duke of Aquitaine last autumn in the wake of the bombing of Canterbury and the Battle of Hythe, relations between him and Philip hadn't exactly been cordial. David's advisers had feared that Philip might refuse to talk with him as one king to another, preferring to deal with him as the Duke of Aquitaine and thus a vassal to the French throne. That had been one of the many stumbling blocks in the negotiations between them.

Then at Easter, the pope had issued a call for a new crusade. More importantly, Pope Boniface expected David and Philip to crusade together, and it was the frank admission that neither of them wanted to go at all that had ultimately broken the ice and brought them together. While their respective courts had told the world that they were meeting to discuss a possible expedition to the Holy Land, the real point was to put their heads together to find a way to present a united front—and a plan—to the pope. They had to explain—without appearing sacrilegious or irreverent—why they weren't going.

"Such is my hope too," Philip said. "Thank you for traveling so far to meet me. I understand this is your first time on the Continent."

"Yes—"

David's reply was cut off by the sudden extinguishing of all the torches in the bailey, excepting the ones near his head on the wall-walk. Since torches burned in all weathers and conditions—water wouldn't douse them—they wouldn't have all gone out at once unless someone put them out.

Then the unmistakable sound of clashing swords resounded from below, in the midst of which Justin called, "Jump, sire! Jump now! We are betrayed!"

"Justin!" David moved past Philip towards the stairs, intending to come to his captain's aid, but before he could take more than a few steps, Philip gave a suppressed cry. David spun back and cursed to see the French king clutching at the arrow shaft sprouting from his left shoulder. A red bloom of blood stained his elaborately embroidered shirt and kirtle. Then a second arrow whooshed past David, ruffling his hair and clattering on the stones behind him, having missed killing him by millimeters. David's sudden movement back towards Philip had saved his life.

David had been Prince of Wales longer than he'd been King of England, and his own wife was an excellent shot, so David knew full well how long it took to aim and loose an arrow: well-trained archers could shoot one every few seconds. But even five arrows a minute was too many. From this distance, missing even once was a statistical improbability. Unfortunately, throwing himself onto the stones at his feet would do David little good because there was no railing around the inside of the wall-walk. Both he and Philip were completely exposed to the archer firing from the wall-walk on the other side of the bailey.

Lili had made David swear never to take off his MI-5 provided Kevlar vest except if offered the opportunity of a bath—and then only if the door was locked and he was alone. She had demanded this of him because she hadn't trusted the King of France. But it wasn't the King of France who'd arranged this meeting, who'd garrisoned the castle, and who wasn't here tonight.

It was Clare. And David didn't need Justin's shouted warning to know it.

The decision to step in front of Philip and take the next arrow—or two as it turned out, fired in quick succession, Legolas-style—was one that David made without thought as the only logical next step. Though Kevlar couldn't stop an arrow all by itself, the interior ceramic plate, which protected his chest, would.

And did.

The first arrow struck David with breathtaking force and drove him backwards into Philip. The second one had him flailing his arms and lolling his head in hopes that these dramatized death throes would be enough to convince the assassin that if David and Philip weren't dead yet they soon would be. Above all else, David needed the arrows to stop coming.

Then Philip showed he'd been doing some thinking of his own. Despite the wound in his shoulder, his arms came around David's waist, and, with an athleticism that rivaled the best Olympic gymnast, he leaned back into the crenel behind him, flipped up his legs, which forced David's upwards as well, and rolled backwards with David through the gap. The two men turned a complete somersault, ultimately falling feet first towards the river that flowed below them.

As they fell, David kept a tight hold on Philip's arms so that when he *traveled,* Philip would come with him. But to David's surprise and dismay, no black abyss appeared to save him from the dangers above and below. Avalon failed entirely to appear. There was only the same watery blackness of the river, flowing relentlessly and unchanged to the sea.

2

Westminster Castle, London

Near Midnight

12 June 1293

Lili

Lili sat up with a start, her heart pounding in her ears. She'd felt those arrows hit her chest, and her pulse had thudded along with Dafydd's as he'd fallen from the battlement. She could almost believe that she'd been miraculously transported to Aquitaine for a short while, instead of sleeping here in their big, canopied bed, empty but for Alexander beside her. The baby lay completely relaxed, as babies do, on his back with arms and legs spread wide. At nearly six months old, Alexander had long since rejected the restrictions of infant wrappings. He slept under any blanket at all only because she would wake every so often to cover him.

She slipped off the bed and went to the window, built into the curtain wall of the King's Tower. Similar to Chateau Niort, Westminster Castle perched on the bank of a river, though in this case, it was the Thames. From her window, once she opened the shutter, she could see straight down into the water flowing sluggishly past, heading towards the English Channel a hundred miles away.

Leaving the shutters open, since it was a warm night and she liked the fresh air, she turned back to Alexander, who rolled over and whimpered. He stayed asleep, however, so she looked back to the water, thinking of Dafydd falling into it. He was strong and could swim, so she didn't fear him drowning, but she would never forget the feel of those two arrows hitting his chest.

The only light in the room came from the moon, which would be full in another week and shone brightly down, leaving a square of light on the floor. As her heart finally slowed its pounding, she was able to think more calmly about what she'd experienced and witnessed. Why Dafydd hadn't *traveled* to Avalon she didn't know any more than he did, but she felt certain that he lived under the same moon she did. The thought was comforting to her, rather than dismaying as it had been to Dafydd.

It wasn't quite midnight yet. As was often the case, she'd fallen asleep while nursing Alexander to sleep. She could hear the wet nurse stirring in the next room, where she slept with her own son, Sion, who was near to Alexander in age. Most of the time Lili fed her baby herself, but as Queen of England, there were occasional times when she couldn't be with him when he was hungry. Because Alexander was a prince of England, he also had his own nanny, though Lili had given her the night off.

"What is it, Lili?" Bridget, Lili's twenty-firster friend, stepped through the doorway. While Dafydd was away, Bridget and her husband, Peter, had come to visit, taking a short holiday from their wool business and their spy work for Callum in Shrewsbury. Bridget carried a lighted candle and raised it higher. "I heard you cry out just now."

Branwen, Lili's maid, had died suddenly a month ago from an illness the twenty-firsters called *cancer*. It had spread throughout Branwen's body, weakening her and opening the way for pneumonia to take hold. Not even the best efforts of the Llangollen physicians could help her once her lungs had filled with fluid. Branwen hadn't confided to Lili that she felt ill until it was too late. Despite many interviews and much hard thinking, Lili hadn't yet settled on anyone to replace her lost friend.

"I—" Lili closed her eyes, shaking her head slightly. "I had a dream of Dafydd."

"Just a dream or—" Bridget paused a moment as she looked carefully at Lili, "—something more?"

"Yes. It was more than a dream." Lili opened her eyes to meet Bridget's green ones. They were full of concern. "I know

Dafydd is far away in Aquitaine, and I know it sounds mad, but I *saw* him."

"Is he okay?"

"He's alive."

Most of the other twenty-firsters would have dismissed out of hand the possibility that Lili might have the *sight*. Lili found it refreshing that Bridget was taking her seriously. In fact, Bridget was taking her more seriously than even Lili herself might have before she had this dream. It had been so long since she'd experienced any kind of vision or premonition that she had wondered if she'd ever had the ability at all. Branwen had believed this lack to be a result of living in London for so long. *There's no room in the city for the spirit,* she'd told Lili more than once.

Bridget moved farther into the room. "Do you want to tell me about it?"

So Lili told her everything she could remember. From the vision, she knew that Dafydd believed Gilbert de Clare to be the mastermind behind the assassination attempt, which was both terrifying to think about and made so much sense that Lili wondered how it was possible that they hadn't suspected him of evildoing months—if not years—ago. She thought back to the time before Dafydd's coronation when they'd spied on a meeting of Nicholas de Carew, Edmund Mortimer, and Gilbert de Clare in one of the chambers right here at Westminster

Castle. She'd told Dafydd to leave them to their plots because he couldn't possibly control his barons in everything, and at that time they were conspiring on his behalf.

She blamed herself for not recognizing the extent to which Gilbert de Clare lived and breathed intrigue. Clare was a proud nobleman, with a heritage that time and again had elevated him to a position just short of the throne. He'd stood at Dafydd's side for the last five years. He'd watched other men challenge Dafydd and fail. What had made him decide that *his* time was now? The answer was beyond Lili.

Bridget looked gravely back at her. "Gilbert de Clare is dangerous."

"I know. Perhaps it was an underlying fear of his power that kept us believing in his fealty all this time. We wanted to believe in it."

"I haven't ever liked Clare," Bridget said flatly, "and I have no trouble believing that if one of David's barons was going to betray him, he would be the one to do it." Now that Bridget and Peter were married, and Peter was the captain of the Shrewsbury town garrison, it was an open secret that Bridget's shop was a clearinghouse for news from around the country. Even so, as a woman, she was more effective at her job than a man would be—and the whole point of her not returning to Avalon was for her to *do* her job. "We must do what we can to stop him."

"First of all," Lili said, "we don't even know if what I saw has happened or will happen. As far as we know, Clare hasn't done anything wrong. We can't convict him because I had a dream of what the future holds. I have no proof of any kind against him except what's in my heart."

Bridget laughed without humor. "In Avalon, movies have been made about people being convicted for crimes they haven't yet committed, but you're right." She studied Lili for a few heartbeats. "At the very least, you must tell Carew what you *saw*."

"Must I? Can I trust him? He could be as much a part of this as Clare. He's Norman too."

"I may not have been here very long, but I've learned a lot in a short amount of time. We can trust Carew. He and Clare have hated each other since birth and have worked together recently only because of David."

Lili allowed herself to feel a bit of amusement. "You have learned a lot."

"You have Peter and me, but you need the help of at least one man who isn't a twenty-firster," Bridget added. "Besides, Carew is in the Order of the Pendragon."

"So is Clare!" Lili generally called Dafydd's counselors by their first names, but she hadn't ever grown comfortable referring to Gilbert de Clare with such familiarity. "He has heavily influenced the names that have been put forth for membership. Who knows how many he's corrupted?"

Bridget shook her head. "I think you overestimate his reach."

"I fear that I do not. Half the people in the Order could be loyal to him rather than to Dafydd by now." Lili threw out a hand to encompass the whole of Westminster Castle. "Dafydd took the majority of his most loyal men with him. The garrison here could be made up entirely of Clare's men for all we know!"

Bridget looked at her sideways, not willing to argue further, but her eyes glinted, telling Lili that there was a great deal more going on behind her calm exterior than she was currently saying.

And the truth was, Lili didn't want to argue. Bridget was right that they needed help, and they didn't have very many options. Dafydd and most of his men were in Aquitaine. Callum and Cassie were in Shrewsbury, awaiting the birth of their first child. Bronwen had become a mother for the second time a few weeks ago in Wales, where both she and Ieuan had wanted the child to be born. Lili had intended to travel to them, but a sudden sickness had overtaken both Arthur and Alexander just at the point she meant to have left, and they had ended up not going.

That left Nicholas de Carew as the last man standing—and she was lucky to have him here at all. His wife and children were in Somerset, no doubt missing him as much as Lili and the boys were missing Dafydd.

Lili dressed quickly and then told the wet nurse that she would be gone for a while. Alexander was sleeping. Now that the baby was older, she could expect a good four hours of sleep from him at this time of night. Bridget had woken Peter while Lili was dressing, and the three of them hurried down the corridor that ran inside Westminster's curtain wall, to the Queen's Tower, which had been given over to Nicholas and his staff.

One of his men stood outside the door. At the sight of Lili, he bowed and, without questioning her presence, knocked. "My lord?" He spoke to the closed door.

Nicholas replied, and the guard opened the door to poke his head inside, albeit without admitting Lili yet. In retrospect, she probably should have sent Peter to Nicholas to ask him to come to her instead of going to him herself. Then again, it really didn't matter. Either option would have invited comment and was unusual enough that there would be talk about it belowstairs.

Another minute passed, and then Nicholas himself pulled the door wide, admitting the trio into the sitting area. The room was brightly lit with many candles, which emitted a friendly glow. Nicholas's bedchamber lay adjacent. This suite of rooms was slightly smaller than Lili's in the King's Tower, but since Nicholas's wife and children were not with him, Lili didn't need to worry about waking anybody else. Thus, once the guard had shut the door and returned to his post, Lili explained about her dream and Dafydd's belief in Clare's treachery.

Nicholas listened in complete silence, with his arms folded across his chest and looking down at the floor. When she finished, he looked up and simply gazed at her without comment.

"I know how foolish this sounds, even to my ears," she said, by way of apology. Now that she'd laid her fears before her friends, she couldn't help but doubt herself in the same way Nicholas had to be doubting her. Peter probably felt it too, but he'd been too polite to say so, at least to her.

Nicholas dropped his arms, and his expression gentled. "With David gone, it's natural that you should worry about him. Dreams are often a confused mix of thoughts and ideas that we don't even know we have—" He stopped, one shoulder lifting in an unasked question.

"I know what you're thinking. What I experienced might have been only a dream. You are absolutely right that I miss Dafydd and feel unsettled. I know as well as you the number of times Dafydd has put himself in danger. This family makes a habit of it. But you also know that my *sight* has been true before, and that Clare is capable of betrayal and deceit. More than capable."

"Queen Lili is right." Where it had been rare for Branwen to speak to any noble other than Lili, Bridget was far more forthright.

Nicholas now directed his gaze not towards Lili, but at Peter. "Say the queen is right. Should we have seen this coming?"

"Six months ago, rumors and warnings from various sources suggested that Clare might be working with the King of France," Peter said. "Bridget shared what she had with David and Callum, and they decided that the rumors were exactly that. She and I talked about it again last Christmas during the investigation of the ambush of the French emissary and James Stewart."

Bridget nodded. "It did sound far-fetched at the time."

"But you think now, in light of Lili's dream, that we made a mistake?" Nicholas said.

Peter tsked through his teeth. "It could be."

Nicholas didn't argue further, just glanced once at Lili before moving to pace back and forth before the fireplace, unlit as it was June. "*Sight* or not, a real *seeing* or not, sometimes a dream can bring together bits and pieces in a person's mind that he has been unable to put together when awake. Even if what you *saw* hasn't happened, perhaps we should be looking instead at the intent of the dream." Nicholas stopped his pacing to look at the others.

"Which was to show us that Clare is no longer loyal," Bridget said.

Peter's eyes gleamed, and he spread his hands wide. He wasn't one to talk unless it was necessary, but he had experience investigating crime and espionage, both in Avalon and in this world. "What is the downside of following up? If it was just a dream, we have lost nothing by entertaining the possibility of treachery. If Clare has indeed betrayed us, then the sooner we move, the better off we'll be."

Nicholas rubbed his chin, clearly more accepting now that Peter, the other man in the room, had concurred with Lili. "I suppose I could make a few discreet inquiries."

"Of whom?" Lili said. "We aren't in a position to trust anyone in the Order, not with Clare having as much influence as he does."

"My lady," Carew said, "if Clare is plotting treason, we four here are hardly enough to overcome whatever he's planning, not with Arthur and Alexander to protect. We need someone we can trust outside our usual circles."

Peter looked rueful. "We don't have many allies in the Church."

The new Archbishop of Canterbury, Robert Winchelsey, had not been Dafydd's choice. An austere man in his late forties, he'd been confirmed in February with great enthusiasm by Pope Boniface. Winchelsey disagreed with Dafydd on just about everything to do with religion and politics, from taxation, to freedom of religion—to the idea that Winchelsey and the Church had to listen to, respect, or obey Dafydd at all. Winchelsey agreed with Boniface that the Church should be the cornerstone of all spiritual *and* temporal authority.

"Archbishop Romeyn remains in Italy," Nicholas said, "so, no, I don't think we can look there."

"One of us could speak to our Jewish friends," Bridget said. "They've never trusted Clare."

"For good reason," Lili said.

Nicholas snorted. "The massacre at Canterbury didn't help."

Lili bit her lip. "Who else in London isn't a possible companion to Clare?"

"What about your brother? He has been nothing but accommodating since he took over Temple Church." Peter was referring to Godfrid de Windsor, Carew's bastard younger brother, who'd adopted the old family name of Windsor rather than Fitzcarew because, as Nicholas had once told Lili, if his family didn't want anything to do with him, he didn't want anything to do with his family. He was the new master of Temple Church, the Templar seat in London. "He was one of the people who warned us months ago that Clare might not be all that he seemed."

"I can speak with him." Nicholas blew out his cheeks in a puff of air. "It will give him a chance to tell me *I told you so!*"

"Even if Godfrid is loyal, how can he help us?" Bridget said. "He's stuck in London just like we are."

"His men aren't, though," Peter said. "Godfrid has access to hundreds of men and resources in France and Aquitaine—far more men and resources, in fact, than Clare can marshal. He can get word to his brethren that David might be in peril."

Nicholas nodded. "He can warn the commanderies in France to be careful of Clare, whose men might be hunting David throughout the Aquitaine countryside. Godfrid also can have his fleet warn us if Clare attempts to cross the Channel to England."

"Even were Clare to do so, we still can't arrest him," Lili said. "As far as we know right now, I had a dream, and he's done nothing wrong."

Nicholas's laugh caught in his throat. "For a moment there, I forgot what we were basing our anxiety on." He studied Lili a moment. "You're sure?"

"Yes," Lili said, and suddenly she was. "If you lay out what I've told you, will Godfrid believe you?"

"I don't plan to lay out what you've told me." Nicholas gestured to Peter and Bridget. "He will know from his own sources that two of David's spies are visiting. I will tell him that we have reconsidered the information he gave us last year and now believe the king's meeting with France to be a trap. Once I name Clare, Godfrid will immediately understand that we can't go to the Order of the Pendragon for help, nor can we rely on the fact that David is the Duke of Aquitaine."

Nicholas eyed Lili. "I must warn you that Godfrid might not agree to help. Previous English kings, Edward among them, rubbed shoulders with the Templars in the Holy Land, but the Order has rarely concerned itself with temporal politics. He is a Templar first, English second."

"I know," Lili said. "Perhaps Godfrid will be willing to make an exception in this case."

"We must also warn Callum and Cassie at Shrewsbury," Bridget said. "It would be better to send word to all of David's barons, but I don't see how to make that happen because we can't use the radio for this. We have no idea how many of our men Clare has bought. If he was smart, he would have started at the radio stations."

Before traveling to Avalon last Christmas, Dafydd had already shifted gears away from his quest for a telegraph and moved straight to radio. Compared to laying wire for telephones and telegraphs, radio was *easy*, relying on relays and antennas that were producible with technology available to them in this world.

And, as it turned out, among the numerous gifts from MI-5, for which Mark Jones had traded himself, had been a box of old (to the twenty-firsters) CB radios, transistors, and transmitters with mini-solar kits to run them. Tate had included them as a by-the-way, and nobody had realized the treasure they'd been given until Bridget and Peter had taken the time to go through the boxes.

Oddly, it was Rupert Jones, a reporter who'd hidden himself aboard the bus before it left Caernarfon, who'd been instrumental in making the network viable. Dafydd had been able to broadcast a May Day greeting to all of London last month. What's more, only two weeks ago, he in London and Callum in Shrewsbury had been able to send and receive messages from Llywelyn in Caerphilly.

"I thought that was what the radio was *for*," Nicholas said, sounding slightly exasperated. Lili could understand, since quick communication had been the entire point of the network and now, all of a sudden, they were back to communicating in what Dafydd would call *the old-fashioned way*.

"Peter and I will go to Shrewsbury," Bridget said.

Lili gazed at her friend. The journey was a long one, but Bridget had traveled it recently and knew what she was suggesting. In fact, her clear eyes and level head tonight had given Lili a new respect for her. They hadn't known each other very long, but Bridget's short visit to London had made her a closer companion to Lili than almost anyone but Bronwen, Lili's sister-in-law. Yet up until now, all of their discussions had been focused on everyday things—the children or their husbands or politics—or Avalon. Lili was ashamed to have given little thought before this about the person Bridget was inside. She'd come to Lili's world and chosen to stay. What did she lie awake thinking about in the wee hours of the morning when she couldn't sleep?

"*You* can't, Bridget." Nicholas was dismissive. For all that he'd lived under Dafydd's banner for ten years, he was fundamentally unchanged in matters of women. "I have twenty men I can send with Peter."

"Who might that be, Nicholas?" Lili said. "If Clare can betray Dafydd, how many others can too? Would he have had the foresight to woo some of your men with promises of wealth and a higher station? Can you trust every man-at-arms in your retinue? Can we trust *any* men at Westminster with what we fear?"

Nicholas put out a hand. "Surely it can't be that bad—"

Lili cut him off. "Clare is the wealthiest man in England. He has more men and resources than anyone—perhaps more even than Dafydd. We can't take anyone's loyalty for granted."

Nicholas narrowed his eyes at Lili. He didn't have a satisfactory answer to any of her questions, so Lili turned instead to Bridget, whose eyes were very bright. "You're sure you're ready to do this?"

"Are you sure of what you dreamed?"

Lili nodded.

Bridget smiled. "Then I am too."

3

Near Midnight

12 June 1293

David

David and Philip hit the dark water, which loosened Philip's arms from around David's waist, and the two men plunged into the depths separately. As David's boots touched the riverbed, his knees bent, and he surged to the surface, coming up twenty yards downstream from where they'd gone in.

Philip had surfaced too, and both men gasped for breath, struggling to stay upright in the swift current. The weight of their clothes pulled them down, though without mail armor, neither were in danger of drowning. David sent a look upwards. No heads were silhouetted against the light of the torches that lit the battlement. David was still shocked that he wasn't looking at the twenty-first century Chateau Niort, but there seemed little doubt that they were still in medieval Aquitaine.

Though they'd risen to the surface near each other, during the subsequent seconds that David had been fighting the current, Philip had been pulled away from him and was struggling in the water more than David. With long strokes, David reached Philip, grasped him around his waist, and turned him onto his back so he could float better.

Philip didn't protest. That he hadn't drowned meant he could swim a little, but staying afloat seemed to be the extent of his abilities.

"You took those arrows for me," Philip said. "Why aren't you dead?"

"I have good armor." David didn't want to waste energy—either his or Philip's—talking. One of the two arrows that the archer had shot at David had caught in the fabric of his shirt. With impatient motions, he worked the arrowhead out, though once he did that, he didn't know what to do with it. The arrow was three feet long, and if he tossed it towards the near bank, Clare's captain might find it, which wouldn't do at all. If the man had any sense, he would send men looking for their bodies along the riverbank, and if he discovered the unbloodied arrow, he would know that David, Philip, or both had survived the attack.

In the end, David snapped the arrow in half to make the wooden shaft a more manageable eighteen inches long and shoved both halves down beneath the strap that bound his right boot to his foot. Since he had no other weapon, maybe it would come in handy later, and he was tall enough that it rested comfortably against the side of his calf.

David expected to have huge bruises tomorrow where the arrow points had hit him, but today he was just happy to still be breathing. Philip, however, lacked David's Kevlar vest and had been wounded by the arrow that had struck him. He was bleeding and in pain, not to mention big and heavy. History called him *Philip the Fair* or *the Iron King*, which wasn't too far off in David's judgement, since he weighed a ton. History wasn't talking about Philip's weight, of course, but his resolve.

Philip was the French king who'd stood up to Pope Boniface at the beginning of the next century, who'd had him murdered, in fact, and who'd wiped out the Templars in 1307 as a way to avoid paying back the money he owed them. Historians always liked kings who got things done and were decisive. David had to admit, whatever Philip's faults and motivations, he'd carved out a place for himself in history.

"They're up there looking for us." Since Philip was on his back, he had a better view of the battlements than David. They'd come a hundred yards from the castle by now and the glow from the torches on the wall-walk were all David could make out from a quick glance back. Then they swept around a bend and were hidden from view of the men on the tower.

The river was called the Sevre de Niortaise, translated as the *weaning of Niortaise*, whatever the heck that was supposed to mean, which at the moment David didn't care. All that mattered was that the river had run right up against the edge of the curtain wall, to the point of starting to undermine it, the same as at David's castles in Rhuddlan in Wales and Westminster in London. Thus, when Clare's men had shot their arrows into David's chest, and Philip had made them fall head over heels, the river had been there to catch them.

It was some consolation that at midnight it was so dark that anyone looking over the battlement of the chateau would have been hard pressed to see their heads in the water, even had David and Philip been directly below them. The archer who'd shot at them, or perhaps a companion or two, would have had to run around the wall-walk first, and most of Clare's men were fighting David's and Philip's. Still, the farther downstream he and Philip were able to float, the safer they were going to be.

Over the years, David had made a personal study of battlements and their time travel potential. He had been in a hundred castles since he'd come to Wales in 1282. Especially since Dover, he'd made it a point to circumnavigate their defenses when he could in order to determine where the best place to fall might be so as not to kill himself if the time traveling didn't work. While David had chosen to stand in that particular location on the wall-walk because of the view, he'd also stood at the best spot for *traveling*.

Falling through the crenel had genuinely been the last thing on David's mind as he leaned through it to look down at the water, but if he had been thinking about it, he would truly have expected to time travel. And yet, inexplicably, the great gaping blackness hadn't come. Apparently, his life hadn't been in enough danger for that. Truth be told, Philip's quick action had ensured that the archer hadn't been able to fire off another shot, and, as it turned out, the arrows that had hit David hadn't come close to touching his skin.

He'd always suspected that his time traveling wasn't as simple as he'd pretended all these years. Since that first day at Cilmeri, he'd put himself in all kinds of danger, accidentally and on purpose, and the time traveling had always come through for him. It would have been a relief in a way to have found himself in the twenty-first century, because he could have dealt with Philip's shoulder and then either left him (wouldn't that have been a devious way to deal with Philip's impact on history?), or returned with him—presumably arriving at the exact place and time he needed to in order to stop Clare from taking David's kingdom.

In a way, David's failure to time travel had loosed him from his moorings—much like coming to Wales for the first time at the age of fourteen had done. That day, his predominant emotion had been fear. Although part of David was supremely ticked off that the time traveling hadn't happened, he also felt a little exhilarated to realize he didn't know as much as he thought he did.

Putting his questions aside, David focused on swimming, pulling Philip into the center of the stream, which was the swiftest portion of the river. France, like England, had experienced a rainy spring, so the river was high, but because it was June, they wouldn't freeze to death from the temperature of the water. Since one arm was occupied with keeping Philip above water, David was forced to swim with a modified breaststroke. Though he was clearly a better swimmer than Philip, he was out of practice and had never enjoyed swimming much anyway, beyond splashing around in a community water park. So when a log floated by him, David caught it and shoved it at Philip so he could hang onto it with his uninjured arm.

This country was truly a foreign place to David, and he had no notion what obstacles might lie ahead. He couldn't see anything of the land around them, and even though he'd surveyed the landscape from the castle and noted that it was mostly flat, that wasn't to say they wouldn't find themselves swept over a waterfall if he wasn't careful.

As Philip had noted, David had never set foot on the Continent before this week. The few days it had taken to ride from Bordeaux to Chateau de Niort, which had been built by

David's Plantagenet predecessors as part of their control of the Duchy of Aquitaine, were the only days he'd ever spent in France. But while David didn't know the general geography of Aquitaine as well as he knew Britain, he knew that La Rochelle was somewhere to the west.

In the aftermath of Hythe, David had regained a significant territory that had been lost to the French crown at the Treaty of Paris in 1259, including Angoulême and the western portion of the county of Poitiers. Unfortunately for David, he'd entrusted the entirety of his defenses and the governance of the Duchy in the last months to Clare, as a way to distract him from his holdings in Ireland, which up until now had been David's primary concern.

A bad mistake.

"They're going to be searching for us," Philip said. "We have to get to French territory. We'll be safe there."

"Are you sure about that?" David said. "Clare's man shot you first. I imagine that all of your men are dead, as well as mine. Clare wants my throne. Who's usurping yours?"

"I don't know."

David's head was close enough to Philip's that he could hear him grinding his teeth. He also had accepted without question David's assumption that it was Gilbert de Clare who'd betrayed them.

"Meanwhile," David continued, "your lands are miles away, and while Aquitaine might be technically in my possession, nobody knows me here. It isn't as if we are dressed like kings either, or at least I'm not."

Philip had no answer to that, so David continued to struggle in the current, keeping Philip and himself afloat. Finally, his lips turning blue and his limbs no longer able to bear the cold, David hauled Philip onto a sandy spit on the south side of the river. Both men collapsed, exhausted. David couldn't help but agree with Philip in his instinct to keep to the north bank of the river and head to France. But while traveling in that direction might present a possible source of aid, David thought *he* was right about Philip's rival. Someone in the French court was working with Clare. That meant retreating to Paris wasn't the answer. While it was true that Chateau Niort lay on the south bank of the river, so did David's way home.

"I should have known something was wrong when Clare wasn't on the dock to greet me when I arrived," David said. "I apologize, Philip. Clare was my man. It is my judgement that was faulty in trusting him."

"We all trust where we shouldn't." Philip groaned as he rolled onto his back and flung his good arm across his eyes. "Clare will be in London, awaiting word of your death and mine." Then he cursed in French, the word cut off by a gasp of pain.

David dragged himself up to kneel beside his companion. "Let me take a look at that wound." Though it had been the arrow sticking out of Philip's shoulder that had prompted David to stand in front of him and take the next two, he hadn't actually gotten a good look yet at the damage.

"It's nothing."

Ignoring what he viewed to be a *pro forma* objection, David ripped Philip's shirt at the shoulder to reveal the bloody mess beneath it. "The arrow shaft broke off in your shoulder, probably when you hit the water." David grimaced in sympathy at what that must have felt like. As he explored the wound, he was careful not to irritate the sensitive tissue around it more than he had to.

"Can you cut out what's left?" Philip said.

David's mother called this battlefield medicine, and nobody liked it. If David left the arrowhead inside Philip's body for even another hour, the wound could fester. It could fester anyway, especially given their stint in the river. David was also a little worried that the archer might have dipped the tip in poison, though perhaps if that had been the case, Philip would have died already. Regardless, the arrowhead needed to come out. Right now, however, it was plugging a hole in Philip's body, so when he pulled it out he needed to be ready to staunch the wound.

David shifted slightly so he wasn't blocking the moonlight from shining on Philip's shoulder. Even with that light, however, it was too dark to see more than the outlines of what he had to do, and he ultimately was forced to probe the extent of the damage with his fingers. Each time the metal head moved even a millimeter, Philip flinched, and David winced in sympathy.

But then he sighed in relief. "I don't need to cut it out. There's still a little bit of wooden shaft attached. I think I can grab it."

A pair of pliers would have been really nice since David's fingers were slick with Philip's blood, but pliers were (sadly) not part of his regular attire. Taking a chance that the flow of blood was slowing, David let go of Philip's shoulder for a second in order to pull his tunic over his head and fold it to form a bandage. Then he retreated to wash his hands the best he could in the river. Returning to kneel beside Philip, he gently grasped the truncated arrow shaft. "When is your birthday, Philip?"

"June 14th—*aaahhh!*"

With a quick jerk, like ripping off a bandaid, David pulled out the arrowhead. He'd known when Philip's birthday was and had simply been looking for a distraction. Then David pressed hard on Philip's shoulder with the cloth. It was good that Philip was lying on his back, because gravity was working for him rather than against him.

Philip held out his right hand. "May I have the arrowhead?" His voice was more gravelly than normal, but he hadn't passed out, which boded well for the future. Their journey was only just beginning, and they had a long way to go.

"Sure." David was happy to give it to him. Like the arrow shaft in David's boot, keeping the arrowhead was preferable to tossing it behind him into the river or dropping it on the bank. It wouldn't do to leave behind any evidence that they'd been here. Clare's men would know that the arrowhead had been pulled out of a living man.

After Philip stowed the arrowhead in his pocket, David had him press his own hand to the wound. That left David's hands free to tear off Philip's bloody sleeve so he could use the fabric to bind his shoulder. The wound was in an awkward place, but David managed to wrap the cloth under and around Philip's shoulder and tie it at the collarbone.

"It hurts like the devil." Philip lifted his head slightly to eye the wound. "And it's bleeding still."

"That's often a good thing, according to one of my physician friends," David said.

"*Sacre Dieu.*" Philip rested his head back on the sand. "How many times have you saved my life tonight?"

"It was you who got us off that battlement." David swiveled on the ball of his foot to observe their surroundings.

"We need to keep moving. Clare's men will be searching for our bodies."

"We can't let them find us." Philip moaned every time he moved, but with David's help, he managed to reach his feet and stood in the sand, swaying. At least he hadn't gone into shock. Focusing on the urgent needs of the moment—from flipping them over the battlement to staying alive in the river—might have saved Philip's life more than David himself had—aside from David taking those two arrows for him.

"France and England have been ever at odds." Philip shook his head, but the moon was bright enough to show David the small smile on his lips. "I should have known meeting with you was a bad idea." As before on the wall-walk, he was making a joke. David was impressed that he could.

"Come on." David ducked under Philip's right arm and put his left arm around the French king's waist. "We'd better get moving. I intend to make Clare regret our meeting even more than we do."

4

13 June 1293

David

"Is someone trying to depose you to take the throne in your stead, or is he thinking that he will govern as regent? I'm not sure what the rules are for succession in France." While David was focused on their immediate survival, a significant part of his brain was working on the larger problem. He forced himself to relax and listen to his surroundings as they crouched beneath an old oak, his eyes searching and his ears perked for any sign of pursuit. Unfortunately, because the river wended its way sinuously across the landscape, they weren't as far from the castle as he felt they ought to be.

"I'm being deposed so another can take the throne," Philip said. "My sons are the same age as yours. They are not ready to rule, and nobody would go through this much trouble for just the regency."

"I wouldn't put anything past Clare," David said, "and my sons wouldn't be the first young princes to lose their lives at the hands of their regent."

David spoke these words calmly, even as his heart was screaming at him. Beyond Clare's treachery, what was preoccupying David most was concern for how quickly news of his death would reach England, and if he could possibly get home first. In his mind's eye, David had no trouble picturing Clare walking into the hall at Westminster and telling Lili he was dead. The very idea was torture. She wouldn't want to believe Clare at first, hoping perhaps that David had time traveled to safety, but if David didn't return within a few days— or at least get word to her within a week—she would have no choice but to accept his death.

"Regardless," David added, "I am very lucky that Clare chose this moment to betray me."

Philip's expression was a mix of astonishment and utter skepticism. "How are you lucky?"

"I didn't come to Aquitaine with a full complement of advisers. Most of my closest companions remain at home—and none of them are going to go down before Clare lightly."

Philip's brows came together. "I noticed that lack and wondered."

David gave a wry grin. "I left some at home on purpose, due to other commitments, but for the rest ... we sailed down the Thames to the Channel, and then turned south, making for Bordeaux. But we'd only reached Dover when many of my people, including my squire and manservant, went down with an intestinal ailment that laid them so low they couldn't possibly sail any farther. Rather than put off the meeting with you, which had taken so long to arrange, I continued with those who could still stand." David shrugged. "At the time, I figured it would be okay to have so few men with me, because Clare's men would meet me at Bordeaux."

"They surely did that." Philip's laugh was mocking.

"We have to assume, Philip, that all of our men are dead. The only way Clare is going to get away with the outright murder of two kings is if he leaves nobody who isn't loyal to him alive as witness to what happened."

"Even then, those men who perpetrated the act might find their lifespan shorter than they hoped." Philip canted his head. "You realize that the archer used a longbow, not a crossbow. He was English."

"More likely, he was Welsh." David gripped Philip's good arm and helped him to his feet. He was ready to be done thinking about the larger picture because it was making him want to puke. "Let's move."

A road ran parallel to the river, not far from their stand of trees, and they turned onto it. On the whole it was probably a safer strategy to avoid the roads, but they could always get off it if they heard someone coming. The night was clear with a bright moon, and stars splashed across the sky in a way that David hoped he would never grow tired of seeing.

"What is your plan—to walk all the way to the sea?" Philip said between puffing breaths.

"Pretty much."

"La Rochelle is forty miles from here!" Philip said.

"If I'm not mistaken, it's your shoulder that's wounded, not your legs," David said.

Philip made a guttural sound, implying disbelief, but although he was keeping his right hand pressed to his left shoulder, he was, in fact, struggling along without the assistance he'd needed earlier. Eventually, he would grow weak from pain and loss of blood, but as long as his legs still worked they could keep moving.

"My plan is to ask the Templars for help," David said. "They've stationed the bulk of their fleet at La Rochelle, and the commanderie there is the largest in the region."

Philip gave a low groan that had nothing to do with the pain in his shoulder. "Asking for help from the Templars would not be my first, second, or third choice."

"That would be because you owe them money and haven't kept up with the payments."

A Templar such as Pierre de Villiers, the La Rochelle master, was on a par with David in terms of power and resources. If anywhere in Aquitaine was safe from Clare, it was their stronghold. The Templars had never had much of a presence in Wales, and hardly any Welshmen had become Templars. The order had always been predominantly French and Norman, which was why David hadn't had much to do with them before he'd become King of England. The Order of the Pendragon, David's own secret society, had been enough to be going on with—or so he'd thought.

Over the last year, however, David had begun reaching out personally to the Templars. Pope Boniface wanted David to go on crusade, and the Templars' entire aim was to win the Holy Land for Christendom. Thus, it seemed like a good idea to be on civil terms with them. It was during those initial overtures that the Templars had told David that Clare might not be as loyal as everyone supposed.

By now, David's relationship with the Templars had matured to such an extent that, before David had sailed to Aquitaine, Carew had taken him aside and offered him a password, the use of which at any Templar holding would gain the speaker instant help, no questions asked. David didn't think Carew himself had any premonition of what was to come—the man lived as solidly in the here and now as anyone David had ever met—but he was cautious, particularly about leaving David to his own devices. The password had come from Godfrid de Windsor, Carew's own half-brother and the current commander of Temple Church in London, since its former master was ill, perhaps to death.

It seemed to David that if there was ever a time to use that password, it was now.

The sky had grown darker over the last few minutes. Clouds had come in, skittering with the wind to hide the moon and stars, but David could still see Philip narrowing his eyes at him. "I'm not going to England."

"Fine. You can sail to wherever you think you'll be safe." It seemed pointless to argue with Philip, in large part because a lot could happen in forty miles, including their deaths. David lifted his chin to point ahead of them. "What is that village?"

"I do not know. It's your land."

"I had never set foot in Aquitaine before this week, and you know it." David shook his head. "I'm afraid to ask for help. We have to assume every town in the region is controlled by Clare's men, not mine."

"We still might be able to find horses. Or steal them." Philip groaned again, and now he leaned into David, who ducked under the French king's right arm and put it across his shoulders as he had done when they'd left the beach. If Philip's strength was waning already, they were never going to make La Rochelle.

They needed help, no question, but as David had said to Philip, he was worried about where to get it. If he were alone and uninjured, he would have simply kept moving. He could walk forty miles. Philip, despite David's sarcastic comment about his legs being uninjured, could not.

When they were thirty yards from the first house in the village, David pulled Philip into some woods to the south of the road and set him down against the base of a tree. Then he went forward alone. The village consisted of a cluster of homes surrounding a green. At this time of year, the animals that belonged to the villagers were left outside in a corral rather than brought into the houses. Each house was simply built of wood and clay with thatch roofs with a hole in the center to let out the smoke from a central fire.

Nobody was stirring, but then a dog barked and a man holding a lantern came out of the first house. He held it up, revealing himself to be at least thirty years older than David, a little hunched, with a scruffy beard and unkempt hair. He wore breeches, a wrinkled shirt, and no shoes. "Who goes there?" Except the man said it in French, *Qui est là?*

Aquitaine had been a war zone for as long as it had existed. With Philip wanting the country for himself, and the village so close to the border with France, David shouldn't have been surprised that a villager would be alert to visitors in the middle of the night.

David put up his hands. "I am a traveler, seeking aid. I have a wounded companion, who needs bandaging." Soaked as

David was from the river and without armor or sword, he looked more like a vagabond than a king. He also didn't have any money, which was a stupid oversight that he swore here and now that he would never make again.

The man screwed up his face, squinting at David. "You're not from around here." His breath was as sour as his tone.

David's accent had given him away. "I'm English." It was close enough to the truth.

The man gestured with his chin to the east. "The chateau is just there. You would be better off seeking aid from them. We have nothing here and cannot help you."

"But—"

Hoof beats sounded on the road—the first David and Philip had encountered since climbing out of the river. The horses were still some distance away but coming from the east.

David ducked his head. "I will take your advice and leave you be." Without another word, David ran back the way he'd come, his feet pounding as loud as he could make them along the road to give the half-blind peasant a clear idea where he'd gone. Then he dove into the woods and pulled up in front of Philip. "Come with me and don't speak."

They didn't have time to flee, so they had to deceive instead. David helped Philip along a narrow trail, having had a sudden inspiration that moving closer to the village rather than farther away might bring them within what the villagers thought was a safety zone. If the peasant gave him up, Clare's soldiers would start looking for him farther to the east.

They ended up in a ditch amongst some bushes, a stone's throw from the village entrance. The villager stood exactly where David had left him, still holding the lantern, which was a blessing because it meant he had no night vision and couldn't see anything beyond the circle of light. Not that he likely could have anyway.

After another minute, four riders approached, torches held high, and even though it had to be nearly one in the morning by now, more people in the surrounding huts stirred. A second man came out of his house, followed by a half-dozen more peasants, all men. The second man said something to the villager who'd greeted David, and though David couldn't make out the exact words, it sounded cutting. The villager gave up his lantern to this newcomer, who appeared to be the headman of the village, and took a step back. Then, lantern in hand and buttressed by a handful of his fellow villagers, the headman went forward to greet the riders.

"We are hunting two men, traitors, one English, one French," one of the riders said without preamble. "They attacked Duke David and King Philip of France as they were meeting at Chateau de Niort. Both assassins were wounded, but they escaped the castle by diving into the river."

So I'm an assassin now. It wasn't quite as good as being a pirate. Beside David, Philip cursed softly under his breath and then said, "Clever."

"Have any strangers passed this way?" the rider added.

"No, my lord," the headman said, "not that we have seen."

David held his breath in expectation that the villager would correct the headman, but he didn't.

"How is the duke?" said another peasant.

"Both king and duke are dead," the lead rider said. "Set a watch. I will return before dawn."

At the headman's nod, the four horsemen continued through the village, and the several men who'd gathered at their arrival conferred for a moment before splitting into pairs. It looked to David as if they were going to patrol the margins of the village and along the road, but not yet into the woods. The man who'd greeted David went back inside his hut.

"We have to go now." David got Philip upright and moving south. Within fifty yards, the woods grew sparse and soon gave way to fields. He helped Philip over a stone wall and across a pasture of grazing sheep. Only then did he breathe more easily.

"Clare has no royal blood," Philip said, as if their conversation of earlier hadn't been interrupted by some wound bandaging, stumbling about in the dark, and nearly being caught by Clare's men. "How can he think to take the throne?"

"After me, he is the richest, most powerful man in England, with a private army of men who will fight for him, especially if they believe I am dead. What if Clare were to suggest that France was responsible for my death? There's nothing like a good war for uniting people behind their king."

"As you discovered to my detriment not long ago," Philip said sourly.

The war had been entirely Philip's fault, of course, but this admission might be all the apology David was going to get. Since his people had won at Hythe, he didn't see a need to chastise Philip about it today. "It would be especially true if Clare manufactures proof that your replacement had me murdered."

What he decided not to point out, thinking that Philip wouldn't understand, was that the people of Hythe hadn't repelled Philip's invasion for David at all. They'd done it for themselves and for England. Overlords like Philip and David's Norman barons were pretty much out for themselves and their own power and prerogatives.

The Normans had conquered England not because they cared one tiny bit for the people, but because they wanted the land and the power that went with ruling. David had grown used to the power he wielded, but he liked to think that he didn't need it. Philip wanted the whole of what would one day be France under his control because he wanted power and money. He had never been interested in what his people thought or in their welfare.

Contrast that attitude to Wales, where every rock, tree, and mountain was holy to the Welsh, lord and peasant alike, and by which terms his father had defied David's predecessor, Edward: *Even should we so wish ... never would our nobles and subjects consent in the inevitable destruction and dissipation that would surely derive from submission to these terms. It would surely be more honorable, and more consonant with reason, if we should hold from the king those lands in which we have right, rather than to disinherit us, and hand over our lands and our people to strangers.*

David had been King of England for only five years, but he thought he had the measure of his people now: the Saxon underbelly of the Norman conquest—the English people—felt as strongly about their lands, language, and laws as the Welsh did. No *Frenchie,* as the men of Hythe had called Philip, was going to take their identity from them if they had any say in the matter.

This was, of course, the attitude that Clare would call upon in taking the English to war against France to avenge David's death. What David hadn't quite figured out was how Clare could have colluded with a French baron to assassinate

Philip and then turn around and start a war against that same French baron, who would now be King of France. Maybe both lords viewed a little war—a few skirmishes, maybe a sea battle—to be a small price to pay for a throne.

"Similar parties to that one have ridden in every direction from Chateau Niort," Philip said. "Perhaps a man has been sent to Paris with word of my death, and another to London with news of yours."

David grimaced. "Every homestead and hamlet we encounter between here and La Rochelle might be closed to us by now."

They reached another wall, and Philip leaned against it breathing hard. He glanced at his shoulder. Even in the dim light, David could see the blood continuing to seep from the wound.

"We need to keep moving, David, before I'm unable to ever move again."

5

13 June 1293

Bridget

As she walked through the darkened castle with Peter, Bridget's heart thudded in her chest, less with fear than with excitement. Maybe it was a product of reading so many adventure stories as a child, but from the time she was small, she'd loved moments like these. Something was happening. As when she and Peter had investigated the attack on James Stewart and the French emissary last Christmas, she was glad to be a part of it.

Peter felt the same way. It was one of the things that had brought them together.

Three weeks ago, after Lili had decided that she couldn't travel to Wales for the birth of Bronwen's son, Bridget and Peter had come to London, in preparation for David's departure for Aquitaine. Peter had wanted to go with David, but David had convinced him to stay behind, as one of the few people he could absolutely trust at Westminster. Peter had agreed in large part because it was the same request David had made of Peter last Christmas, and David had been absolutely correct to ask Peter to stay.

Bridget was a modern woman, sprung from a world in which the *sight* played no role. But she had been around Lili long enough to believe that she really could *see*. And given all the times David had guessed right about something, she was pretty sure that he could too.

Bridget shivered. It was only by chance that she'd been awake and near the door when Lili had cried out. If she hadn't, Lili might have gone back to sleep and not shared her dream—maybe not until the morning—maybe not ever.

"We knew something was going on with Clare, and we dismissed it, Peter. How could we have done that?"

"I'm kicking myself, believe me. The Templars warned us. We had whispers from around the country. We even had chatter within the Order of the Pendragon, and we did nothing."

"I'm wondering now if Clare didn't encourage Amaury de Valence to ambush the French emissary as a way to distract us from what he himself was doing," Bridget said.

"I'm not wondering," Peter said. "The idea of the *sight* makes me uncomfortable, but if Clare has betrayed us, it makes a whole lot of other things that have gone on recently make sense. He has been hiding his true self for a long time now. It was a mistake not to take his interests into our calculations."

"David could have paid for that oversight with his life," Bridget said.

"Not according to Lili." Peter stopped and turned to Bridget. "Why do you believe her? You don't think her dream was just a dream?"

"You didn't see her, Peter. She was like a ghost there for a minute. And you know she's been right before."

He took in a breath. "Well, if nothing else, it gets us out of London and back home where we belong."

Bridget smiled. Her husband had grown up in the city, but he was a country boy at heart. "It's just too bad we can't simply ring up Callum and tell him what's going on."

Peter snorted. "I'm afraid I'm fresh out of mobile phones."

That was an inside joke between Bridget and Peter. Not a day went by that they didn't wish for a way to talk to each other in real time. If they had phones, David could have called for help all the way from Aquitaine. Unfortunately, communication with France was still restricted to homing pigeons, and they weren't necessarily the most reliable of creatures.

"Maybe we should talk to Rupert before we go—tell him what's going on. He's loyal to David, and maybe he could think of a way to get word to Callum, Llywelyn, and Math." As the newsman for the crown, Rupert broadcast the events of the day from Lambeth station, which lay across the river from Westminster Castle and was powered by a waterwheel in the Thames.

Peter shook his head. "We shouldn't. I don't doubt Rupert's loyalty, not really, but even if he could get a message all the way to Shrewsbury, there are too many relays in between and too many men manning them."

They reached the stable, which was deserted at two in the morning, only to find Lili had arrived ahead of them.

"I thought you were nursing Alexander?" Bridget said.

"He's asleep again." Lili looked Bridget up and down. "You do make a very fine man-at-arms."

Bridget smiled. She was dressed from head to toe as a low-born soldier, meaning that her cloth was poor, her armor was merely a leather jerkin, and she carried an axe in her belt instead of a sword. That was just as well. Peter had taught Bridget to use an axe for self-defense, rather than a knife or sword, because she'd taken to the axe most easily. Probably her Scottish heritage showing.

The bulky, ill-fitting outfit did hide her curves, which weren't all that easy to hide normally. The heavy cloak and knitted cap over her fiery hair helped too. She was dressed this way to present the image of a man with no money but one who could defend himself if he had to. Peter was dressed similarly, though of a slightly higher station, and wore a sword belted at his waist.

"At least we don't have to worry about Callum believing you." Lili took her by the shoulders. "Clare will stop at nothing to gain power. Don't underestimate what he might have in store for you out there."

"I won't."

Lili looked at Peter. "Take the high road and don't stop unless you absolutely have to."

"If a rider left from Chateau Niort in this same hour, he has over three hundred miles to ride to reach Dover, plus a voyage across the channel, while we have not even a hundred and fifty," Peter said. "Your vision has given us a four-day head start on anything Clare might have planned."

"And if my dream wasn't a true *seeing*?" Lili looked worried for the first time.

"Then Bridget and I will have made a swift journey home," Peter said, "and we will look into Clare's activities anyway."

Bridget took a chance and hugged her friend. "And if you're mistaken, we will all just be grateful when David returns home safely."

"That is what we all want and need. I—" Lili stopped.

Bridget looked at her curiously. "What?"

"You are the first Englishwoman I have ever felt close to," Lili said. "I have been the Queen of England for five years, and yet I have kept all of my ladies-in-waiting at arm's length. If you hadn't been here, I would have had no female friend to turn to."

"It's hard to adjust to a new place, even if you aren't the Queen of England," Bridget said. "I have never known what to say or how to talk to anyone who isn't from Avalon—except for you. And now I'm riding away and leaving you alone."

Lili managed a smile and returned Bridget's hug. "The sooner you leave, the sooner you can come back."

Bridget nodded, though she wasn't sure she meant it. She didn't like London; she didn't want to come back. It was Lili who had committed to spending much of her life here because she was married to a man who'd become the King of England despite himself. "When David gets back, you might consider telling him how much you hate London. The court is wherever the king resides, you know." She smiled. "I'd tell him, in particular, that Shrewsbury is quite beautiful this time of year."

Lili laughed. "I remember."

Then Bridget looked intently into Lili's eyes. "As long as David is alive, Clare has failed."

"It still leaves David floating down a river in the middle of Aquitaine with a wounded King of France," Lili said.

"That is true," Bridget said. "But given your *seeing*, we can't sit by and do nothing. He really is in trouble. Even though he is hundreds of miles away, we will do everything we can for him."

6

13 June 1293

David

"When was the last time you traveled this far on foot?" Philip said.

They'd been walking for hours, through fields and woods, and across creeks, avoiding every settlement out of fear that their false identity would have spread far and wide by now—and that if they were seen and captured, they would be killed before their true identities could be revealed. They had turned west as soon as David thought it was safe to do so, and could only hope that La Rochelle was, in fact, getting closer.

"It's been a while," David admitted. "My sister had to do something like this ten years ago after the English burned down one of my father's castles."

"You speak of the English as if you yourself aren't one of them."

David laughed under his breath. "I wasn't then."

"Tell me of this journey your sister undertook."

Clouds had blown in as the night had worn on, to the point that David thought they would have to stop because of his inability to see the path in front of them. They'd persevered in part because they were going so slowly that any obstacle came into focus long before it became a problem, and because David was afraid that if Philip lay down, he wouldn't rise again. Now, however, the sky was turning a murky gray with the coming of the dawn.

While Philip was functional, his wound was still bleeding to the point that David had needed to change his bandage twice more. The French style of clothing at this time was to wear a long shirt covered by a kirtle that fell to the knees. Philip's undershirt was of better quality than most, which meant it was holding up well to a soaking in the river and then being pulled tight as a bandage. David's ministrations had reduced the garment to something that looked more like a modern t-shirt, but Philip still wore his long kirtle over the top, so he looked respectable. Once David had given up his tunic, he didn't really have any more cloth to rip, other than his breeches, which he was hoping to keep intact.

Throughout the long night, David had found himself splitting his time between elaborate calculations as to how far they'd come and evaluating how much blood Philip had lost compared to what was left in his body.

And because of his fears about Philip's chances, David told the story Philip asked for. "The English had tried to kill my father, and they were hunting him."

"That was at this place called *Cilmeri*, yes?"

David nodded. "We'd made it to Castell y Bere, and that was where my father and I left my sisters, Anna and Gwenllian, thinking they'd be safe, in order to wage war on Edward, my predecessor."

"But they were not safe."

"No. A small company of soldiers snuck deep into Wales. They bribed the captain of the guard, and he let them in the front gate. They slaughtered the garrison and burned the castle."

"Your sisters were not there, however." Philip obviously knew something of the story, because it wasn't a question.

"She had spied out the English, learned of their plans, and fled in the night with baby Gwenllian, a wet nurse, and a stable boy."

Philip's expression was strangely satisfied. "If she can do it, I can do it."

What David didn't tell Philip was that during Anna's journey, there had been a moment where she'd had to accept that the eighteen miles left to go could have been eighteen hundred for all the difference it would have made. David and Philip had come perhaps ten of the forty they needed to cover but, unless David found medical treatment for Philip or a faster means of transport, whether they had three miles to go or thirty, the French king wasn't going to manage them.

"I know who seeks my throne," Philip said all of a sudden. "Your story has given me insight."

"Who?"

"My brother, Charles."

David almost laughed, and he would have if he and Philip hadn't been under such strain. "How did my story help you to that conclusion?"

"King Llywelyn's brother, Dafydd, was the one who gave the information about Castell y Bere to the English."

David stared at the French king. "How do you know that?"

Philip shrugged. "I don't remember. It was a long time ago, but isn't it obvious, given what came after?"

David shook his head. "It's comforting to know that it isn't just the Welsh kings who can't trust their families." Welsh history was full of rivalries among brothers, and Philip was right that David's uncle, Dafydd, had been only the most recent example. Before David himself had come to Wales, Uncle Dafydd had attempted to assassinate David's father. He'd been thwarted by a snowstorm and the guilty conscience of one of the conspirators. If Philip was right that Uncle Dafydd had sold out Castell y Bere, it was only one more betrayal out of many.

"Why do you name Charles in particular?" David said.

"He has always objected to having been born second. He is two years younger than I and thinks himself more capable." Philip looked at David out of the corner of his eye. "He wants a throne, any throne, and resents my insistence that he curb his ambition."

"Jealousy is the most poisonous of emotions," David said. "So is lying to yourself, and they seem to go together a lot of the time."

Philip grunted, whether in agreement or pain David didn't know until he said, "Is that what you think of me? That I reached too far because I listened to the wrong people and chose to believe what they told me?"

"Didn't you?"

"I know you English think our court is full of pretension and excess, but if I reach too far, it is because God has given me the authority to rule."

"He hasn't given you the authority to rule England," David said, "or Aquitaine."

Another grunt. "My brother and your Gilbert de Clare seem to have convinced themselves otherwise."

David couldn't disagree. Aymer de Valence, who'd plotted with Red Comyn last Christmas to undermine David, was rotting in the Tower of London because he had convinced himself that David was weak and distracted. He was far from the only discontented lord within David's or Philip's domains. Even if David made it home in time to stop whatever plot Clare was hatching, there would always be another disaffected baron and another plot. It was a constant struggle to maintain a balance between using the power he'd been given as king, and following the path he'd laid out at the start to use power differently. Just thinking about it made David tired.

It occurred to David, now that Clare's duplicity was clear to him, that Clare could have easily been behind Valence's scheming. Valence, Comyn, and Fitzwarin were proud enough that it would have taken only a few subtle—or not so subtle—suggestions that the time was ripe for rebellion to set them on their chosen course. Then, once David and Callum were distracted by Valence's overt and poorly planned treachery, Clare had the freedom to work unhindered on his much more dangerous and complicated scheme.

David and Philip reached yet another stone wall at the edge of a farmer's field, having soaked themselves to the knees with early morning dew. Listening hard, David held up a hand so Philip would stop and listen with him.

The French king halted and leaned against the wall with a low groan. Then his head came up, having heard the hoof beats that had gained David's attention. "I hadn't realized we were so close to a road."

"Me neither. Let's move a little farther, and I'll check it out." David helped Philip over the wall and propped him against a nearby tree. Then he hastened through the brush and foliage towards the sound.

A plan was forming in his mind. Philip couldn't walk the thirty miles they had still had to travel, but if he could ride—

David crouched in the dirt and grass beside the road, listening to the hoof beats pounding along like David's heart. They resolved into a single horseman coming towards him from the east. David couldn't see the crest on the man's surcoat from here, and he warred with himself, knowing that the quickest way to acquire the horse was to take it by force. But his cursed sense of rightness told him that he couldn't simply assault an innocent man. As it was, if there had been more than one rider, David would have assumed they were Clare's men and stayed hidden.

David took a breath and stepped out of the ditch to stand in the middle of the road, his hands up and out at his sides. Given the hour, he didn't want to appear threatening to the rider or he might race right by. David faced the same problem as before at the village: he wore no armor or sword, and showed no allegiance to any lord. He was also damp from the river and grimy with sweat and dirt.

The rider slowed at the sight of him, and then he reined in, still some fifty feet from David. He wasn't wearing colors David recognized. "What do you want?"

Now that it came to it, what he needed was the man's horse, and David had been naïve to think the man would just give his horse away. But he had to ask. "I have a wounded friend, and I was hoping you might help him to the nearest village."

"Did you now?" The man's tone softened, though that didn't make it more friendly. "A wounded friend, did you say? And who are you?"

David had a bad feeling about this, but if he was going to get real help, it was as the duke, not a simple traveler. "The Duke of Aquitaine."

The man guffawed. "He's dead. I'm thinking you killed him."

"No!" David took several steps backward. "I mean you no harm, and you will be richly rewarded for helping me."

"Yes, I will." The rider pulled his sword from his sheath and spurred his horse at David.

With a curse, David dove back into the woods the way he'd come. He didn't feel like he had a choice, since this man was clearly influenced by Clare's lies. Countering a man on horseback when he had neither sword nor knife was a losing proposition at best. The only way to survive a charging horse was by running away. David couldn't survive such a ridiculously one-sided game of chicken.

By now, they were within a half-hour of dawn, so it was light enough to see a little bit, even in the thick woods. The horse would be far faster than David, so David didn't have much room to maneuver. Thirty yards from the road, he spied the tree he was looking for and swung up into the branches. It was an oak tree located to the left of the path. David had noted it on the way to the road because he still had a kid's-eye view of trees, always looking out for good ones to climb.

The rider charged after him, hardly slowing as he entered the woods. David crouched on the branch he'd chosen, about eight feet off the ground, blocked from the rider's view by the tree trunk and many leafy branches. Just as the rider went by, not as warily as he should have, his eyes peeled for David's running form ahead of him, David launched himself from the branch.

He caught the rider around the shoulders, and the two men fell to the ground on the far side of the path. They landed with a *whuf* and a cry from David as pain shot through his chest. He'd been so fired up until that moment that he'd forgotten about the damage the two arrows had caused. His chest felt a lot more than bruised now.

The man lay underneath David, the wind knocked out of him, and David took the opportunity to speak to him again. "I don't want to hurt you. I really am the Duke of Aquitaine."

"The Duke of Aquitaine is dead." The rider rocked his hips back and forth, trying to throw David off. "And you killed him." He threw out an elbow which caught David in the jaw, and instinctively David fell back slightly, which gave the rider enough space to scramble away.

Cursing, David surged upward too, throwing himself at the man again and knocking him to the ground so that he lay on his left side in the dirt, and David again pressed down on him with the full weight of his body.

Because the man's sword had fallen in the brush three feet away, both men went at the same instant for the knife at the rider's waist. David's opponent got his right hand on the hilt first, but David grasped his wrist with his own right hand, pressing down on the knife, determined to prevent the man from drawing it.

David's chest ached, and he feared that the trials of the last day had left him weaker than he should have been, while this rider was strong and just as determined to live as David. "I don't want to hurt you! I just need to borrow your horse!"

The rider wasn't listening. Reaching up with his left hand, he clawed at David's face, and when David reared back to avoid his fingernails, the man got his knife loose from its hilt.

With a quick twist of his hips, he reversed their positions, and David ended up flat on his back in the path with the man straddling him. David bucked and kicked desperately, while at the same time trying to keep the man's knife away from his chest. The man had both hands on the hilt now, pressing downward with all his strength, while David pressed upwards, his hands on the man's wrists and both men grunting and straining with effort.

"Please. I am. The Duke. Of Aquitaine."

The man only pressed down on the knife harder.

Gritting his teeth, knowing he had no choice but to finish this before his strength gave out completely, David let go of the man's left wrist, which he'd been holding with his right hand and brought up both knees with sudden force, jackknifing his body so that the man was knocked forward. That brought David's chest closer to the knife, and the rider plunged the point downwards. But the move also allowed David to access the arrow he'd been carrying all this time on the outside of his right boot. Thus, at the very moment the tip of the man's knife hit the ceramic plate in David's Kevlar, he drove the point of the arrow with all his strength into the man's neck.

* * * * *

With what felt like the last of his willpower, David got Philip astride the horse, and they began moving west again. David had claimed the sword and armor of the man he'd killed, as well as one of his two knives. He gave the one they'd fought over to Philip, even though he wasn't in any shape to use it, and kept the man's boot knife for himself. He'd done no more with the body than drag it off the path into the surrounding brush, but he'd reacquired the arrow and had transferred it to the horse's saddle bag. Characteristically Welsh in its fashioning, it was still the best and only proof David had that the man who'd shot him hadn't been French.

David walked beside the horse, leading it, though he kept glancing up at Philip every few seconds to make sure he remained seated. Rather than feeling relief now that things were looking up, rage clogged David's throat. The anger wasn't at the man he'd killed. He'd been doing his duty. It was at Clare, and at Philip—and if he were honest, at himself. It was he who'd led his company to Chateau Niort. It was he who'd been too trusting and allowed Clare's men to murder his friends and companions. Grief for Justin rose up and threatened to overwhelm him, and David furiously tamped the emotion back down. He had thought he'd come to terms with what this world required of him, but he'd been wrong about that too.

Philip cleared his throat. "You did what you had to do."

"I know."

"I, for one, am grateful."

David ground his teeth, wanting to argue that if Philip hadn't sent his spies to Canterbury, none of this would have happened. Canterbury Castle would still be standing; there would have been no battle of Hythe; and he wouldn't have had to kill that man in this godforsaken region of Aquitaine.

But that wouldn't be true. Philip's men had supported Lee's efforts to undermine David's rule, but Lee could have turned to someone else for aid—Philip's brother, Charles, for example—or simply gone ahead and blown up Canterbury Castle on his own.

And it wasn't as if good hadn't come out of it. Since then, David had stood up to the pope; he'd found an ally in Archbishop Romeyn; the people of Hythe had turned back the subsequent French invasion, to the great honor of England; David had gone to Avalon and back, returning the bulk of the bus passengers to the modern world; and Lee had died.

Philip tried again. "Clare deserves a similar fate."

David took in a breath and let it out, feeling his shoulders sag. Philip—and Clare—were men of their time. They had done only what they knew how to do. Back when Wales had fought England for its sovereignty, David had gone to equal lengths to further his father's interests.

He looked up at the French king. "I know that too."

7

13 June 1293

Carew

Bridget and Peter had an important task in riding to Shrewsbury, but really they were just messengers. Lili had entrusted the responsibility for David's safety to Carew, and though he had attempted to sleep after their midnight meeting, he'd lain awake until the early hours of the morning wondering if he'd lost his mind to approach his brother with a *seeing*. Godfrid was a churchman after all. Perhaps he would view Lili's dream as from the devil rather than a gift from heaven.

Then reason reasserted itself. Carew was David's loyal servant. He'd chosen that role years ago and never had cause to regret it. In fact, he'd been rewarded for his loyalty beyond all expectation. It would be foolish of him to falter now. He would go to his brother with the story that spies had reported a possible plot headed by Clare, and he hoped that the Templars would be ready to aid their king in his time of need.

On the surface, Carew's request was a simple one, but his relationship with his brother was complicated. The two men had experienced numerous ups and downs and, until David had asked him last year to pursue a relationship with the Templars, Carew hadn't seen his brother in more than five years.

Godfrid had been born a bastard a year after Carew himself had been born. Among the Welsh, as long as a father acknowledged his son, illegitimacy was of no matter. But Carew's father had placed himself fully in the Norman camp. While the family had Welsh blood, his father subscribed to Norman law, which gave short shrift to children born outside of wedlock.

With an English mother, Godfrid had spent his life walking a very narrow path—a knife edge, even—between Norman snobbery and English aloofness. There had been times, particularly in their younger years, when Godfrid and Carew had been inseparable, and other times, starting in their middle teens, when Godfrid's resentment of Carew's position, and Carew's (to be totally honest) lofty superiority had driven them apart.

To his credit, Carew's father had done what he could for Godfrid, which in the end had been a great deal. Rather than give Godfrid directly to the Church, Carew's father (also named Nicholas) taught both boys warfare, and then he'd arranged for Godfrid to serve in the household of another Marcher lord, though not the same one to whom he'd sent Carew. Godfrid had been knighted at the age of twenty-five, at which point his father had bought him a commission with the Templars.

Unlike monks, the Templar order had no novices. A man came to the order as a knight already or joined as a sergeant and was never knighted. As Godfrid would never inherit land of his own, the Carew lands being under Marcher rule rather than Welsh, this was the best that could be hoped for. The very best.

At the time of Godfrid's acceptance into the Templar ranks, Carew had actually been jealous, thinking that nothing could be more noble than fighting for Christ in the Holy Land. His father had been unsympathetic, however, just as he'd been eight years earlier when Carew, at the age of nineteen, had begged to fight with King Edward in the ninth Crusade. Nicholas senior had refused permission, and by the time Carew was twenty-one, Edward was on his way home to be crowned king.

At the time, Carew had cursed his father's stubbornness. He had believed that, had he gone with Edward as Gilbert de Clare had done, he would have won honor and glory for the Carew name and improved his family's fortunes and position with the crown of England.

But in the end it had been Godfrid who'd gone to the Holy Land and won renown for himself. He'd been at the fall of Acre in 1291 and barely escaped with his life. He was battle scarred and respected among the Templars, and thus among soldiers throughout Christendom. Upon Godfrid's return to England, it had been Carew, as the elder brother and the one who'd stayed behind, who'd made the first overtures to initiate an adult friendship between them. Godfrid had been open to him, if wary. Since then they'd met a dozen times more. Carew liked to think that the initial wariness in both of them had given way to genuine pleasure. What he didn't know was if they were friends enough now for him to ask the kind of favor Lili had requested. As resolutely as any monks in Christendom, the Templars answered to God, not to David.

As Carew stood in the foyer to his brother's quarters, adjacent to the round Temple Church, which had been modeled after the Holy Sepulchre in Jerusalem, he found his stomach clenching with uncharacteristic anxiety. He'd grown accustomed in the last few years to the day-to-day interactions with dignitaries from across Europe. He thought he'd grown out of the nerves that used to overwhelm him, and he laughed at himself to realize that it was a meeting with his brother that had made him more nervous than he'd been in years.

As a Templar master, it was within Godfrid's purview to make even important men within the royal court wait up to an hour to see him. The current Archbishop of Canterbury certainly would have, but after only a quarter of an hour, Godfrid appeared, striding towards Carew with bright eyes and a smile. His appearance was nearly the exact opposite of Carew's: dark where Carew was light, stocky and muscled where Carew was tall and lanky.

"Welcome brother!"

The two men embraced.

Then Godfrid frowned as he looked at Carew. "Nobody has provided you water to wash or offered refreshment?"

Carew shook his head, which prompted Godfrid to turn on the hapless monk, who'd admitted Carew to the receiving room, and roundly chastise him for his neglect. "This is my brother and the Lord High Treasurer," he said, naming Carew's Office of State. The monk wore a black tunic with a red cross, indicating that he was a sergeant of the order. Godfrid wore the characteristic Templar white tunic with its red cross, which was specifically reserved for knights.

Before Carew had come to Temple Church, he'd gone over some of the reports he'd received over the last few months about the Templar Order. While their losses in the Holy Land had been grievous, two years on, their numbers were once again approaching the four hundred knights and two thousand sergeants they'd had before the fall of Acre. He found it likely that this sergeant was one of the new recruits.

Then Godfrid turned back to Carew and gestured that they should walk together. "I'm glad you have come. I have a letter from the Grand Master in Cyprus that I hope you will deliver to your king."

As Carew walked beside his brother, he marveled at the way the two of them not only looked different, but had turned out so differently too. Godfrid lived for war and, somehow, Carew had tied himself to a king who hated it and would move heaven and earth to avoid it if he could. Carew had fought battles, certainly, but not often and—despite his desire to travel to the Holy Land when he was nineteen—without conviction. It may have been that King Edward had sensed this lack of resolve, and this was part of the reason Carew hadn't gained a higher standing at court like the Clares or the Bohuns.

It wasn't that Carew was weak or wasn't known among his peers for his fighting skills. It was rather that—inside—he hated the accompanying dirt and the sweat, the long hours on horseback, and sleeping on the ground. Godfrid, on the other hand, appeared to revel in it all. Carew's stomach twisted. If Carew had been a little more like Godfrid and a little less like himself, perhaps Clare wouldn't have been able to run wild through King David's domain.

As he looked at his younger brother, Carew's smile turned rueful. He'd become too fastidious in middle age, and he needed to curb that tendency if he expected to maintain favor with the king. In keeping with his predecessor, David despised the pomp and fashion of royal life and didn't admire men who embraced it as much as Carew did.

They reached Godfrid's receiving room, and Godfrid immediately went around his desk to a cubby hole behind it to pull out a sealed letter, which he then handed to Carew.

"Plans for the retaking of Jerusalem are continuing apace! To think we will have the return of Arthur on our side when we do it. We can't lose." Godfrid was referring to David, of course. The legend of Arthur, and David as the embodiment of everything he'd stood for, had taken on a life of its own. Whether English, Norman, or Welsh, the people of Britain had all been raised with the story and claimed King Arthur as their own. Godfrid was no exception.

Carew took the letter his brother gave him, but he hesitated as he did so. When the two men were younger, this would have been the moment when Carew would smile gravely in order to imply superior knowledge and reassure Godfrid that he had everything well in hand.

But today he didn't, and he decided that it was time his brother knew how very much things had changed between them. Still with the letter in his hand, Carew grasped the top rail of a spindle chair near the unlit fireplace and walked with it to Godfrid's desk. He flapped the hand that held the letter at Godfrid, and the older brother in him took over for just a moment. "Sit. I have something to tell you." Carew himself sat in the chair he'd brought.

His forehead furrowed, Godfrid obeyed Carew, sitting in his ornate chair behind the desk. It was clearly Godfrid's usual chair, one worthy of the station of a Templar master. Carved and cushioned, it was in appearance more like a throne than a chair to work in, though work in it Godfrid did. The desk in front of him was piled with stacks of paper, each carefully arranged in rows, and even as Carew watched, his brother carefully aligned the papers in one of the piles more neatly.

Carew himself had never mastered the art of orderliness in his business affairs, preferring to leave such things to his steward, and he was pleased to see that a certain level of haphazardness had been introduced to the room by a small stack of papers that had been tossed on the floor and cascaded across the wooden boards.

There was no point in avoiding the issue at hand, since it was the whole reason he was here. "As much as I would like to give your letter to the king, I fear it is not possible right now."

"I know that he is in Aquitaine, meeting with the King of France about plans for the crusade," Godfrid said, "but when he returns—"

"That is what I must speak to you about," Carew said, "and I don't want to continue another moment as we have been if it gives you any misapprehension about why I'm here. I fear that unless we do something to aid the king—you and I do something, I mean—he may never return."

"What?" Godfrid leaned forward. "What has happened? Tell me quickly."

"As you yourself told us once, Gilbert de Clare may not be as he appears. We have indications that he plans to betray the king," Carew said, all in a rush. "We are asking for the assistance of the Templars to aid King David if—or when—he seeks your assistance."

Godfrid's eyes narrowed. "Who is *we*? Is this request from the Order of the Pendragon?"

That was the Templar part of Godfrid speaking. While concerned about the danger to David, Godfrid knew as well as Carew that his obligations were first to his order, not to the king, no matter how much he personally might admire him. Fortunately for Carew—and in large part because of Carew's own efforts—it was the crown of England that had developed a relationship with the Templars, not the Order of the Pendragon, a fact for which Carew was infinitely grateful now.

"No." Carew was anxious to get back to the more important issue. "No. This is coming from me, as Lord High Treasurer and adviser to the king. I fear to involve the Order of the Pendragon because Clare is a prominent member. I find it likely that he has been suppressing any information that might expose him for what he really is. Thus, I cannot turn to the

Order for help because I do not know anyone within it I can trust."

Godfrid nodded, apparently willing to accept Carew's assessment at face value. "Where is this betrayal supposed to occur?"

"Aquitaine. As you probably know, Clare has made all the arrangements for the meeting between King David and the King of France."

"What could I possibly do to help from here?"

"You could contact your brethren across the English Channel and warn them of the danger and to be on the lookout for David, who may be roaming Aquitaine without retainers, injured and in need. I know you have pigeons capable of the journey. Your ships sail from Portsmouth to La Rochelle daily."

Godfrid's expression turned skeptical. "We brought you a warning about Clare over six months ago, and you dismissed it."

Carew hung his head. "I know. But we believe now that you were right." And then, because Godfrid still looked skeptical, and even a little disgruntled, he took a chance that his brother's initial reaction to the news of David's peril indicated that his belief in the legend was more than skin deep. He looked into Godfrid's eyes. "Last night Queen Lili dreamed that King David was shot with arrows and fell from the battlement of Chateau Niort into the river below."

Godfrid surged to his feet, scattering his neat piles of paper everywhere. "Why did you not say so before? The queen believes this dream was a true *seeing*?"

"Yes."

Godfrid left the desk and paced to the window to look out at the busy London morning passing by. After a moment, he turned back to Carew. "I will do anything and everything within my power to aid the king. Since it is the Templar Order that brought the suspicions against Clare to you in the first place, my men will readily accept the possibility that circumstances have changed and that our information has been proven true."

"That is as much and more than I could have hoped for," Carew said.

Godfrid eyed Carew with pursed lips. "You cannot be unaware that we owe King David a debt."

"Do you?"

Godfrid scoffed. "The knowledge that his physicians have brought to our infirmaries has transformed them from places men go to die to centers of healing. That reason alone would justify my aiding him." He shook his head. "I only wish I'd given him, as I gave to you, the password that would allow him entrance into any Templar holding. Why didn't I?"

Carew found himself clearing his throat awkwardly. "You gave it to me, Godfrid, and that was enough. I knew at the time that to do so was a violation of your trust, but before the king sailed for Aquitaine, I passed it on to him."

Godfrid was silent a moment, and then he sat himself back into his chair and regarded his brother. "Under the circumstances, I forgive you."

Carew raised one shoulder in a half-shrug. "The decision to give it to him was impulsive, but I must tell you that even after I'd done it, I couldn't regret it."

Godfrid grinned. "So you have the *sight* now too? I find having a Welsh brother far more interesting than the Norman one you used to be."

8

13 June 1293

Bridget

B ridget and Peter stood together at a crossroads, gazing northwest towards Shrewsbury, even though there was nothing at all to see in the dark, the fog, and the rain, beyond the twenty feet the torch illumined. Bridget had always hated driving in fog. The only consolation here was that they moved so much slower on horseback that they never outran what they could see. A horse whickered in the distance from someone's farm. Otherwise they were alone with the puddles.

They had come a terribly long way—nearly a hundred miles of almost constant riding, a feat Bridget wouldn't have thought possible before she took up the challenge that Lili's *seeing* had laid out. They'd changed horses four times at David's strongholds between London and here, wherever *here* was. That was the only thing that had allowed them to keep going through the last six hours of pouring rain and ferocious wind.

"We should rest a minute," Peter said. "We're both exhausted."

"We don't have time. It was bad enough that we stayed at Kenilworth for as long as we did." Bridget said, a little more tartly than she meant to. She put out a hand to her husband. "I'm sorry. You're right. I am tired. And I hurt everywhere."

"We rested because we could do nothing else. If we hadn't, we wouldn't have made it this far. We still have miles to go. If we are too late, it won't be because of a lack of trying." Peter grimaced as he dismounted. "We'll take ten minutes and then ride on. We have forty miles to go. If we get fresh horses at Bridgnorth, maybe we can reach Shrewsbury by four in the morning."

Bridget took in a breath, summoning patience. Peter was right. She'd spent these last months since their marriage working on getting him to tell her what he thought when he thought it, so it would be counterproductive to argue with him when he was actually doing what she wanted—just because she didn't like what he was saying.

They moved off the road, more in accord. And for all that the weather was miserable, Bridget found herself not minding it as much.

"I can hear you smiling." Peter said as he trudged along beside her, leading the horses and using the long torch as a walking stick. His other hand held his horse's reins. "Why?"

"I'm happy." Bridget tucked her hand into his elbow, realizing as she did so that she missed touching him. The formality of the English court at Westminster had required that they keep their distance from one another outside of their bedchamber. It wasn't like that at Shrewsbury, where people knew them and accepted their strange ways. London was like a different country—huge and foreign—and even the way they spoke English was different.

Peter smiled too. "Any adventure with you is a good adventure. No offense to David, wherever he may be."

"He wouldn't be offended," Bridget said, "especially since it's his fault we're together—"

A thundering of hooves sounded along the road behind them, intermingling with the drumming of the rain on their hoods. At first Bridget thought it was actual thunder, but then Peter motioned with the torch, hustling them through a gap in the stone wall to the south of the road. He dropped the torch on the ground and hastily suffocated the light with dirt.

Then they stood stock still among the few trees that lined the wall between them and the road. The riders were carrying torches, many of them, without which Bridget couldn't have seen her hand in front of her face. It was a company of forty men at least.

"Clare's men." Bridget recognized the chevrons of the Earl of Gloucester. "Lili was right."

Peter made a rumbling sound in the back of his throat. "It could be coincidence."

"You hate coincidences and don't believe in them."

He gave a low laugh. "I've been taught not to trust them. Where there's smoke, there's often fire."

The riders passed by in a torrent of churned mud and pounding hooves. Only twenty yards down the road, they took a fork to the left instead of the right-hand one that Bridget and Peter would be taking to Shrewsbury.

"Where are they going?" Now that the soldiers had passed, Bridget felt the fog and the darkness settling over them again. Peter felt for the torch and shook off the dirt. A lesser man might have had difficulty lighting it, but he'd become an expert in the year and a half he'd lived in the middle ages. She knew for a fact that he'd practiced. "Hereford. That road leads to Hereford." Peter stabbed the end of their torch into the ground with angry force and lit it.

Bridget tried to picture the maps of England and Wales that David put up on every wall space available. It was a standing joke among David's friends, followers, and admirers that *the king loves maps.* "That means Humphrey de Bohun. Do they ride to him as friend or foe?"

"That's a lot of men to send to someone who's your ally," Peter started walking back to the road, "unless Clare is sending men to support Bohun's takeover of this region."

A snake twisted in Bridget's stomach. She was back to hating the fog and the rain, and her earlier joy was gone.

9

13 June 1293

David

"You must leave me behind, David," Philip said. "You are the Duke of Aquitaine. You must take the horse and ride to La Rochelle. Then you can send men back to me."

"I wish you'd stop suggesting that." David gazed at the abandoned barn and wondered if it was worth checking out. Last night had been clear with a bright moon, but this evening it was pouring rain, and they were soaked through—again—and darkness would engulf them at any moment. They weren't as far north here as in England, but the sun would set within the half-hour, so they would run out of light soon. If he was to tend to Philip, he'd rather do it while he could still see something. He didn't think fumbling around in the dark and the rain with a wounded man, pursuit or no pursuit, was a winning proposition. Not that this barn was going to be ideal. If the roof leaked, they might be better off continuing to walk.

"We've been over this. Clare's men are telling everyone I'm dead, which means nobody is going to believe me when I tell them who I am. And with the death of my men at Chateau Niort, I don't know a single soul in Aquitaine I can trust. Anyway, splitting up is not the answer. I'd be leaving you to your death."

Philip made a disgusted noise. "You are too noble for your own good."

"I have heard that before." David spoke absently, since he'd walked ahead to push open the gate. The structure was more of a shelter than a barn, with what country people in Oregon called a split rail fence instead of walls, thus allowing the free flow of air through the building. The thatch was thick enough that the roof wasn't leaking, and now that David breathed in the smell of the hay, he realized that it was fresh. The shelter wasn't abandoned after all. But as it was empty of enemies at the moment, David couldn't ask for anything more.

He went back into the rain. "We passed a village a quarter-mile back. Maybe they have a healer. At the very least, food would be good. You need something better than dry bread if you are going to maintain your strength."

"If you ask for bandages and food, they'll wonder why you didn't just bring your wounded friend to the village."

"I'll tell them my friend could go no farther, so I found a dry spot in which to leave him," David said. "It is the truth, after all."

Philip cleared his throat. "I could go farther."

David didn't dignify that statement by responding to it. They still had a good way to go too. From the trail where David had killed that man to the southern approach to La Rochelle had to be a distance of at least thirty miles. The twenty they'd covered since then had been the longest miles of David's life, full of constant anxiety and fear of discovery. Had Philip been healthy, they could have reached safety by now—if the Templar commanderie was, in fact, a safe place. But even with a horse, Philip wasn't doing very well. On top of everything else, he'd developed a fever. The last thing he needed was more travel.

David had spent enough time around wounded men to know that some bruising and swelling was normal with an arrow wound, but Philip's wound was inflamed, puffy, and looking far worse than it should. David feared that dirt had gotten into it. Worse would be if David had left a grain of metal or a fragment of bone behind. If Philip was to survive, the wound would have to be probed again, but David had neither the skill nor the tools to do so. Philip needed a healer.

If they were very lucky, the Templar healer at La Rochelle had done a stint at the hospital in London and learned some of the new methods. Philip hadn't wanted to call upon the

Templar commanderie in La Rochelle for aid, but if they'd ever had a choice about it, they didn't now.

"We're going in there?" Even exhaustion couldn't diminish the sneer that formed on Philip's lips.

"A man's home is his castle, be he peasant or king," David said, badly mangling the quote, not that Philip knew it or cared.

Philip snorted, but when David helped him from the horse, he staggered willingly enough into the barn and collapsed onto a mound of hay with a sigh. When he was settled somewhat comfortably, David untied the bandage around Philip's shoulder to reveal a wound far more inflamed than when he'd last seen it. In a way, David was glad the night was coming on because his stomach turned at the sight of what he could see.

"I'm going to die, aren't I?" Philip's eyes were fixed on David's face.

"You are not going to die, not if I have any say in the matter."

"Your eyes say different."

"The Templars have been given the remedies for infection discovered by healers in England. By tomorrow, you'll be on the road to health."

"You gave my ambassador the knowledge too." Philip had closed his eyes against the pain, and David couldn't blame him. He was trying to be gentle, but every touch must have been excruciating. "Why?"

David was focusing so hard that at first he didn't understand the question. Then he paused, his brow furrowed. "You're asking me why I didn't withhold what we know? Why would I do that?"

"Every dead Frenchman is one fewer soldier to fight," Philip said.

David shook his head, not mystified so much as saddened by the cynicism. He didn't really know how to answer Philip without becoming angry, so he took one of the last scraps of cloth, this from a spare shirt in the saddle bag taken from the dead man, and went back outside for a minute to let the rain soak it. Then he returned so he could clean Philip's wound.

Either Philip had grown accustomed to the pain, or he had a better handle on it, because he didn't even wince. Despite—or maybe because of—David's anger, David was working extra hard not to hurt him.

After five silent minutes, Philip said, "You are not as I imagined you to be."

"How is that?" David said.

"Before Hythe, I was led to believe that your compassion for your people was a weakness that I could exploit. I was told that you cared so much for them that you neglected to do what was necessary to maintain power. But then we were defeated at

Hythe by a motley army of peasants. Until today, I didn't understand how such a thing could be possible. Now I see that my advisers misunderstood you completely."

Everybody liked to hear nice things about themselves, and David was no exception. He warmed a bit at Philip's assessment, not disagreeing because Philip was absolutely right, at least about the motley army composed of the citizenry of Hythe.

"I see how you worry for your family. You care that people will take the news of your death hard, and it eats away at you. You are unlike any lord within my experience."

"I've heard that before too," David said.

Philip continued as if David hadn't spoken. "From across the Channel, one might make the mistake of concluding that a man who has done nothing but gain more and more power since he was fourteen years old would be driven to upend Clare's plans because he treasures his throne as his God-given right. That would be natural. In our fraternity of kings, we all think this way. But it seems to me that you want power in order to keep it out of the hands of less able men and because you know that only with power can you improve the lives of your people.

"You despair that Clare will overturn all the good you've done in England during your reign. You hate the idea of Clare's rule because you believe his vision for England is colored by self-interest. As far as I can see, you have no self-interest."

"I have no interest in dying," David said dryly.

"But you could live without being king."

David ducked his head in acknowledgement of the truth of Philip's words. "I would never have chosen to be King of England for myself. It was my father's dream. In fact, we fought about it more than once. When I first considered accepting the crown, it was because doing so would mean that Wales was finally free of England. And then I began to care about the English people too. In the end, I took the throne because the barons and the people asked it of me. I couldn't turn my back on their need."

"And, again, you mean what you say." Philip snorted and shook his head, even though it clearly pained him. "My priests tell me you're barely a Christian, and yet God favors you. How is that? From where does your strength come?"

"I am a Christian," David said, slightly offended. At the same time, he knew the source of Philip's query. *God wills it!* was a common cry at the beginning of battle, as if God would ever favor a leader who went to war as easily as European Christians did. Then he added, knowing that his words would make no sense to Philip but not caring, "I'm also an American, and we tend to be absurdly—and perhaps stupidly—confident that we know best."

"Sometimes when you speak, I have no notion of what you're saying." Philip's eyes remained fixed on David's face. "As I said, you are like no king I have ever known."

David finished bandaging Philip, uncertain what to say or if he needed to say anything at all. He could hardly return the compliment Philip had paid him because Philip was exactly like most lords David knew. Up until today, which admittedly had been humbling for them both, Philip had simply been fortunate enough to be born to a higher station than anyone else in his country and had been more ruthless in holding onto what he had.

Then again, Philip might not see his analysis of David's character as positive, and Philip hadn't mentioned the related reason why David had no intention of giving up his throne to someone like Clare: he'd become a control freak. Maybe he'd always been one, but there hadn't been as much scope for the tendency when he was a fourteen-year-old freshman in high school.

Because the mail and padding underneath would never dry while he wore them, David stood and began to strip off his borrowed weaponry and armor, biting back a moan as he worked his way out of the padding. His chest hurt from the arrows and from whatever further damage he'd caused himself by falling on top of the man he'd killed. He was glad to leave the

Kevlar vest on, per Lili's instructions, so he wouldn't have to see what he'd done to himself.

Fortunately, the dead man's change of clothes, which David had found in his saddle bags, fit well enough for one evening. He put them on. Only after he was dressed did he finish his conversation with Philip.

"You make me sound like a better man than I am." David gestured to his transformed appearance. "I go to the village dressed like a common man, to be treated like one, because I don't dare go as myself. In just this last day I have learned how accustomed to power and my ability to wield it I have become. Out here, I have none, and I hate it."

Without waiting for Philip's response, if he meant to make one, David bent to tuck the dead man's blanket around Philip's shoulders. "I will return as soon as I can. I swear it." Then he threw his newly acquired cloak over his shoulders, pulled up the hood, and went out into the rain.

David approached the village, which was larger than the one they'd first tried, with some trepidation. He watched the outside of the inn for fifteen minutes before deciding he couldn't wait any longer and pushed through the door. He would have preferred to look like a knight, but the dead man's tunic, declaring his loyalty to an unknown lord, was covered in blood. This was the best way David knew to change his appearance, since Clare's men would never believe that a king would dress like a commoner.

"Evening." While the tavern keeper's greeting was civil enough, his look said otherwise, and several other inhabitants of the common room glared balefully at David before looking away. That wasn't quite the reception David was used to, but it was how he should have expected them to treat a stranger.

"I need food." David put a single coin, taken from the dead man's purse, on the bar. "Enough for several meals." He decided in that instant that he didn't dare ask for bandages or a healer.

"What are you doing out in this weather?"

"My mother's sick and can't cook."

"Haven't you heard the news?"

"No."

"The Duke is dead! The countryside has been roused in search of the two assassins who escaped. I've been kept hopping all evening."

That was disappointing but not surprising. Clare's men were bound to have made better time than David and Philip. But as the tavern keeper wrapped up the food, David grumbled to himself about his decision not to push on, fearing the price they might pay for losing so much time in sleep. And yet, Philip truly could go no farther today. Despite the manhunt, David still couldn't take the horse and leave Philip, not even on the promise of sending help, since he couldn't guarantee that help would ever come.

"I'll be on my way then. Thank you." David stuffed the food into his pack, realizing as he did so that the tavern keeper had wrapped the bread and cheese in a rough cloth. It wasn't suitable for a bandage, but he could put it to use as a sling. Then, as David turned towards the door, it opened to reveal two men in Clare's colors, dripping water everywhere.

"What can I get you?" The tavern keeper raised his hand to the newcomers, welcoming them to the bar.

David hastily threw the hood from his borrowed cloak over his head and sidled to the side, his eyes averted. Both the tavern keeper's behavior and David's were in keeping with how men of their respective stations would treat two men-at-arms: welcome, even obsequiousness in the tavern keeper's case and wariness in his.

The men-at-arms walked to the bar, and David edged his way among the tables before slipping out the door into the darkened street. Several other armed men were just leading their horses through the inn's gate towards its stable yard. They glanced at David, but he simply raised a hand and said, "Ugly night," in French.

It was enough to cause a snort of laughter and a passing, "God go with you," from their leader.

Ten seconds later, David was loping his way past the borders of the village and onto the road that would take him back to where he'd left Philip. He had deliberately not ridden the horse because he didn't think a commoner such as he appeared to be would have one.

When he reached the hut, after a bit of frightening stumbling about, Philip was awake, his eyes agleam in the dark. David settled in front of him to help him drink and provide him with some of the food he'd brought.

"My first concern," Philip said, "after I remove my brother's head from his body, must be retribution against the men who plotted with him, else my ability to maintain power will forever remain a question."

When David didn't answer immediately, Philip added, "Do you disagree? Tell me, David, what payment for what he has done will you exact from Clare when you return to London?"

"You think I will hesitate to hang him because of a misguided love of all humanity?" David said. "You misunderstand me again. Love, compassion, and fairmindedness are important in a king, but they are not enough—not nearly enough—for him to rule effectively."

"If not these three, then what?"

It never ceased to amaze David how few lords truly understood leadership. His father understood it, of course, and it was his father's words to him ten years ago that he echoed yet again. "Justice, Philip. It has always been about justice."

But then he looked away and didn't say the rest of what he was thinking. Regardless of what he outwardly confessed to Philip, his gut was telling him that hanging was too good an end for Clare. And it scared him that he couldn't tell if he thought that because of his professed desire for justice or because of the boiling anger inside him.

10

After Midnight

14 June 1293

Callum

"What are we going to name the baby if it's a girl?" Callum smoothed the blanket over Cassie's belly. At eight months pregnant, she couldn't sleep enough, but sometimes, she couldn't sleep at all either, and he'd woken a few moments ago to find her staring up at the ceiling.

"Something everyone can pronounce," Cassie said, "including my grandfather." If the baby was a boy, they planned to name him Gareth, meaning *gentle spirit*, after Cassie's grandfather's Indian name.

"I suppose I'd be in trouble if I suggested Addfwyn or Mwyndeg." Callum laughed and clasped his wife's hand.

They'd waited a long time for a baby, first because it seemed smart not to have kids when they were in Avalon and looking to return to this world, and then once back, the timing had seemed all wrong. Eventually, they'd come to the conclusion that the timing was always going to be wrong, in which case, there was no time like the present.

"Women have been doing this childbirth thing since the beginning of the beginning, you know." Cassie took his face in both hands and kissed him. "I'm going to be fine."

"You're going to be especially fine because Rachel arrives early next week." The baby wasn't due for four weeks, but Callum believed in being prepared.

"My lord!"

Callum frowned, and Cassie released him. "You'd better go. It sounds urgent."

Callum swung his legs out of bed and reached the door in two strides, anxious to find out what had Samuel, Shrewsbury's sheriff and Callum's right-hand man, waking them up in the middle of the night.

Callum pulled open the door, and Samuel almost fell into the room, since he'd swung his arm to knock again only to find the door was no longer in his way.

"Sorry." Samuel's voice dropped to a normal volume. "Peter and Bridget have returned."

"That can't be good," Cassie said from the bed, though she made no move to leave it.

"Give me a moment, Samuel." Callum shut the door and gathered up his clothing.

"You don't know what this is about?" Cassie said.

"Not yet." He tugged on his boots.

She flopped back onto the pillow and flung an arm over her eyes. "It has to be bad if Samuel is banging on the door at three in the morning."

It probably was three in the morning too. Cassie tended to be unerring in her estimation of time.

"I will find out and let you know."

"Okay." Cassie rolled onto her side and repositioned the pillow more comfortably under her head. There was a time when she would have been right there beside him to find out what was the matter. She liked being in the thick of things. But pregnancy had taught them both detachment, and in this case it was for the better. Like any good soldier, Cassie would sleep when she could, and she trusted that Callum would let her know if she was needed.

Back in the corridor, now booted and cloaked because even if it was June the castle was cold, Callum followed Samuel down the stairs to the great hall, which was brightly lit. If the lord was up, the castle was awake too. Breakfast would be served at any moment.

Bridget and Peter were already there. Their dripping cloaks had been hung on a rack before a blazing fire. Callum had slept through the storm, but now that he was upright, he noted the wind howling outside and the rat-a-tat-tat of rain on the glass windows on the west side of the hall.

As he'd come through the doorway, Bridget was bent over at the waist, working her hands through her wet curls to untangle them, and Peter was removing his boots in order to shake water out of them. They'd been talking quietly with Jeffries, whom Samuel must have roused before coming to see Callum. Jeffries had stopped by for a visit on his way south to collect Rachel from Buellt, where she'd gone to see Bronwen and her new baby. He would be bringing her back to Shrewsbury, where they'd stay until the birth of Cassie's baby.

All three stopped what they were doing when Callum approached and came to a halt in front of them.

"What's going on?"

Bridget and Peter looked at each other, revealing uncharacteristic uncertainty, and Callum felt a tinge of exasperation. They'd arrived in the middle of the night, so it had to be important. He took a step closer and softened his voice. "Just tell me."

"Carew believes that the rumors from six months ago that Clare was plotting against the king have merit," Peter said. "In fact, he and Lili believe that Clare has made an attempt on David's life at Chateau Niort in Aquitaine."

"They *believe*? What does that mean?"

Again Peter and Bridget exchanged a glance before Bridget took in a breath and said, "Lili had a dream of him being pierced by two arrows and falling from the battlement in the company of the King of France. Because of David's Kevlar, he was not hurt, though King Philip took an arrow in his shoulder."

Callum rubbed his face with both hands. Probably because of the hour, his brain wasn't working properly, and he hadn't heard correctly. "Lili had a dream?"

"A *seeing*," Bridget said.

Callum glanced at Jeffries, who raised his eyebrows and shrugged.

"You rode all the way here because Lili had a vision?" Callum rocked back and forth on the balls of his feet.

"Yes." Though a moment ago Bridget had seemed nervous about telling him what was going on, in the face of Callum's skepticism she was perfectly calm. "We couldn't trust the radio because we don't know how many men Clare has bought."

The communication network David had established throughout the country had two aspects. The radio stations operated as one-way broadcasts, which were relayed around the country through antennas built on the highest hills in England. A village could receive that broadcast as long as it was within line of sight of an antenna and provided it had a working radio.

By now, at least one village in every district had one. Westminster Castle itself had been fitted out with the speaker scavenged from the bus, from which the news of the day blared out every evening.

The second component to the network was two-way communication, and it also worked through the antennas, but required that both parties were tuned to the same frequency and had hand-held radios or walkie-talkies, much like lorry drivers used for decades before the advent of the mobile phone. Its existence was almost wholly attributable to the gifts from MI-5. And because they were government issue for military purposes, they weren't subject to the artificial wattage limits of civilian CB networks of the twentieth century.

"Has he taken over the stations?" Callum said.

"Not yet," Peter said, "not that we know, but if he owns the men who run them, we could hardly speak openly about his treachery."

"I realize that what Bridget and Peter are saying doesn't make sense, Callum," Cassie's voice came from behind him, and he turned to see her enter the room with a blanket wrapped around her shoulders, "but we should listen to them anyway."

Bridget shot Cassie a grateful look, and the two women embraced.

"You were supposed to be trying to sleep," Callum said.

"Emphasis on *trying*. I gave up." She released Bridget and moved closer to Callum in order to put her hand on his arm. "We should know by now that there is more in the universe than we can understand with our five senses. We were worried about Clare last year, and we dismissed our worries. Maybe we should reexamine the evidence."

Callum squared his shoulders. The traditions of Cassie's people and Lili's people, though separated by five thousand miles and a thousand years, weren't far off from one another and, in fact, were far closer in spirit than the English customs in either era. At the very least, the accusation that Clare had arranged for an attempt on David's life was too serious to ignore just because he didn't like the way the information had been acquired.

The Templars had warned them about Clare late last autumn, and that warning had been augmented by chatter from Callum's spy network. He could admit a mistake when he made one: he had allowed himself to become distracted by the machinations of Valence and Comyn. In his defense, they'd been quite a distraction.

"You are saying that David is alive, though. Right, Bridget?" Cassie said.

Bridget nodded. "Lili said he was uninjured, and he landed in the river that runs by the chateau."

Cassie bit her lip before speaking again. Callum knew what question was coming next because it was on the tip of his tongue too. "He didn't go to Avalon?"

"No," Peter said shortly. "At least Lili doesn't think so."

Cassie nodded and returned her gaze to Callum. "We have to hold Shrewsbury."

A hundred and fifty years ago, Shrewsbury Castle had surrendered to King Stephen during the civil war between him and his cousin, Empress Maud. Stephen had besieged the castle for several days before it fell, after which he'd tarnished his honor by executing the entire garrison, a total of ninety-three men.

Callum hoped that Gilbert de Clare wouldn't want to invest the resources in bringing an army to bear on Shrewsbury, since it was only one English town. At the same time, if Clare thought David was dead, he would move quickly to consolidate his power, and in so doing, eliminate or co-opt everyone who'd ever stood for David, including Callum, Humphrey de Bohun, and Edmund Mortimer, all high-ranking barons in David's kingdom and rulers of extensive lands, with power bases in western England and the March.

That meant that Bohun and Mortimer were Callum's natural allies. Callum couldn't judge right now whether or not David was alive, or even if Clare was a traitor, but he could remain true to David's cause. With the aid of the other barons,

Callum could have a genuine chance to hold a swath of territory from Chester to Hay-on-Wye. And yet, if Callum chose to hold Shrewsbury against Clare, he would be risking the lives of every citizen he was supposed to protect.

"Say any of this is true," Callum said. "How does Clare hope to rule in David's stead, since if David dies, Arthur is the rightful King of England."

"I don't know," Peter said. "Maybe Clare and the Archbishop of Canterbury have done a deal."

Callum grimaced at the likelihood of that. David hadn't exactly gone out of his way to placate the Church and Pope Boniface recently, so Callum didn't know that Arthur could, in fact, count on the Church's support.

He let out a breath. "We have to act on the information as if it's true. The consequences of learning of danger to David—and all of us—and not acting are too dire."

"That's what we thought too," Peter said. "That's why we rode all this way."

"What do we think Clare's next move will be?" Jeffries said. "And what can we do about it this far from London or Aquitaine?"

"Maybe nothing for Lili or David, not right now," Callum said. "But we can be ready if Clare comes for us."

11

14 June 1293

Gwenllian

As she peered between the slits in the golden fabric in front of her, Gwenllian decided that one of the good things about being eleven was that she was still young enough to be overlooked, but she was finally old enough to understand her elders' conversations without having to ask what they were talking about and give away the fact that she'd been eavesdropping.

And Gwenllian was very good at eavesdropping.

Today, before Gilbert de Clare had arrived with his news that Dafydd was dead, killed in Aquitaine by the French, she and Arthur had stationed themselves underneath Lili's throne, hiding behind its wide, golden skirt, not realizing when they'd chosen their hiding spot what horrible news they would soon be hearing.

Not that Lili hadn't warned Gwenllian about what Clare might be planning and what he might say if he ever did arrive at

Westminster. Lili would have liked to prevent him from entering the castle at all, but it was a public space. Parliament met in the hall adjacent to the receiving room in which they were sitting. Since Clare was a member of Parliament, it would have been difficult to keep him and his men out.

Though he didn't seem to be there now, Rupert Jones had his news office down the corridor. Had Lili barred Clare from the castle, the snub would have been all over England in a hot minute (to use a phrase Gwenllian had learned from the twenty-firsters).

Gwenllian didn't believe Dafydd was dead any more than Lili did. Next to her own papa, he was the bravest, smartest man in the world. In a hoarse whisper, she told Arthur as much. He might be only four years old, but he wasn't stupid. Arthur hadn't even been listening when Clare had started talking, but the hubbub in the room had caught his attention, and he had stared at Gwenllian with wide blue eyes and trembling lips.

She shushed him and told him that *of course* his father wasn't dead. He hadn't gone to Avalon like he always did whenever he was in danger because he hadn't been in *that* much danger. Gwenllian hugged him and reminded him about his mother's *seeing,* without telling Arthur that she was having a hard time holding onto hope too. Clare seemed so *certain.*

When she peered again through the slit in the fabric, Clare's face was drawn and white, and he looked like he hadn't slept. In fact, he seemed nearly as unhappy as Lili with the news. Clare even wiped a tear from the corner of his eye, but then he blinked and straightened. As a great lord, he wouldn't want to be caught weeping. Gwenllian had seen it though, and she suspected that Lili, sitting above her, had too. Not much got past Dafydd's wife, particularly when it came to what other people were thinking or feeling.

Apart from Lili—and Gwenllian's own mother, of course—it was Gwenllian's experience that adults were often wrong about what was really going on at any castle. They would assume that orders were obeyed, for instance, or that all the people who worked in the kitchen or the stable didn't know everything there was to know about their secrets. Dafydd wasn't as bad as some adults. He talked to her like he talked to everyone—with big words and ideas she didn't understand most of the time. That was okay with Gwenllian. There were worse things than being the sister of the King of England.

The other good thing about being almost eleven instead of an all-grown-up thirteen was that she wasn't expected to prance around in a dress that prevented her from running, and now that Lili was so preoccupied with Alexander, it meant that if Gwenllian and Arthur gave their nurse the slip, they had the whole of Westminster Castle at their disposal.

Which was how they'd ended up beneath Lili's chair for Clare's audience.

"How did he die?" That was Sir Nicholas de Carew, standing to the right of Lili's chair. His voice was deceptively level. She couldn't see his face, but she knew without looking that his jaw was like a block of stone and his eyes had narrowed to blue chips under his blond eyebrows.

"His castle was infiltrated by men from France at the behest of King Philip's brother, Charles. King Philip is also dead." Clare bent slightly at the waist. "I am so sorry, my queen."

Again, Gwenllian was confused about what was happening because Clare really did sound sorry, and his voice had a hitch in it when he said Dafydd's name. Gwenllian bit her lip. Could Clare be right, and Lili wrong?

Clare continued speaking. "I fear I have more bad news. We have indications of a credible threat against you and the boys as well, and we fear that the French have bought someone—one of your men or a trusted ally—inside Westminster."

"Where did that news come from?" Carew said.

"I have spies of my own, Nicholas," Clare said wryly. That tone was more normal than not for him. Then Clare turned back to Lili, his amusement gone. "I have taken the precaution of reassigning your guards and much of the garrison. Westminster will be guarded by my men for the time being."

Lili's voice was thick with tears, but she spoke through them. "Lord Clare, really that isn't necessary—"

"I believe it is. My queen, I beg you to take steps to protect yourself. I must speak with Parliament, to inform them of David's death, and then we must decide how we are to counter this threat from France. It would greatly ease my heart if you would confine yourself to the Tower until such a time as I can either apprehend the traitors or ensure your safety elsewhere."

"I'm sure I'll be safe—"

"Please, Lili," Clare said, using her given name as if she was a beloved niece. "For me."

Carew cleared his throat. "I will stay with her." He put his feet together, and though Gwenllian couldn't see him bow, she knew he had.

"Make sure to keep the children with you too," Clare said. "Gwenllian and Arthur are under the throne."

At first, Gwenllian thought she'd misheard him, but when she looked towards him, he was peering at her with an amused expression. Angry because she'd been the one fooled instead of doing the fooling, she nudged Arthur. She didn't want to be locked in the Tower of London, and for all Clare's sweet words, she didn't believe that any of this was for their own good. Lili couldn't be wrong, and Dafydd couldn't be dead.

"It's time to play hide and seek!" Gwenllian scooted out the back of the throne, pulling Arthur after her, and then ran with him for the rear door to the room.

Arthur loved hide and seek, and he ran with her, his little legs and arms pumping enthusiastically. After months of exploration, Gwenllian knew all the back ways and passages at Westminster Castle far better than Clare or the men he sent to chase her. She spared a thought for little Alexander, wishing she could keep him safe too, but Alexander was still nursing, so taking care of him was something she couldn't help with very much.

They ran down a corridor, up a back stairwell, through a series of connecting rooms on the third floor of the keep, and then they were out the other side into another long corridor. Gwenllian heard pounding footsteps along the passage and said a bad word—one that she'd heard one of the guardsmen say but knew she wasn't supposed to use. She said it again anyway and grabbed Arthur's hand, tugging him into one of the stairwells. They went up the steps and came out on the floor above.

"No, no, no!" The sight of men running towards her, this time from both directions, caused her heart to race even more than it already was. It was as if they knew where she was going to go before she went, and that thought made her even more angry. Arthur wasn't having fun anymore either. His face was screwed up as if he was about to cry. He was too heavy for her to carry anymore, but she picked him up anyway and then struggled up the last few steps to the top of the tower.

And that was when she realized she'd done exactly the wrong thing. She'd trapped herself and Arthur at the top of the keep.

Gwenllian looked through a crenel to what lay below her. Clare had confronted Lili in the receiving room, which was adjacent to the outer courtyard. The moat that ran past the west tower didn't extend around the whole castle, so only hard earth was below her. She thought about trying to *travel* to Avalon, but as she stared at the ground, she knew she couldn't risk Arthur's life on the chance that he had the same magic in him that his father had.

One of Clare's goons (Gwenllian loved the word goon. Her vocabulary had grown a lot since coming to live with Lili and Dafydd after Alexander's birth) came out of the stairwell and stopped. Gwenllian had nowhere to go, so he didn't even need to grab her. "This is for your own safety, princess."

Arthur, meanwhile, sobbed into her neck. When he was in full spate like this, it was best to let him cry it out, so what came next was up to Gwenllian. She gathered herself up and lifted her chin to project her voice in her best imitation of her mother. "You're scaring him!"

The man didn't appear to be dissuaded, since he grasped her by her upper arm and urged her towards the stairwell door. "This way."

Gwenllian's shoulders fell. There seemed no way for her to fight the soldier—or even to argue with him. He was as tall as Clare and wore mail armor. Punching him wouldn't hurt him, and she'd left off her belt knife this morning in order to play with Arthur. Even if she did manage to poke him in the eye, she was still carrying Arthur and had nowhere to go but down the stairwell anyway.

Despite the armor, the soldier moved so quickly down the stairs that she found herself struggling to stay upright as her boots slipped off the stone treads, especially with the Arthur's weight throwing her off-balance. The soldier took them all the way back to the receiving room where she found Clare and a handful of men guarding Lili.

Lili held Alexander in her arms. Neither his nanny nor his wet nurse had joined them. Maybe they were some of the people Clare didn't trust. Lili held out her free arm at the sight of Gwenllian and Arthur and gestured them into the circle of it. Wrapping them up in a hug, she bent to whisper in Gwenllian's ear. "It's going to be okay."

Gwenllian wanted to believe her.

Then Lili looked back to Clare. "I want to hear more about what happened to Dafydd. How do you know he's dead?"

Clare's shoulders rose and fell. "My queen, I'm sorry. My men were there."

Gwenllian looked up at Lili. "Aren't you going to tell him about—"

A strong hand came down on Gwenllian's shoulder, stopping her words. Lord Carew stood next to her. He didn't say anything, but the hard look in his eyes told her that the last thing he or Lili wanted Clare to know about was Lili's vision.

Fortunately, Clare's attention had remained on Lili, and he held out a hand to her, indicating that it was time to move. "I assure you—as I will assure Parliament when it convenes—that the French will pay for what they have done."

"You will lead our troops?" Lili started forward at Carew's urging. Gwenllian hoped he had a plan, because hers were all used up.

"Who else?" Clare said. "For the second time in nine months, France threatens to invade. We must have immediate leadership."

"You seek the throne, Gilbert?"

"My dear." Wide-eyed, with his hand to his chest, Clare stopped and turned to Lili. "The throne belongs to Arthur."

Through her natural mother, Elinor de Montfort, Gwenllian herself was the great-granddaughter of King John. For the first time, she wished she were older, because then she could have gone before Parliament and argued that *she* instead of Clare should be the one to lead England until Arthur came of age. She knew from listening to adult conversations how important royal blood was for claiming the throne, though Dafydd had never claimed to have royal English blood any more than Clare did. Dafydd did have plenty of royal Welsh blood, which seemed to have been enough for everyone.

Lili pressed her lips together and followed Clare through the doorway. Gwenllian was walking beside Lili, so she heard Carew's words when he leaned down to whisper in Welsh in Lili's ear. "Don't fight them for now. We'll find a way out of this. I will get word to our Templar friends somehow. They will help."

"They were supposed to have helped Dafydd already." Lili's lips barely moved as she answered.

"The only possible way that Clare could be standing before us today, in this hour, telling us of David's death, is if it was his man who shot those arrows at David and Philip, just as you dreamed. The fact that he wasn't there himself to witness it, as he had promised to be, is enough to convince me that he had a hand in it, despite his apparent sincerity today."

Gwenllian felt much better all of a sudden, and she thought Lili did too because she gave a jerky nod. "I wish I knew if Bridget and Peter reached Callum. And what of Bohun? Against all expectation, he has been one of our staunchest allies, and yet I left him to deal with Clare on his own."

"We could do only so much. If Clare is as smart as he appears to be, he will have taken over the radio relays and bent them to his own purposes," Carew said. "For now, they are as much on their own as we are."

The guards closed in on their little group and, under the guise of guarding them, with Clare leading the way, herded them into the bailey of the castle. Gwenllian's back was aching more than ever, but Arthur had wrapped himself around her— his arms around her neck and his legs around her waist—and she didn't want to make him more upset by putting him down or giving him up to someone else. Since Lili was already holding Alexander, there wasn't anyone to give him to anyway.

To Gwenllian's surprise and relief, Clare didn't head across the bailey towards the castle gate but turned the other way to walk deeper into the castle grounds. Earlier, when Clare had suggested they go to the Tower, Gwenllian had thought Clare meant the Tower of London, because everyone just called it the Tower. Clare however, had simply meant the tower that housed the king's quarters at Westminster.

Geoffrey de Geneville, Dafydd's ambassador to the French court, met them at the entrance. He canted his head to Clare. "It is done. Our men are in place."

"The queen thanks you, Geoffrey. It is good to know that all is well."

Geoffrey's expression blanked for a moment at Clare's words, but then he recovered and said, "As well as can be expected under the circumstances."

Clare nodded, a little shame faced. "My apologies. I was referring only to the security of the castle." He gestured to Lili. "I would appreciate it if you could continue to see to the comfort and safety of the queen and the children. They are not to be disturbed so they can mourn King David in peace."

"Of course, my lord."

Carew and Lili passed Geoffrey and Clare, who were still conferring, and crossed the ground floor room of the King's Tower. With Gwenllian hard on their heels, they entered the stairwell that would take them up to the chamber level.

Carew bent to Lili again. "My dear, Arthur isn't safe here. Is there any way for him to travel to Avalon as his father has done so often in the past? It might be that you're wrong about what happened with David, and he is already there. That could be why Clare thinks he's dead."

Lili started up the stairs. "You imply that Clare had nothing to do with it, Nicholas."

Nicholas grunted. "Lili—"

She cut him off, finally answering his question. "We don't know if Arthur has the gift of *travel*."

Gwenllian was straining so hard to eavesdrop on what they were saying that she almost tripped over her own feet. The stumble did give her the opportunity to get closer, just at the point that Carew lifted his chin to point briefly back down the stairs at Gwenllian and Arthur.

"As long as David's sons live, they are the rightful heirs to the throne. Clare may not be actively seeking the throne now, but he would take it if offered—and we don't know that Parliament won't offer, especially if he has the support of the Archbishop of Canterbury. I would have the boys hidden away in Avalon, to return when they were needed, as Llywelyn arranged for David when he was an infant in order to protect him."

Lili gave a brief shake of her head. "We can't risk Arthur's life."

"All your lives are forfeit," Carew said in an even lower voice. "You know that. Maybe not today, but soon. Even if Parliament doesn't offer Clare the crown, he will quietly remove you from Westminster, and nobody will ever hear from you again."

"I know. I know," Lili said. "With his behavior today, I see now that there is nothing he wouldn't dare."

Gwenllian was starting to shake. Any fool could see that they were in trouble, but for Clare to have decided to murder them—to murder little Arthur—was nearly impossible for her to get her head around. Carew seemed very sure of it, however, and that meant Gwenllian had to be sure of it too. Carew might be half-Norman, but he'd stood by Dafydd and her father even when the odds had been stacked against them, and this wasn't the time to be disbelieving him.

Carew was still shaking his head at Lili as they entered the king's apartments. Clare and Geoffrey had caught up by then and entered the chamber right behind Gwenllian.

Lili turned to Clare. "I really don't think this is necessary."

"It really is, my dear. We can't lose you and the boys too."

His words made Gwenllian angry again, which was better than being afraid, and she almost sneered at Clare. But she had lived all her life in a royal court and knew intrigue and plotting, even if it had never been directed at her. Her anger did give her courage, however. She saw now that Lili was right: the fact that Clare could plot against Dafydd one day, and then come to Westminster and express sincere grief the next, meant there was nothing he wouldn't dare to do.

12

14 June 1293

David

David woke Philip at first light, having by some miracle spent the night without encountering a soul. Maybe Clare's men couldn't see in the dark any better than David could and had called it a night too. It was too much to hope that they'd given up.

"This is not how I imagined I would spend my birthday," Philip said.

"We were going to have cake," David crouched beside him, checking his bandages, "and I hoped it would be a chance to celebrate the new treaty between us."

"We still have to talk about that," Philip said.

David tsked through his teeth. "Some other time."

While Philip had slept for a full eight hours at least, David had stood guard, though he'd dozed on and off despite his best efforts to stay awake. The combination of food and rest and another change of bandages had brightened Philip's eyes, and he appeared to be in a little less pain. Consequently, five hours later, they had actually made reasonable time—two miles an hour perhaps instead of the one mile an hour the day before—and it wasn't quite noon when the pair came to a halt on the outskirts of the village of La Rochelle.

David helped Philip down from the horse, and they crouched together on the edge of a small knoll south of the town. David cupped his hands around his eyes to block out the sun, which shone brightly down. The warmth was nice, but the clouds and rain from the night before would have been better, since they made them less likely to be detected. David had learned in his years in England that a man with his hood up against the weather was less likely to be stopped or questioned, and he'd specifically cautioned his own men to beware of men wearing hoods. One never knew what lay hidden beneath a cloak.

Still, David was grateful for the sun, which might even dry him out if it stayed around for a little longer. The padding under his mail hadn't dried much at all during the night. He had been wet almost nonstop for thirty-six hours now—first from the river, then from the rain, and now from sweat. When he finally reached safety again and took off everything he wore to have that long-awaited bath, he'd resemble a prune. Of course, he mocked himself, that was the least of his worries, though if Lili knew of it, she would fuss.

"We should rest at Vauclair Castle. It is just there."
Philip gestured towards the towers. Built of white sandstone,
which was luminous in the sunlight, Vauclair Castle had four
towers, and David's banner still waved from the tops of all of
them. "The men there will recognize you and aid us."

"They don't know me," David said, "I've never been here
before. They are as likely as the villagers we encountered to
believe Clare's men that I am the assassin."

Philip frowned. "Surely you can't doubt the loyalty of the
men in this castle too?"

David laughed softly, though without amusement.
"Surely, I can. Haven't you been paying attention? It is Clare
who garrisoned my castles; Clare who handpicked the men who
met me at the dock."

David hadn't set foot in Aquitaine—especially the
territory here which was newly acquired—until he and Philip
could meet because he hadn't wanted to rub Philip's face in
what he'd lost. Not to do so had been an important concession
on David's part. But of course, it had been Clare who'd
suggested that concession—and since he and Geoffrey de
Geneville had been David's foremost negotiators between the
two countries, and Geoffrey had agreed that such a concession
was vital, David had trusted their judgement.

The French king was still frowning. "I didn't realize the
extent of your mistake until now. I thought we just had to reach

La Rochelle, and we'd be safe. You would see that the Templars were not our only option."

David shook his head. "I trusted where I shouldn't have, but I did it because I was in the midst of negotiations with you."

Then, as they watched, three riders entered La Rochelle from the east and, in so doing, demonstrated perfectly why safety lay with the Templars or nowhere. David put a hand on Philip's good shoulder. "Get down."

They ducked below the level of the bushes in front of them. After a moment, David peered around the side, trying to get some kind of view of the road. Now it was Philip's turn to cup his hands around his eyes and swear under his breath. The men had approached the front gate of Vauclair Castle and were admitted. "They wear Clare's colors."

"They're his men, like every other horseman we've encountered, regardless of what colors they wear." David thought again of the man he'd killed. He didn't even know his name.

"Perhaps the castellan is innocent in this, and the news that you are dead and that the riders hunt your assassins will surprise him."

David raised his eyebrows but didn't actually laugh. "It's a nice thought, but now who is too trusting?"

Philip sighed. "I agree we cannot risk detection by anyone connected to Clare. The Templar commanderie it is—if you are sure that you can trust *them*."

"All the reports out of La Rochelle, even Clare's, indicate that the master was very pleased when his city was once again in English hands. The Templars have found a freedom under the rule of the English Duke of Aquitaine that has at times been absent under French kings."

Philip raised an eyebrow. "Now you're mocking me."

"Sorry," David said.

In fact, from the very beginning of the Templar order, the Templars and the kings of England had maintained a cordial, even mutually beneficial relationship. Temple Church was neutral ground, to the point that the great knight William Marshal had negotiated with the rebel barons there in the lead-up to the signing of Magna Carta. The Templars had remained loyal to King John throughout his kingship despite his many failings. To them, the divine right of kings to rule didn't apply only when the king was a good one.

Philip made a sour face. "The Templars pay homage to nobody but themselves, David. You would be wise to remember it."

"After the last two days, there's a lot I'm going to remember."

Philip muttered a curse as he dropped below the level of the bushes again. "If not for your quick thinking, Clare's plan would have worked."

"Clare's captain knows it too and seems to think that the situation is still salvageable. Containing the plot to Aquitaine is key."

"But once we slip through his fingers ..." Philip's voice trailed off.

"It is my hope that we are about to do exactly that. Clare cannot be so omnipotent as to have bought the Templars too."

They took a moment to rest on the ground under a nearby tree. David had filled the water skin several times throughout the course of the day, and now he silently handed it to Philip again. While the French king drank, David put the back of his hand to Philip's forehead as if he were one of David's sons. He was burning up. The fever had him shivering, even in the June sun. Philip grimaced and pulled the black cloak, the one David had used the night before, tighter around himself.

The cloak also hid his wound, which had soaked through the latest bandage. It might have soaked through the wool cloak too, but David couldn't distinguish the dark red blood from the black fabric without looking closely, which he decided he didn't need to do.

Up until the arrival of Clare's men, David had been thinking that it might be a good idea to leave Philip here, as he'd done back at last night's shelter, so he could approach the Templar compound alone and try the password Carew had given him without putting Philip at risk. But Philip's skin had a grayish cast to it that was worrisome. He needed attention, and he needed it now. Maybe having a sick man with David would be the tipping point to gaining admission to the commanderie—and reveal a previously unnoticed compassion among the Templars. Regardless, after an arduous journey, they were almost there and, blood or no blood, either Philip was going to find healing in the Templar commanderie, or David was going to die trying to get it for him.

"I don't want them to know who I am," Philip said.

That suited David just fine. "We don't have to tell them who you are. In fact, I was hoping we wouldn't have to."

"What makes you think they'll let you in?" Philip said, in a last ditch effort to change David's mind. "We have little money and no authority. These are warrior-monks, not mendicants. They don't give sanctuary to just anyone."

"They will give it to me," David said, "whether or not they know I am the Duke of Aquitaine."

Although Philip looked at David warily, for once he didn't argue or ask for clarification, and David didn't give it. If the password didn't work, David would look like a fool, but he'd rather not share more than he had to with Philip. For all the amiableness of their conversations, David had come to see that the French king lived up to his historical reputation. He was hard and ambitious and, quite frankly, not to be trusted in the long run to look out for anyone's interests but his own—even if in the short run his and David's aims aligned.

In fact, Philip reminded David of Humphrey de Bohun when he'd first met him. In those days, Humphrey had cared only for his own interests and would do anything to further them. He'd changed in the last few years since David had become King of England, almost as if the sharp edges, which the dog-eat-dog world of the March required in order for him to survive, had been worn down and softened, revealing a more vulnerable man beneath—a man he'd spent his adult life trying to hide. David's mother had assured David it was there, because she'd seen it. A few years of David's honesty and justice had been required to convince Humphrey that it was safe to show it again.

Which explained completely why David had worked so hard to keep Philip alive when it would have been far wiser and certainly expedient to eliminate him from the equation. And it also explained why David had all but ignored Clare's dubious past: until the day any of these men proved himself false, David felt it was necessary to accept him for the man he appeared to be.

In the coming weeks and months, many of David's barons and advisers were going to argue that he should have recognized Clare's duplicitous nature long ago, and that he had been naïve and stupid. Maybe they were right. If David lived to return to England, lots of people were going to be telling him *I told you so.* But even with the circumstances in which he now found himself, he could do no less for Philip than he'd done for Bohun or Clare.

"Only a little farther now." David boosted Philip onto the horse and hoped that his words weren't merely wishful thinking. If they were going to reach the commanderie, they had to pass through La Rochelle and that meant coming under the gaze of the men on Vauclair's towers.

They set off down the grassy slope and came out onto a narrow track that would take them into the town. With a population of a thousand, La Rochelle had its foundation as a sea port, but the economy had been augmented by the building of the castle and, of course, the presence of the Templars.

From La Rochelle, the Templars sent trading vessels to the Levant in order to connect with the Silk Road that led across Asia, thus creating a network of goods from Ireland to China. Although the fraternity of warrior-monks had been founded to take the Holy Land from the Saracens, by 1293 the Templars were one of the richest private organizations in the world, with interests in trade, banking, and politics. No wonder Philip would move to wipe them out fourteen years from now.

Since the fall of the Holy Land to the Muslims, a fleet of twenty ships had berthed permanently at the port. This meant that the town was also home to twenty crews— Templar knights, sergeants, and servants—who needed food, clothing, and materials, all supplied to them by the inhabitants of La Rochelle.

"We've been seen." Philip spoke the warning in a low tone.

David had been studiously ignoring Vauclair Castle, as if by looking at it or giving the men who manned it an acknowledgement of any kind, he would increase the chance of someone on the battlement alerting the castellan of their presence. Now, he glanced in the direction Philip indicated. The castle lay a quarter-mile to the north of the Templar commanderie. A half-dozen men stood high up on the tower battlements.

Even from this distance, it was possible to see several gesticulating in their direction, and David had no trouble imagining what they were saying. Unfortunately, David and Philip still had several football fields to go to reach the gate of the commanderie. But David wasn't helpless by any means, and he endeavored to tip the odds of making it to the commanderie in their favor.

First, he veered away from the middle of the road until he was following the north side of the street, which ran from east to west. Because the houses along the street were high enough that the angle was wrong, he concealed their progress from the watching eyes at the top of the tower. Unfortunately, the change of position also meant that David couldn't see what was happening at the castle.

Second, he gave up on leading the horse and swung himself onto the horse's back behind Philip. They were two large men, and it was too much weight for the horse to carry very far, but he could carry them to the front gate of the commanderie. It was the only way David and Philip were going to get through the Templar gate in one piece.

"Come on!" David spurred the horse, which leapt forward.

Almost immediately, the line of houses ended, and they emerged from the narrow road on which they'd been traveling into a green space that gave them a direct line of sight to the castle—and vice versa. A small company of riders, six or eight at most, emerged from underneath the gatehouse and started towards them.

"*Mon Dieu*," Philip said, each word accompanied by an obvious gasp of pain. "We're not going to make it."

The horse's gait was causing him to bounce up and down. If David hadn't been so near to panic, he would have been wincing too in sympathy. "Yes, we are. We have come too far to falter now." Sensitive to the moods of humans, the horse whinnied and readily quickened its pace.

David wasn't going to stand for anything less than freedom. He'd survived the fall from Chateau Niort's battlement without time traveling, which meant that he was going to keep on living, come hell or high water. All along, Clare may have viewed him as a jumped-up Welsh interloper, but he was sorely mistaken if he thought David was going to be killed that easily. He had a family that loved him, and a country that needed him. Two countries. Three if he included Aquitaine. And he didn't think it was vanity or hubris to say so.

Although initially the riders had left the castle gate at a trot, shouts and pointing fingers from the men at the top of the castle battlement caught their attention. Once the lead rider realized how close he was to his prey, he urged his horse into a gallop.

Meanwhile, with sixty yards to go, David didn't care if Philip was barely holding on as long as he wasn't actually falling off.

Forty yards.

David knew now that they were going to make it to the door. Whether or not they'd be admitted was still an open question. A stone wall encircled the whole commanderie, and it was guarded by two great wooden doors, which were armored with iron fittings, iron nails driven through the boards every few inches, and iron panels like the scaly hide of a stegosaurus. David didn't have time to wait for the doors to open. Even if the gatekeeper saw him coming, it would take too long for him to swing the gate wide.

Instead, David made for the wicket gate inset into the left hand door, slowing the horse before he barreled into it. The small doorway was only four feet high, meaning the men would fit but not the horse. Thus, David dismounted almost before the horse had completely stopped and pulled Philip down after him. Inset into the wicket door was a small barred window that the gatekeeper could open without jeopardizing the security of the commanderie. Somebody on the wall-walk must have been paying attention because the gatekeeper pulled open the window and poked his nose through the bars before David had to pound his fist on the door.

"Who are you?" The gatekeeper was a gray-haired, gray-bearded man in middle age, with bright blue eyes that looked at David with curiosity. Then they tracked to the region over David's left shoulder. David didn't need to turn to know that the man's eyes had fixed on the men riding towards them.

"Stop! Don't let them in! Those are wanted men!"

Trying to speak calmly despite the fact that what he really wanted to do was reach through the window and shake the gatekeeper, David put his face right up to the opening so that the gatekeeper would be looking only at him. *"Et mortuus est in Golgotha."*

Translated into English, the passcode said, *He died at Golgotha,* referring to the place where Jesus was crucified.

As Carew had promised, the gatekeeper didn't blink, question, or hesitate. He pulled open the wicket door. David had his arms wrapped around Philip's waist, holding him upright, and he half-carried/half-dragged him across threshold.

Then with only seconds to spare, the gatekeeper slammed the door shut in the faces of Clare's men.

13

14 June 1293

Callum

"Someone is here, my lord, from Clare." Samuel came to a halt in front of Callum.

Callum, Cassie, and Jeffries had been sitting to one side of the high table, taking a moment to eat and speak a few words to each other. They'd spent the six hours since the arrival of Bridget and Peter frantically preparing for exactly this. Callum had called in his men from some of the surrounding areas, outposts which he regularly patrolled. He'd sent for goods and supplies from outlying towns as well and personally inspected the entire perimeter of Shrewsbury Castle's walls while Peter inspected the town's. If Clare was to lay siege to Shrewsbury, the more men and resources Callum had inside the town the better. Unfortunately, this was far sooner than Callum had thought Clare's men would come, and they weren't ready.

"How many men does he have?" Callum stood, straightening his tunic as he did so.

"Twenty," Samuel said.

"Not enough to really challenge us." Though she remained seated, Cassie took her feet off the chair, where she'd been resting them to counter the swelling of her ankles in late pregnancy. "What's his plan?"

"I suppose we should find out." Callum looked at Samuel. "Send a runner to Peter to let him know that Clare's men are here, and then I guess we let them in." He turned to Jeffries. "See to the men, as we discussed."

"Yes." Jeffries disappeared through a side door.

"We're still allies," Cassie said. "It's only because of Lili's vision that we're even half-prepared."

"We shall see what kind of treachery he has in store for us." Callum took Cassie's hand and walked with her to the front of the hall. "Are you ready?"

"As I'll ever be."

Two minutes later, Samuel ushered Clare's captain and his men through the front gate. The rain had stopped, though the clouds hung low in the sky and the bailey was full of puddles. Callum had deliberately arranged for only a half-dozen members of the garrison to show themselves around the perimeter of the bailey. He wanted to hear what Clare's captain had to say before he threatened him.

Clare's captain bowed and introduced himself as Robert de Valles. Tall and thin, he had a supercilious air that immediately put Callum off. "I bring grave news, my lord. We have received word from Aquitaine that our noble King David has been murdered by agents of Charles, the brother to the King of France."

A sudden shiver went through Callum. *Lili really did have the sight.*

Callum didn't know what he thought about that. It went against his logical mind to believe in anything supernatural. But then—he'd been forced to believe in time travel too, so he supposed dreams that were true weren't much of a stretch. Even Anna, David's sister, had dreamt true *seeings* of her mother when she'd first come to Wales. Maybe there was something in the air in this universe that made such things possible.

All Callum knew was that without Lili's vision, he would have been standing before Valles, in uncertainty and deep grief, facing the complete loss of not only his close friend but everything they'd worked so hard to build.

Callum cleared his throat and tried to appear as if he was fighting back sorrow. "Why didn't Queen Lili send me a message by radio?"

"My lord Clare felt that it would be better if you didn't have to learn of King David's death by such impersonal means."

Valles worked at his v-shaped beard, twisting it to a fine point. "My lord Clare only wishes that he could have come himself to tell you the news."

Cassie came down the steps so she could talk to Valles without shouting. "How did Clare learn of David's death in Aquitaine if he is in London?"

That was the question of the hour, but Valles was ready for it. "Pigeon."

Callum grimaced. If David was attacked on the evening of the twelfth, the only way Clare could have a man here, on the morning of the fourteenth, was if a pigeon had been sent immediately from Chateau Niort. The risk of a pigeon messenger going astray was high, which meant that Clare had been lucky. Callum didn't like to see that in anyone but David.

What was also clear was that the only way Valles could have reached Shrewsbury in such a timely fashion was if he'd been sent west days ago and been simply waiting for confirmation of David's death.

"Why was Clare in London in the first place? Wasn't he supposed to be in Aquitaine with David?" Cassie said, innocence in her voice, though the question she asked was calculated.

"He was delayed in traveling to Aquitaine."

"Lucky for him." Cassie frowned at Valles, her face a block of ice, and the temperature in the bailey on this warm June morning dropped precipitously.

Callum made slight motion with one hand in Cassie's direction, asking her to subside. "Have you dined? Perhaps over a meal you could tell me more."

"I know nothing more than I have said, my lord, and I am not here to dine." Valles paused, his eyes on Callum, searching. "I am here on the behalf of Earl Gilbert to ask for your support for his leadership."

It was as if Valles had dumped a bucket of cold water over Callum's head. "Clare seeks the throne?"

Valles made a dismissive motion. "Of course not. Arthur is the rightful heir to the throne, but my lord Clare is concerned, with King David dead, that the barons will fight among themselves for power. Someone must step forward. At the very least, Parliament must appoint him regent immediately if we are to counter the French threat."

Clare might claim that he didn't want the throne, but Callum was starkly reminded of the actions of King Stephen a hundred and fifty years ago. Upon the death of King Henry I, who'd died of eating too many lampreys (which sounded implausible enough to make one think that the king had been hurried along to his death), Stephen had raced for the French coast and a ship for England. Once Stephen made it to London, his kingship had been a foregone conclusion, since it was his brother, the Bishop of Winchester, who'd done the crowning. In so doing, Stephen had put himself ahead of Henry's daughter, the rightful heir to the throne.

The result had been nineteen years of civil war and anarchy in England. Clare would know that history, of course, and would want to avoid it by preempting any objection to his rule before it could fully form. David was a strong king by pretty much any standard. Clare would be the same—even more so because he was ruthless in a way David wasn't.

"You are certain that France is responsible for the assassination?" Callum said.

"We have no doubts. Charles of France is a treacherous snake." Valles held out a hand to Callum. "Can Earl Gilbert count on your support?"

"For England, yes," Callum said. "I cannot offer my support to Clare for the regency, however. Not without meeting with him first."

"You want it for yourself." Valles nodded. "My lord Clare assumed you would feel that way, but he wanted to give you the chance to ally with him. What I do now is for the good of England."

And with that, Valles sprang without warning upon Cassie, pulling her back against him with an arm around her neck and a knife to her belly. Valles men responded too, forming a circle around them, swords out and ready.

"It will be better for you and your lady wife if you come quietly." Valles had a definite note of triumph in his voice.

Callum's own men had all been on guard, all warned that Valles might not be what he seemed, and all of them pulled their weapons from their sheaths too. Callum noted the eyes of some of his men flicking this way and that, looking for a way to turn the tables on Valles and his men. Each had hidden knives or darts up their sleeves. Callum wore them too as a matter of course, but with Cassie in peril, they could not use them.

Instead, he sheathed his sword, put up his hands, and said, "Hold!"

His men subsided as instructed, but they didn't sheath their swords.

Valles lifted his chin. "You will put down your weapons or your lady dies."

Nobody obeyed. This wasn't quite the scenario Callum had planned for, but it was close enough that he could adapt. "If you kill her, your own life is forfeit. You know that."

"If you fight me, you will lose men, and your wife will die anyway."

They were at a stalemate. Valles gave a quick nod in Callum's direction. "I beg you to reconsider. Come with me to London. Clare desires your friendship and counsel."

Callum gestured to Cassie and his men. "What of my wife and my men?"

"They will stay here, under the protection of my company, as assurance that you will keep your word. Tell your men to stand down."

"Release my wife, and I will do as you ask."

"You will go to London?"

"I swear it."

Finally, the castle's warning bell clanged loudly from one of the gatehouse towers. *Awake! Awake! To arms! To arms!* At the same time, Jeffries and the bulk of the garrison filed along the top of the wall-walk, the archers among them with bow in hand and arrow nocked. In ten seconds, Valles had gone from twenty men against a half-dozen to being outnumbered three to one.

That moment of distraction was all that Cassie needed. With the expertise of the MI-5 agent she was, she twisted away from Valles, but instead of seeking the safety of Callum's arms, she upended Valles. In a split-second, he was on the ground with his own knife, which Cassie had relieved him of, at his throat.

"Put down your weapons." Cassie's voice rang out amidst the clamor of surprise and shock.

With their position reversed, outmanned and outmaneuvered, Valles's men obeyed—without Callum having to unholster his gun, which had definitely been an option, or spill a single drop of blood.

Jeffries relieved Cassie of Valles, allowing Callum to gather Cassie into his arms. "Are you all right?"

"He was never going to hurt me. He should have known better than to come in here with so few men."

"If we hadn't been forewarned of Clare's treachery, I might have given him my assurances," Callum said. "Nobody would have had to get hurt."

Cassie snorted. "Nobody did get hurt—well, except for Valles's pride at being bested by a pregnant woman."

Samuel halted in front of Callum, though he shifted from one foot to the other, looking unusually awkward. "I apologize, my lord. If I had been more observant—"

Callum made a chopping motion with his hand, cutting Samuel off. The big Englishman had been the first to obey Callum's command not to attack, knowing that if he did as Valles ordered, the others would follow. Cassie's life had been at risk, and there was nothing else he could have done. Callum had instilled in all of his men the idea that it was far more honorable to live to fight another day than to die because of pride. In Callum's view, putting pride above running an earldom was a shortcut to no longer running that earldom. David wouldn't thank him for that.

SARAH WOODBURY

But figuring out what David *did* want him to do was suddenly far more urgent. Lili really had been gifted a vision, even if Callum himself didn't have a clue how that was possible. He'd never had that mystical surety that Cassie claimed from her Native American ancestors or Lili from her Celtic ones. What he did have was people to protect. If David lived, he was going to come home to find that Shrewsbury still stood for him. And if he didn't live, Shrewsbury would become the easternmost outpost of the Kingdom of Wales, the border of which was only seven miles away.

Callum could have cursed himself for ever trusting Clare, who had a history of changing sides in war. Nearly thirty years ago, as a young man, he'd fought on the same side as David's father, Llywelyn, and Simon de Montfort in the Baron's War, even putting his name to a pact that would have divided England and Wales among the three of them. Then, at a moment when Montfort's rule stood on a knife's edge, he'd changed allegiance, betraying all the Marcher barons he'd allied with, including his foster father, Humphrey de Bohun (the current Humphrey's grandfather), and putting his considerable resources at the disposal of King Henry and Edward.

The current Humphrey's father had lost his life at Evesham because of that betrayal. At the time, Humphrey had been sixteen to Clare's eighteen. The eldest Humphrey de Bohun, having buried his son, had gone on bended knee to

Henry in order to regain his lands, but Callum knew that none of the Bohuns had ever forgiven either Edward or Clare for the outcome of that war.

It was odd to think that the three Humphrey de Bohuns—grandfather, father, and son—had seen more clearly than any of them.

14

14 June 1293

David

"Those men are wanted for the murder of the Duke of Aquitaine!"

It wasn't clear to whom the rider was speaking—perhaps to the guards on the tower of the gatehouse. In his quick glances over his shoulder, David hadn't recognized any of the men chasing him, so he hadn't been able to tell if they were the same riders he and Philip had encountered at the village right after they'd come out of the water.

The gatekeeper himself stood with his back to the wicket door, pressed against it as if he, a lone man, could prevent Clare's men from battering it down if they chose to try. The black tunic with a red cross he wore indicated that he was a sergeant in the order and not a knight. Watching *Kingdom of Heaven* twenty times in the year before he'd come to this world hadn't prepared David for the variety and complexity of monastic orders and their attire, but he knew that much.

They had entered a central paved courtyard, laid with white tiles adorned with a great, central Templar cross. Facing away from the gatehouse, the three other sides of the square consisted of a stable to the left, a huge stone church directly ahead, and what appeared to be barracks and a cloister off to the right. Like the white paving stones at David's feet, everything was worked in stone and finely crafted, with great attention to detail, down to the little carvings of shields and crosses on the walls as decoration, a match to the symbol on the tiles.

Nobody had yet arrived in the courtyard to see what the fuss was about, which was either because the Templars had no curiosity at all or because they had a level of discipline that David envied. If he'd been standing sentry somewhere on the battlements, he'd be wondering what was going on and tempted to take a few steps to find out. But no head appeared from around the stonework above the gate, and the wall-walk that encircled the interior of the curtain wall was empty of observers.

"We are also supposed to have murdered the King of France, I might add," David said in a dry tone to the gatekeeper. "Naturally, we didn't do it, but we do know who is behind the plot, which is why those men are so anxious to capture us."

"The Duke and King are dead?" The gatekeeper had the look of a man who few pieces of news could faze, but David's had surprised him.

"Many untruths may be spread throughout Aquitaine and France in the coming days and weeks, and that is one of them. Neither is dead. Don't believe they are, no matter how certain the man who tells you." David gestured with his head to indicate the men beyond the gate. "Like them."

Whether from Avalon or this world, people thrived on gossip, and news could spread quickly around the countryside like a game of telephone—aided and abetted by the riders who'd been following David and Philip for two days. Without any media to counteract the gossip, lies would be believed and could ferment for months and years in little villages and hamlets before people finally learned the truth.

The gatekeeper gave David a steady look, which David returned unflinchingly. He wasn't telling the gatekeeper that he himself was the Duke of Aquitaine. It was more that he meant for the man to look into his eyes and see truth. And it seemed that the gatekeeper did believe him, or maybe it was simply that David's password promised him not only entry but no pressing questions or explanations by the man who admitted him. As David and Philip were now captive inside the Templar compound, those questions could be put to him by the master.

After a slight narrowing of the eyes and a quick nod of the head, the gatekeeper moved away from the door enough to swing closed the metal grid that supported it on the inside. The riders outside were still shouting their objections to David's disappearance, but the gatekeeper ignored them and drove the lock home. Since the walls on either side of the door were made of stone, and iron rods were shot through them and mortared, the door was as sturdy as any door could be. It was such a relief to be safe that David let out a breath. Clare's men, complicit or not, weren't getting to them right this second.

Still not having spoken more than a handful of words, the gatekeeper stood with his hands on his hips, looking from David, who loomed over him, to Philip, who, if anything, looked even grayer than before. Philip swayed slightly, opened his mouth to speak, but closed his eyes before he could.

"He's passing out!" David had been holding Philip up. Awake, with his feet under him, he wasn't too much of a burden, but an unconscious Philip was too heavy to be held. David went down on one knee in order to lay Philip on the ground and then looked up at the gatekeeper. "This man needs the infirmary."

Proving himself as capable as first impression had implied, the gatekeeper gave a sharp whistle. After a moment, two younger men, servants or squires since they didn't wear the cross, hastened out of one of the buildings that surrounded the courtyard.

One of the newcomers nudged David aside so he could care for Philip, and David let him. The Templars were knights, destined to fight for the Holy Land, but also monks, and the two roles meshed well for David's purposes. Monks were known for their herbs and healing, and Templar monks worked hard to perfect the healing arts because men in their order routinely went into battle and were wounded.

The second man the gatekeeper had called disappeared for a few minutes before returning with a stretcher and men to carry it. They loaded Philip onto it and headed off into the nether regions of the commanderie. At a gesture from the gatekeeper, David followed, and he had to assume that word of the arrival of two strangers, one of them wounded, would reach the master, whether through the gatekeeper or one of the other guards.

The four stretcher bearers took Philip along a covered walkway that formed one side of the cloister, out a back door, and then along an open flagstone pathway to the infirmary. Even in June, a fire burned in a grate, vented out the back of the building by a half-chimney, and the room was warm.

The infirmarer, this man dressed in Templar white, with a long gray beard, greeted them. "Over there."

Of the ten beds in the room, only three were occupied, and Philip was maneuvered onto one of the free ones. The infirmarer then dismissed all but one young man, who seemed to be his aide.

Then the infirmarer sat on the edge of Philip's bed and gently began the process of removing the bandages and inspecting the wound. David watched in silence. He'd already done everything he could for Philip, and this man clearly knew his business.

The Templar spoke into the silence. "I understand that you arrived with a password. Am I not to ask your name?" He turned to look up at David. "Or his?"

"You can call him Jacques," David said.

The Templar grunted a laugh. "Of course I can. Well—" He leaned forward to inspect the wound, which he'd bared, and then took a wet cloth from the bowl of water his aide held and began dabbing at the blood. "I believe the master would see you now."

David turned to look behind him. A Templar knight, dressed like the infirmarer in the full regalia Templars were always supposed to wear, stood in the doorway. He appeared to be in his mid-thirties, with the nearly black hair, brown eyes, and olive skin of someone from more southern parts of Europe.

"I am Henri. I will escort you to the master."

David nodded, internally bracing himself for what was to come. He honestly didn't know in this moment if he was going to tell the commanderie's master, Pierre de Villiers, the truth. Would Clare have gone so far as to woo him, convince him that David was an ineffective king and would never support a new crusade like the Templars hoped? Certainly, Clare and Villiers had met. Because the Templars were focused on victory in the Holy Land—possibly at all costs—they might be buyable. David had placed his trust in the wrong man, and now he was more than a little wary about trusting anyone else.

It would have been much better for David if Clare's captain had continued to believe that he and Philip had been mortally wounded when they'd fallen into the river, and their bodies hadn't been found because they'd been swept out to sea. Even if he'd already sent word to Clare that David was dead, he would certainly need to inform Clare now that David was alive. Somehow, David had to convince Pierre to aid him in beating the news home.

Henri took David through the main hall and along a corridor to a closed door. Barred and blackened, it was nearly as formidable as the main gate. Henri knocked, received a faintly heard permission to enter, opened the door for David, and gestured him through it.

David found himself in a reception room—more of an office, really—not unlike his own, which testified yet again to the wealth and power of the Templars. The room contained a large table that served as a desk, several chairs, and a grate in which a fire was burning brightly. The window opened onto a garden surrounded by a high wall that formed the perimeter of the Templar holding. Pierre stood before the window, looking out, with his hands clasped behind his back.

David took two hesitant steps into the room. Henri didn't enter with him, and it wasn't until the door clicked shut that the Templar master turned to study David—still in silence. David didn't speak either, not because he didn't feel like it was his place or because he felt somehow inferior to the older man, but because he was taking the measure of Pierre too. Gray-haired like most of these Templars seemed to be, Pierre was tall and thinner than looked healthy on him, as if he'd recently lost a great deal of weight. Templars weren't as ascetic as other monks, since they could be called upon to fight at any moment, which was difficult to do well on an empty stomach. Pierre, David guessed, had recently been ill—and might still be.

After another few heartbeats of study, Pierre gestured towards a chair on the other side of his desk. "Please come forward into the light and sit. My eyes aren't what they used to be."

David settled himself into the cushioned chair, which wasn't a luxury he would have expected from a Templar, even a master. The place where the arrows had hit his chest really hurt, and he let out a low groan as he leaned back. He was bone-tired, and acknowledgement of that fact almost had him standing up again out of fear that if he sat for more than a minute, his muscles would lock, and he wouldn't be able to move again today.

Pierre sat too—with a similar groan and a sigh. "Getting old isn't for the faint of heart."

Given what David had just been thinking, that was worth a laugh, though to do so hurt his chest too. Pierre sounded so much like Bevyn, so he answered him with Bevyn's words. "It is the price we pay for living."

"Ah." Pierre's eyes brightened as he looked at David. "A philosopher. I've heard that about you, my lord."

David froze.

Pierre patted a pair of glasses on his desk. "I have you to thank for these."

David felt himself stuttering. "Have-have we met?"

"I attended your crowning alongside the master of Temple Church."

David shook his head. "That was a busy week. I'm sorry to say I don't remember."

Pierre flicked his fingers as if it were no matter. "Much has happened since then."

David felt like saying, "You can say that again," but refrained. He didn't have a read on Pierre yet and was afraid of putting a foot wrong.

"I was invited to Chateau Niort to dine with you the evening King Philip arrived, but I have been—" Pierre paused a moment before continuing, "incapacitated."

David hadn't been told any of that, and he wondered how differently that night would have gone if Pierre had been at the chateau. Maybe Clare's captain would have blithely murdered him too.

"I heard the news of your assassination not two hours ago from my own men. The news grieved me sorely, for the sake of my Order as well as the people you rule. Your death would bring disorder yet again to Aquitaine—and to England." He gestured to David. "But here you are alive and on the run. Why did you not seek sanctuary at Vauclair or any number of your castles between here and Chateau Niort? Surely Charles's influence doesn't reach this far?"

David gave a rueful grunt. "Is that what you heard—that the man behind the assassination was Philip's brother, Charles?"

Pierre nodded. "You're saying he isn't?"

"Oh, he might be behind it all right, but he had help on this end from Gilbert de Clare, who I would peg as the actual mastermind. Did you hear what those men who were chasing us said? They accused us of murder."

"Who are you supposed to have murdered?"

"Ourselves!" David laughed. "It's an ingenious plan, actually. Clare's captain must have been hoping we'd be executed on sight, long before we could prove our identity."

"You say *our*? Then—"

"Yes. My wounded companion is Philip, the King of France." There didn't seem to be any point in hiding his identity, now that David's was out of the bag.

Pierre leaned forward, his gaze intent. "By your very presence, I believe you that there is a plot against you, but do you have any proof that Clare is behind it?"

"Are not the words spoken by Clare's men enough?" And then David explained all the reasons why it had to be Clare who'd orchestrated everything. With each item he listed, David found his anger rising again, and he fought to tamp it back down.

"I kept one of the arrows the assassin shot at me. It is Welsh-made, loosed from a longbow rather than a crossbow." He looked straight into Pierre's eyes. "Do you believe me?"

Pierre held David's gaze for a few seconds and then nodded. "Do not fear, my lord. You have come to the one place in all of Aquitaine where you are safe."

David breathed more easily. He'd poured out everything he knew to Pierre because he'd needed to do so. His welfare was entirely in Pierre's hands, seeing how he was captive in a Templar stronghold. If he couldn't trust this Templar, he had nowhere else to turn. "I had hoped as much. It was my understanding that if you served anyone, it would not be Gilbert de Clare."

"Unfortunately for Clare, he did not include us Poor Fellow-Soldiers of Christ in his calculations, I don't think," Pierre said, using the formal name of the Templars. "The pope has made a similar error."

David leaned forward. "Boniface and Clare are in league together?" He'd been so preoccupied with survival that the idea that Clare had been working with the Church as well as Charles hadn't occurred to him. Boniface couldn't see the future like David could, so he couldn't know that he would die at the behest of Philip in 1303, or that the great writer, Dante, would place Boniface in the eighth circle of hell for questing after temporal power. That was in Avalon, of course, where Boniface wasn't yet pope. There, the papacy had been left empty for two years as a result of bickering over the election. Whether due to David's presence or some other vagary of fate, they'd been stuck with Boniface in this world a little early.

But even without knowing his own future, Boniface could see a threat when it stared him in the face, and both

David and Philip jeopardized his power. He'd begun by threatening to excommunicate David as a way to control him. When that hadn't worked, he tried to co-opt David by calling for a new crusade and putting him at the head of it. That hadn't worked yet either.

Pierre, however, hastily put up his hands. "Not to have you murdered, I don't believe. Not that. But they have met. Clare supports a new crusade and has assured the pope that he does not share your curious religious—" he paused as he appeared to search for the word, "—convictions."

David rubbed his chin. He was speaking to a Templar master, a monk, and a man completely committed to the Church, but he couldn't let that pass. "I desire peace for all peoples, regardless of their religion, and I do not condemn a man for not sharing mine."

"Yes, yes. I know. But we must have Jerusalem."

David canted his head, in apology and appeasement, deciding they'd better talk about something else. "With the events of last Christmas, we did not take the chatter about Clare seriously. That was our mistake for which I apologize and—" he gave a mocking laugh, "—for which it seems I have paid in full."

Pierre accepted the change of subject. "For my part, the directives coming out of Italy are disturbing. Boniface is pressing our grand master, Jacques de Molay, to renew our assault on the Holy Land this year. If we do not, he insists we should disband immediately."

Pierre left *and give up our wealth to Boniface* unsaid, but it was what Pierre meant and what Boniface wanted.

David didn't want to offend Pierre, but he couldn't help asking the question: "Wouldn't taking back the Holy Land be the purpose of your order?"

"Of course," Pierre said, "but God's kingdom is forever. Far better to delay the renewal of our attempt to wrest the Kingdom of Jerusalem from Muslim hands until we have an actual chance of success, rather than waste the lives of good men."

"I can't argue with that," David said, glad to have found a point of agreement. "I gather Boniface can?"

"And has."

The two men were speaking more companionably than David would have thought possible twenty minutes ago. Or ever. But then David noticed that Pierre was fingering the papers on the desk in front of him in a way that made David think he had something else to say. "If there is more, please tell me."

"You yourself met this spring with our new grand master, did you not?"

"I did," David said. Jacques de Molay was the same grand master of the Templars whom Philip would murder in

1307. He wasn't to be confused with Jacques de Molier, the fat French emissary Philip had sent to David last Christmas. Duplication of names wasn't just a Welsh headache. "He wanted my support for the crusade. He seemed very enthusiastic and happy that Boniface had openly called for one."

"He is," Pierre said. "His first objective, however, must be to fortify Cyprus. Only when the island is secure can we use it as a base to launch our attack on the Mamluks. Until it is refortified, any attempt to retake Jerusalem will end in failure. Boniface wants us to attack now, to gain a beachhead at Acre, perhaps—and that success will then force you and Philip to lend your support. It is my understanding that Clare has promised Boniface that he will devote huge resources to the endeavor."

"In exchange for what?" David said.

Pierre shrugged in a very French way. "In light of recent events, Clare might have asked for the throne of England, were anything to happen to you. Perhaps he seeks to rule in the Holy Land itself. Were we to wrest Jerusalem from Muslim hands, it would need a Christian king."

"Clare wants that crown too?" David barked a laugh. "He has a plan for everything."

"Except for your survival," Pierre said. "He didn't count on that."

15

14 June 1293

David

"**M**aster, Sir Beloit, the steward of Vauclair, has come, requesting an audience." Henri's deep voice spoke urgently from behind the door, which he did not open.

Pierre raised his eyebrows at David. "Will Beloit know you by sight?"

"No," David said. "And I do not know where his loyalties lie. It is possible he is in league with Clare."

"I have always found Beloit a fair-minded man," Pierre said doubtfully. "He might be overjoyed to know that the news Clare's men brought is false and that you are alive."

"If Clare has taught me anything these last two days, it is that I trust too easily. Bad enough that we were spotted fleeing into your commanderie. In the last hour, Beloit could already have sent a boat to England to inform Clare that I am alive.

Without the protection of men loyal to me, I am vulnerable to a knife between the ribs anywhere between here and London."

Pierre pushed to his feet and came around the desk, only to pause in front of David, who'd also risen. "You would prefer that your people believe you dead?" He said this in the form of a question, but it was really a censure.

"I'm still hoping I can beat the news home. But if I can't, until I can stand before Parliament in Westminster Hall, and they can see that I am truly alive, I don't see the benefit of a premature resurrection."

"But your wife—"

"I know." David cut him off, sickened at the thought of Lili's grief, as he had been for two days. "But if Clare learns that I am alive, do you think he would be more or less likely to murder her and my sons? *He just tried to murder me.* What would they be to him but a few more casualties on the way to the throne?"

"You are stronger than I had been led to believe. We here thought you'd traded some of your power to your barons out of a need of their favor, but that isn't what you've done, is it?" Pierre paused with a hand on the latch. "As is written in our charter, *a strong man has no need to prove his strength.* The next time someone questions your actions or your character, I will remember that you also adhere to the Templar way."

David still didn't feel like he'd done anything special, except to keep doing what he thought was right even when other people didn't understand or approve of it. Even before he became Prince of Wales, he'd been raised to make his own decisions. He'd found that following a moral code with clear boundaries, ones which he would never cross even when tested, made the rest of his life easier, not harder. He suspected that a Templar like Pierre understood that idea perfectly.

Pierre pulled open the door, surprising Henri, who'd been preparing to knock again. "What is the status of our patient?"

"If he survives the fever, he will live. If his wound suppurates, he may die," Henri said matter-of-factly. "His life is in God's hands."

"As are ours," Pierre said in a manner that sounded reflexive and automatic. He was a monk, after all.

David stepped closer. "If his wound goes bad, how many days does he have to live before his death is inevitable?"

Henri looked at Pierre, but the Templar master canted his head to indicate that Henri should answer. The younger man grimaced. "Though I am not a healer, I would say that with a wound like that he could last as short a time as five days or for as long as a few weeks."

It was as David feared. If he could get to England, he could send Abraham or Rachel to France in time to save Philip.

SARAH WOODBURY

It was equally likely that Philip's fate would be decided before then, but it was worth a shot.

"Thank you, Henri," Pierre said. "Please put Beloit in the reception room and tell him I will be right there."

Henri nodded and departed, leaving Pierre and David alone, both still standing near the open door.

"Beloit thinks you are harboring my murderer," David said. "What are you going to do about that?"

Pierre's eyes crinkled at the corners. "Perhaps a small sleight of hand is in order. We have one or two prison cells here. I will arrange for the temporary incarceration of two of my men, one apparently injured, and see to it that they look like you and King Philip.

"I take it as given that he will be safe here too?"

"Yes."

"How quickly can you get me to England, specifically to the port of Hythe?"

"Four days by ship, if the winds are fair," Pierre said.

"Four days." David ran his hands through his hair, and for a moment despair overtook him. While David had built a radio network with coverage from Dover to Caerphilly, he hadn't yet built the Chunnel.

"It is the same four days it will take for Clare to hear of your death," Pierre said.

"No." David shook his head. "Not quite. His men shot us near midnight on June 12th, and here it is the afternoon of the 14th already. If he sent word immediately, he has a two-day head start."

David chose not to complicate the issue by mentioning the string of radio stations he'd built across southern England, which would allow Clare's men, once they reached Dover, to relay the news of David's death to London instantly. Once he himself arrived, David could use the stations too, if they weren't held against him, which he had to think they would be. In six months, he'd made long strides towards duplicating the modern world's preoccupation with the speed at which information could be disseminated.

David laughed under his breath. Maybe that was going to turn out to be a mistake, on top of all the other ones he'd made, and he'd made many.

Pierre studied David for a moment. "If you are serious about getting home faster, you can get there yourself in three days: two of riding and one more of sailing, with a favorable wind from the south, but it will not be easy."

"Just tell me."

"The Templars have established stations every ten miles or so along every major road through France, including from here to Le Havre. With a pass from me, you can ride as fast as the horses will take you, trading a worn horse for a fresh one every ten miles, which is how far one of our horses can gallop before tiring. The only barrier to how long your journey will take is your ability to keep going."

"How many miles is it to Le Havre?"

"Three hundred and twenty."

David gaped at him. "That's thirty-two changes of horse!"

"If you feel it's impossible—"

"I didn't say that. Has it been done before?"

"No."

David would have laughed again at the absurdity of what Pierre was suggesting if it didn't hurt to laugh and he himself wasn't taking it seriously. In the late eighteen-hundreds in the United States, the pony express sent mail nineteen hundred miles across the west in ten days, though with no one man riding more than a hundred miles. That was only eight miles an hour. With enough fresh horses, three hundred and twenty miles could be done in two days with eight hours to spare.

He scratched the top of his head as he thought. "Okay. I will be traveling through territories controlled by many lords between here and there. They won't stop me?"

"We have arranged unrestricted passage for our people, no matter their mission, through every baron's territory between here and Calais. If you dress as one of us, you will be viewed as one of us. Some might say I violate my own vows by suggesting such a deception, but—" Pierre tipped his head to study David, "—are we not called to crusade together? Do not our interests and England's align, even in the face of the pope's obstinacy? If you do not make England and stop Clare, it might be the end of the Templars."

"You can't be helping me because of the crusade," David said. "As it stands now, I won't be going."

Pierre lifted one shoulder. "One never can fully foresee the paths down which God will lead a man."

David allowed himself an actual laugh, genuinely amused. "No, one cannot."

Then Pierre frowned. "If Clare has been planning your death for many months, then surely he has also taken steps in England to ensure his ultimate victory there. What can you do alone?"

"Just get me to Hythe. After that, I won't be alone," David said.

16

14 June 1293

Callum

Callum came out of the hall and, ignoring the rain that had started to fall again, waved a hand to gather his men to him. Only a few scuff marks on the stones and a fallen lance indicated what had gone on in the courtyard earlier that day. "This is a long way from over, gentlemen."

Peter had been conferring with several of his men near the gatehouse. He made an agreeing motion with his head and approached. "Jeffries told me what Valles said. This is exactly what Lili said would happen. She was right about Clare's betrayal. Could she be right that David's alive and on the run in Aquitaine?"

"I want to believe so," Callum said. "Cassie believes so. One of Valles's men must know something more about David's death. Clare received the news by pigeon, and I want to know exactly what the message said."

"Yes, sir." He headed off to the barracks where Valles's men were being kept.

Then one of the guards standing on the battlement above the gatehouse waved a hand. "Riders approach!"

Since the incident with Valles, Jeffries had glued himself to Callum's right shoulder. "Not again!"

The two men crossed to the northern gatehouse, Jeffries matching Callum stride for stride, reminding Callum of the first time they'd conspired together, back in Cardiff before the bombing. That day they'd been loping across a city street fleeing MI-5 surveillance. The danger they'd been in had concerned them plenty at the time. In retrospect, it was nothing compared to what faced them now.

As they turned underneath the gatehouse, they were met by another guardsman. "Seven riders, my lord. They wear the Bohun crest."

The portcullis was down, but the wooden gate behind it had been left open, allowing them to see through the iron bars to the riders, who halted before the gate. The lead rider's horse danced sideways, and then the rider himself pulled off his helmet, revealing a red-faced and sweaty Humphrey de Bohun.

At the sight of Callum, Bohun dismounted and came to stand before the portcullis, one hand clutching the bars. "You know about David's death?" he said without preamble.

"One Robert de Valles, a captain of Clare's, brought the news." Callum strode forward to meet him. "We have information that suggests David is still alive, however."

"You tell me true?"

"First, what brings you to Shrewsbury?" Callum said.

"You, of course." Bohun left unsaid, *what else, you fool*, which seemed to have been on the tip of his tongue.

"Why me?"

"Because I can't trust anyone else." Bohun snorted. "Are you going to let me in, or shall we really have this discussion at the gate?"

"Your pardon." Callum had needed to be sure of Bohun's loyalty, but his bald assertion of trust coupled with the snide comment were all the confirmation Callum needed. "We've had a bit of trouble here."

The guard ratcheted up the portcullis to admit Bohun's men, who filed into the courtyard, though Bohun himself stopped in front of Callum, who remained in the shelter of the gatehouse.

"Where were you when you got word?" Callum said.

"I was conferring with Mortimer at my castle at Hereford, wasn't I? We had warning that Clare was up to his old tricks, and then my scouts reported that a company of his men was racing for Hereford. Mortimer took our wives and children into Wales, and I came here." Edmund Mortimer's wife,

Margaret, and Bohun's wife, Maud, were cousins, so they were often in company. It wasn't surprising that they'd chosen this week to visit one another—just lucky.

"Clare caught you on the hop." Bohun sounded very satisfied that he and Mortimer had not been.

"What do you know about what happened in Aquitaine?" Callum said. "Did Lili send a messenger to you too?"

"Queen Lili?" Bohun looked puzzled. "No."

"Then how did you hear of David's death?" Callum said.

Bohun looked slightly offended. "I have a man at the Winchester relay, who radioed me as soon as Clare told his people of David's death and that he would be assuming the regency."

Jeffries gave him a stricken look. "You have a man—"

Bohun cut him off with a gesture. "You would have been relying on the king's network, of course, which Clare shut down this morning, starting with the stations in London, to any messages but those he sent himself. I'm sure he wanted to make sure no word reached us before his men did."

Callum cursed under his breath. The centrality of the stations, which had seemed a strength, was proving now to be a weakness. If David wanted to get word to his father or Callum that he was alive, he would have to either take all the stations back or send a rider, just as Bridget and Peter had ridden from London. Should Callum choose to do so, he could still talk to the few lords who had access to the two-way communication system: Llywelyn in Caerphilly, Math at Dinas Bran, and Ieuan at Buellt, but the transmissions wouldn't be private. Other lords farther east into England had radios too, but Callum didn't know who to trust.

"You have your own spy network?" Jeffries sounded impressed.

"I have always intended to survive, come what may, and I am *not* pleased to learn that Clare has made this play for power." As he said the word *not*, Bohun clenched his fist and slapped it into his other palm. Since Bohun himself had made a bid for the throne once, through his eldest son, William, who was to have married one of King Edward's daughters, it was a little rich of him to complain about Clare having a similar idea.

Cassie and Peter approached, followed by two members of Shrewsbury's garrison. They held between them one of Clare's soldiers, a man of about thirty, stocky and muscled, as befitted his profession. His hands were tied behind his back for security's sake.

Callum's eyes went first to his wife. "What is it, Cassie?"

"Gwenllian is in danger too. I just spoke with King Llywelyn. She has been staying at Westminster with Lili for the past several months."

That four members of the royal family were in danger was hardly different than three, but that three of them were children made Clare's actions even more appalling.

Cassie tipped her chin to point at Bohun. "Ieuan reports that your family crossed the border safely and has reached Buellt Castle. Mortimer intends to return to Montgomery to begin preparing his resistance. He hopes to coordinate with us."

Bohun let out a sigh. "Thank you."

Cassie continued, "Llywelyn is marshalling his forces as we speak, but he is wary of Clare's defenses and reach. Clare's stronghold is at Gloucester, fifteen miles from the border— hardly more than the distance from here to Wales. Rather than wait for him to attack, Llywelyn proposes a pre-emptive strike."

"On Gloucester?" Bohun said. "That's bold."

"And on David's castle at Chester, if it has fallen to Clare." Cassie tipped her head. "Our alternative is to wait and be picked off one by one, as Clare has already tried to do. By acting first, we could control the whole of the March from Chester to the Severn Strait."

"We would be a wall of resistance to Clare's rule." Bohun sounded slightly awed.

"With Clare occupied with consolidating his power and a possible war with France, he won't have the resources to counter us if we remain united," Cassie said.

"The people of the March have always supported David," Callum said. "They will stand against Clare if we ask them to."

"You propose we make a Kingdom of the March?" Bohun rubbed his hands, glee in his eyes. His own private kingdom was what he'd always wanted.

Cassie shook her head. "No, Humphrey. Not a kingdom. A chance to give the people a say over who rules them. Hasn't that always been David's vision?"

Callum grinned. "You want real democracy."

"But with David's death—" Cassie broke off, her amusement gone in an instant, and tears pricking at her eyes.

Callum's arm came around his wife's shoulders to pull her to him. "There could be no greater legacy of his rule than what you propose, Cassie. If we offer an alternative to Clare, many barons in England might come over to us."

"It was the people of London who chose David to be their king," Jeffries said.

Cassie nodded. "None of us here have David's power, but we can give the people *and* the other barons the opportunity to make his vision a reality. We can tell them they don't have to follow Clare, and we can not only tell them—we can show them."

"Our first step must be to gather whatever information we can about what Clare is planning." Peter moved out of the shadows. "Torold, here, can tell us what the message to Valles from Clare said."

Torold was looking distinctly worse for wear, tousled with a bruise on one cheek. He wasn't otherwise injured, however, and at Peter's urging, he dropped to his knees on the stones of the courtyard.

"The message said: *King David dead. Proceed as planned.*"

Callum took in a deep breath through his nose. The pieces of this plot were starting to fall together for him, even this far away from the center of the action. "Your words imply that Clare was waiting for the news of the king's death."

"I have reported what I heard, as I was bid," Torold said.

During the brief exchange with the prisoner, Bohun had been muttering to himself under his breath, and now Callum turned to him. "What?"

"It's obvious that Clare had David murdered," Bohun said.

Callum gestured to Peter. "We weren't caught as much on the hop as you supposed. Peter and his wife brought warning from London that Clare hoped to take the throne over David's dead body, and now he appears to be implementing a plan to do exactly that, one that might have been brewing for years."

"His discontent began the very moment he threw in his lot with David," Bohun said. "Clare has always been an opportunist, but murdering the king in order to take his place is another matter entirely!"

"The outcome is the same," Callum said, in his most calming voice, "and my concern for the safety of Lili and the children is the same." He turned back to the prisoner. "Where are you from, Torold?"

"I hail from Tewkesbury." He'd gone very pale.

"Well, Torold from Tewkesbury, you are faced with a choice," Callum said. "You can stay in a cell here at Shrewsbury or you can deliver a message for me to Clare."

Torold looked even more stricken. "I'd rather rot in a cell, my lord, than go back to Lord Clare."

Callum frowned, feeling that he was missing the man's meaning. "Why is that?"

"We—" he made a gesture with his head, which was all he could do since his hands were tied, "—are loyal men of England. We support King David, if he is alive." His eyes went to Cassie. "I would never have wanted to see you harmed, my lady, and I certainly couldn't support any plan of Lord Clare's to murder the king!"

Callum studied Torold, whose expression had turned defiant, as if daring Callum to question his loyalty again. "How many of the men we now hold in our cells share your opinion?"

"All of them!" Then he calmed and amended his assurance, "Except for Valles, of course. I can't speak for him."

Callum raised his head to meet Peter's eyes, as if to say, *what do you think?*

Peter shrugged. "We weren't going to kill them, were we? They can stay here for now." He prodded Torold in the back so that he rose to his feet. "We'll make sure they're fed and put to work."

Callum laughed. This was a better ending to the events of the day than he'd had any right to hope. With a gesture he indicated that Peter should take Torold away. But then, behind him, the guard closed the wooden gate with an ominous thud, reminding Callum that a democratic Britain was still a long way off. For now, Shrewsbury was an island unto itself.

17

14 June 1293

David

By three in the afternoon, David was decked out from head to foot as a Templar knight, wearing dry padding (thank God), new mail armor that actually fit, a borrowed Templar sword, white tunic, and mantle. The clothing wasn't any different in basic shape from what he wore every day as King of England.

But it still wasn't what he normally wore.

To everyone's eyes but his own, he was now a Templar, and that meant something very specific that David wasn't entirely comfortable impersonating. Still, he went along with it, in large part because he didn't have a better idea about how to get to England quickly, and at this late hour he couldn't turn down Pierre's very generous offer to help him.

While the drawbacks to the lack of a good communication system had been staring him in the face for the last two days, there were benefits too. Once he was on the road, riding as fast and as furiously as he could, he would be impossible for Clare's minions to track.

As the company rode from the commanderie, rather than the panicked fear of a few hours before, David found himself with only a feeling of a mild anxiety. In every way the experience was a far cry from the way he'd come into La Rochelle. The men of Vauclair Castle no longer milled about in the street outside the gate of the commanderie, though David felt their sharp eyes staring down at him from the top of the battlement.

Their castellan had already met with Pierre, and by the time David was dressed and ready to ride from the commanderie, the Templar master had showed Beloit the two fake murderers, both looking suitably chastened and ill in their dark and dingy cell. Pierre hadn't promised to give them up to Beloit just yet—not until evidence could be brought against them—but since they were safe in Templar hands, Beloit had gone away satisfied.

Henri rode with the company, keeping just to David's left, almost like one of David's own companions would have. The man who led them was a Templar knight. Yet again, he sported a full gray beard, indicating that he was at least twenty years older than David. When they'd first set out from the commanderie, David had tried to talk to the man, but he had barely acknowledged David's existence. David had tried not to be offended and, once they'd started riding, his irritation at the snub had turned to pity. The captain rode with a stiffness that told David he wasn't sitting comfortably in the saddle. Perhaps he had hemorrhoids like Goronwy (whose were much better these days). It looked to David like the captain was doing everything in his power just to remain seated.

Throughout their journey from Chateau Niort, David had kept his grief at the loss of Justin and the rest of his men in a box on a shelf in his mind. He couldn't grieve them properly and at the same time get himself and Philip to safety. But now, in the momentary lull of leaving the town, he allowed himself to open the box and peer into it. A potent mix of grief and rage flooded through him. Some of those men had served David since before he'd become King of England. Others had been English, but David didn't regret their loss any less. Things had changed in the ten years since David had come to Wales—quite honestly for the better. He didn't want to go back to the days when England was the enemy. They'd all come too far to give up on the dream of peace just because Clare wanted a throne.

His hands trembled on the reins as his emotions consumed him. He fought the anger, just as he'd fought it earlier, and it took him the full three miles from La Rochelle to the crossroads, where the captain ordered his men to peel off onto a side road and stop, to conquer himself.

Pierre had warned David that he would be accompanied for only a short distance before the company would leave him to his own devices. They were a disguise to get him out of La Rochelle, but then they had their own duties—and they certainly couldn't ride the three hundred miles with him to Le Havre. The captain watched his men stop in the center of a little glade of trees. Then he turned to David. With a gruffness that perhaps couldn't entirely be attributed to pain, he said, "Who are you, and what right do you have to wear the cross?"

David blinked at the abruptness of the question and struggled for an appropriate answer that wasn't rude and wouldn't just encourage the captain to question him more. "Your master trusts me, and I suggest you speak to him. Once you do, you may think better of me and of your master's choices. That he made the choice, I would hope, would be enough for you." That was a longer speech than David meant to give, but he couldn't help caring what people thought about him. He'd grown used to being the King of England and the respect it immediately afforded him. It was an awkward feeling to have to earn it.

The captain gave David another long look. Then he clicked his tongue at his horse, threaded his way through his men to take his place at the front, and jerked his head to indicate it was time to go. The men fell into formation behind him, and within five seconds, they were off, heading southeast from the crossroads. It was only as the last man took up his position that David realized Henri wasn't leaving with them. He too watched them go and then trotted his horse over to where David waited.

"I'm with you," Henri said before David could demand what he thought he was doing.

"It was my understanding that I was to go alone."

"Master Pierre thought better of that plan and asked me to attend you." While Henri didn't have the earnestness of a younger man like William de Bohun, he spoke with utter sincerity.

David took in a breath. "Why didn't he tell me himself?"

"He was busy with Sir Beloit, so he left it to me to tell you."

Had Henri known that David was the Duke of Aquitaine and King of England, he might not have been so forthright, even rude, but David had accepted the deception, so he could hardly complain about the result. "It might be dangerous."

Henri looked affronted. "I am a Templar knight."

David's lips twitched. Henri had a point. He was in his middle thirties and may well have seen more battle than David, since his entire way of life was focused on the crusade. He had probably spent more time in the saddle too. Although David made sure to keep himself always in fighting shape, likely Henri was going to handle a three-hundred mile ride better than David was.

"Do you understand what I'm trying to do?"

"You seek to bring word to the queen that the king is not dead and to prevent the Archbishop of Canterbury from crowning Gilbert de Clare in the king's place."

David eyed him. Pierre had told him that much, it seemed, which was good. Henri needed to know that they faced a powerful adversary, and he'd described the barebones of the mission, even if there was a bit more to it than that.

Henri was holding himself very stiffly as he waited for David's reply. Frenchmen had a way about them that made David feel they were always on the verge of sneering. Given that Henri wanted to come with him, David had to assume that the knight's austere expression, rather than indicating disdain, meant that he was anxious about whether or not David would accept him.

Pierre too had seemed entirely truthful in his wish to aid David. The Templar master could have turned him over to Clare's men at any time rather than sending him to Le Havre. David wasn't questioning the aid he received, but he was struggling with the different customs and culture that Pierre and Henri might assume he understood when he didn't. For all that he'd lived in this world for ten years, he was an American man in Templar guise, and it was times like these when the discrepancy between who he was and who he was expected to be was most glaring.

When David still didn't acquiesce, Henri added, "My presence could mean the difference between success and failure. You're wounded—we can all see it, even if you will take no rest."

David frowned. "I'm fine."

"You breathe shallowly at times, and your left side is weak. Besides, Templar knights never travel alone. We should have at least two sergeants and possibly a clerk with us too, but their absence can be explained away by the urgency of our mission."

"Okay," David said simply. He couldn't say no, especially since traveling with Henri would undoubtedly be safer, and it would also mean that if David rested during the journey, he wouldn't have to do it with one eye open. Henri was right about his injury too. David didn't know if his ribs were broken or bruised from the assassin's arrows and his fight with the rider whose horse he'd taken, but they were definitely *something*.

With a jerk of his head, in mimicry of the Templar captain, Henri pointed his horse's nose north and clicked his tongue. David could do nothing else but follow. They'd hardly ridden any distance, however, before David came to see that the only danger he might face on the road would be from Clare's men, were they to discover him. Nobody else would dare.

Because David had headed out of the commanderie among an armed escort of knights and sergeants, he hadn't noticed anything unusual about the way he was treated by the people of La Rochelle. Pierre had wanted the company to look like a regular patrol—and so it was in every respect except for the fact that David rode among them. Any company of soldiers invited deference on the part of the villagers they passed. David had always been treated well by his people: with adoration by some, obsequiousness by others, and genuine respect by many. He felt he'd earned that respect by matching his deeds to his words.

Templars, by contrast, were treated like gods: peasants scurried out of the way as David and Henri passed through their villages. Some bowed from the roadside; some actually knelt. None would look at him. Finally, at the fourth village they entered where inhabitants hurried out of their houses to pay their respects, David asked Henri about their behavior.

"I have been to Jerusalem. I have seen the Holy Sepulchre where Christ's body was placed. My Order keeps Christendom safe from the Saracens." His tone implied that the answer was self-evident, and David should have known it.

It was yet another cultural chasm between David's reality and that of the people he ruled and made David question what he was doing trying to rule them when sometimes he didn't understand them at all.

The patrol that had escorted David out of La Rochelle had put them on the road to the first station at Marans, followed by the second at Moreilles, which was associated with a Cistercian Abbey. David had a soft spot for the Cistercian order because they had supported his father against Edward and the pope, despite him being excommunicated. Henri had obviously been to this Templar station before because he led David unerringly to what amounted to no more than a barn, with living quarters for the station master on one side.

"What brings you here, Henri?" The sergeant who manned the station came out of the barn to greet them as they rode up, wiping greasy hands on a cloth since they'd interrupted his meal. He had a thickness around his chest and shoulders that often came with age and enough to eat. His face was tanned and lined, by age and weather, and his shorn hair was completely gray, indicating that here was yet another older Templar.

"We need a change of horses, and then we will ride onwards," Henri said.

David dismounted and began unbuckling the saddle strap. The man put out a hand to prevent him. "No need for that. I have two already saddled." Then he looked curiously at David. "And who might you be?"

"I'm bound to England with urgent news," he said, aware again of his Welsh-accented French.

"The Duke of Aquitaine is dead." The man bobbed his head. "I heard."

"That's just it. He isn't dead," David said, "and we're at least a day behind in telling it."

The man's eyes widened, and David was pretty sure that the next person who happened by would hear all about it, which is what David wanted. He wasn't ready to proclaim himself, not with Clare's and Charles's men all around him, but he could sow doubt that what Clare's men were telling the people was accurate.

Henri regarded the man stoically, as if he expected no less of the man either, and the result was that he appeared to take David's mission as a call to speed them on their way as quickly as possible. After a long drink of fresh water from the man's well and a piece of cheese between two slices of bread (David had no qualms about introducing the sandwich to Aquitaine while he was at it), they were off again.

They'd ridden a mile before Henri, who'd been in the lead, slowed slightly from a full gallop to allow David to come abreast. He called across the distance between them, both still riding hard. It was the only way they were going to travel three hundred and twenty miles in forty-eight hours. "My lord, how did you come by the news that the Duke is not dead?"

That was the question David had been waiting for. "I witnessed his survival." While he didn't want to lie, it would be better for the time being if Henri didn't know the truth either.

"You were at Chateau Niort." It wasn't a question. Henri was sure of his conclusion.

"I was."

"And the man you came in with. He was there also? He can testify to Clare's duplicity?"

"Yes, he can testify if he needs to. If he lives."

They rode another hundred yards before Henri asked another question. "I am to take it that you have standing in your king's court?"

David smiled grimly. "I do." Though again, without tangible proof beyond a single arrow, specifically the testimony of one of Clare's men, it would be David's word against Clare's. David was king, so he could do what he liked, but he didn't like to rule that way—and he didn't believe in ruling that way. If he was to expose Clare, he needed a lot of luck and more than his own words.

"Will you not tell me your real name?"

"It will be safer for both of us if I do not," David said. "Master Villiers understood that, and believe me when I say that my word will carry weight in Parliament when I tell them that the king lives."

"But you would prefer not to tell me where he has gone." That wasn't a question either, and Henri nodded before David could answer him, apparently satisfied. "It was Master Villier's intention, once we were safely away, to assemble the men of the commanderie and tell them of the plot against Duke David."

When he'd resolved to ride to England alone, David had been fine with letting Pierre determine the moment that he told his people of David's continued survival, but they hadn't discussed whether or not Pierre would explain that it was actually the Duke of Aquitaine who had passed through their commanderie. While the men in the commanderie needed to know to whom they owed allegiance, keeping his and Philip's identities a secret might still be the difference between life and death.

They rode a while more, both men concentrating on the road, though a glance at Henri indicated that he might not be seeing it. His eyes were focused on a spot between his horse's ears, and David saw the moment he came to his conclusion—

"Your secrets are safe with me, Lord Ieuan."

David couldn't help but laugh. How Henri had come to learn of Ieuan's existence, he didn't know. David relied on Ieuan, of course, more than any of his other advisers and friends, with the possible exception of Callum and his own father. Ieuan had pulled together David's knights, men-at-arms, and archers into a fighting force and earned the trust of all of them—or they didn't last as David's companions very long. David was honored to be confused for him, but the lying made him uncomfortable yet again.

David wrestled with himself for a few moments, wondering if it made sense to tell Henri the truth. He might understand being lied to, but part of him would be offended. Ten years older than David, Henri had an air of authority, coupled with a strong sense of righteousness that David guessed wasn't too far off from his own. And yet, the fewer people who knew specifically that David was the King of England the better. He was out in the open with only one companion. Under any other circumstances, every one of his advisers would be panicked to learn of it.

In the end, David opted to tread a fine line between truth and falsehood. "I do not want to lie to you. I am not in a position to confirm or deny what you suspect. Regardless, I greatly appreciate your discretion."

"You have it and more," Henri said.

The miles rolled by underneath them. The first three stations came and went, and as they made fast progress down the road, David realized that he'd been remiss to overlook this unsophisticated way to communicate across great distances. The Templars had, in effect, set up a pony express across Aquitaine, Poitiers, and France. It was, quite frankly, exciting to see.

David had begun a quest for new uses of old technology in order to advance industry in Britain on its own terms, rather than relying on technology from Avalon. Crop yields were up because many of these advances were in agriculture, a field about which David had known essentially nothing before becoming King of England. Most of the ideas for these advances hadn't come from him: the people who used them had embraced the improvements far faster than some of his other reforms. As a leader, David prided himself on looking for intelligent people, encouraging them to share his vision of the future, and then getting out of their way.

What David had failed to appreciate, however, was that the field of communication could also benefit from doing things the old fashioned way. True, it was expensive to maintain stables and horses—and to pay men to man them—but labor was cheap. Besides which, Templars weren't paid. In fact, if a Templar died with money on him, he was posthumously expelled from the Order. For economic reasons alone, as much as the one David was using them for, the Order needed to provide havens for their men.

Suddenly, this particular journey was looking far more doable.

That is, until Henri's horse put his foot in a hole and pulled up lame, and it started raining.

18

16 June 1293

Gwenllian

It had been the worst two days of Gwenllian's life. With nothing to do but mind the boys, she'd been bored silly, and alternating constantly between grief and anger. For the last hour she'd sat in the window seat of the king's quarters with Arthur, while Lili and Carew talked quietly to one another. Built as they were into the curtain wall, the king's apartments were the only ones at Westminster that directly overlooked the Thames, which flowed underneath the walls from south to north as it passed the castle on its way east to the sea.

As it was June, the glass had been removed from the windows, and the wooden shutters were open to let in warm air to heat the cold stones of the castle. Here on the western edge of the city, there was a pleasant breeze, and as it cooled her face, one of her blonde strands that had come loose from its clip lifted off her forehead. Gwenllian had hidden behind these curtains before, though not very often, since it was Lili and

Dafydd's bedroom—and really, who wanted to be caught in here by mistake? When she'd last tried it, Gwenllian heard a bit of news about the King of Scotland not known to the general court, but then Dafydd and Lili had gone all *gooey* (another favorite twenty-firster word), and Gwenllian had fled the instant they'd left the room.

Since they were supposed to be quiet during Alexander's nap, Arthur sat across from her in the waist-high and three-foot deep window seat, playing with a wooden horse, while she stared down at the water as it flowed passed Westminster. Her heart felt as sluggish as the Thames, and each of the days they'd been cooped up in here had seemed to last a week.

A knock came at the door, and then it opened before Lili or Carew even gave permission. Clare and Geoffrey de Geneville stood on the threshold. Clare had come each day to *ease his mind as to how they were faring,* or so he said.

Gwenllian wanted nothing to do with him, and though she wanted to turn her face away, she didn't. He was a like a wild boar, and the last thing you wanted to do with a predator was turn away.

Geoffrey was speaking to Clare as they entered. "Of course, my lord. What is it that you intend to do?"

"I must speak to Parliament," Clare said. "We are facing an imminent crisis that I fear cannot be averted."

Lili was on her feet in an instant. "What crisis is that, Gilbert?"

"As I told you before, I have word that France is preparing an invasion force to take advantage of our disarray," Clare said. "It will launch within days, if not hours."

"Have you sent word to the other barons of Dafydd's death, Gilbert?" Lili said. "Lord Callum and Lord Bohun, for example?"

"I have sent my men. This isn't something they should hear over the radio." Clare waggled his head back and forth as if he didn't want to say more but then decided he had to. "I have ordered the silencing of the radio stations themselves to all but those broadcasts I approve. The people are volatile, and we must do what we can to prevent panic and unrest."

Geoffrey's lips pinched into a thin line, and he didn't look at Lili or Gwenllian. Clare continued speaking. "I trust you are well, Lili, or as well as can be expected?"

"Not really, Gilbert. I would like to leave London."

"Oh my dear, I'm afraid that still isn't possible. Now that we know what the French have planned, it would be too dangerous. You and the boys will surely be a target of French treachery." His sympathetic look was nearly unbearable for Gwenllian to see, and finally she turned her head away. The water continued to flow beneath her, and as she looked first at the river, then at Arthur, and then at Clare, a plan began to form in her mind.

She recalled the conversation she'd overheard between Carew and Lili on the walk from the throne room. It had frightened her at the time, but Clare's growing power had her thinking again about the possibility of escape. *Traveling* to Avalon from the battlements above the main hall had been too scary and dangerous to try, but Clare had brought them to the one place at Westminster where it might be possible.

She could have waited until nightfall, but with Clare speaking before Parliament, she couldn't be sure that any of them would live to see another night. Gwenllian got her feet under her, leaned forward, and took Arthur in her arms. He looked up at her, frowning, but Gwenllian smiled at him and edged towards the open window. As always, nobody paid her any mind, especially since Clare was again gently expressing to Lili his grief at Dafydd's death.

Gwenllian just managed to stop herself from scoffing: Clare wanted power, just like every other Norman baron. Dafydd had lectured *her* more than once about governing, and it was a mantra with him that once a man gained a little bit of power, he would fight tooth and nail—maybe even to the death—to keep it. But then, though none of the Normans glanced at her, when she looked again, Carew had moved ten paces closer, even if his head was turned studiously away and he was looking towards Clare as if he was paying attention to what the treacherous baron was saying.

Gwenllian could tell he was keeping half an eye on her, however. Because of it, she decided she'd better act before she could think too hard about what she was doing and stop herself. After a single indrawn breath, she clutched Arthur to her, faced the river, and crouched over the edge. It was a *long* way down to the Thames. Gwenllian didn't see how Dafydd could have done this so many times, but the fact that he had done it even once and lived gave her courage. Maybe he would be angry with her for risking Arthur's life, but she also hoped that he would be proud of her for doing what had to be done.

She squeezed Arthur tightly. "Hold on, *cariad*."

And then she jumped.

19

16 June 2021

Christopher

"You are not going to spend the summer playing computer games!" Dressed in a dark purple power suit with matching heels, Christopher's mother stood on the slate tiles of the foyer, late for work, which was what Christopher secretly thought was amping up her anxiety. She and his father had stayed up late last night arguing about *him*, of all the crazy things. At midnight, Christopher had put in his earbuds and gone to sleep so he couldn't hear them anymore.

His little sister, Elen, who really wasn't all that little anymore, was already in the car. She'd be dropped off at a friend's house on his mom's way to work. Christopher had asked for the job of keeping an eye on Elen this summer, since at eleven she was too old for a nanny but not old enough to stay home by herself all day, but his mother had scoffed at him and never taken the offer seriously. She didn't trust him.

"I stopped by every store in Radnor yesterday to apply for a job," Christopher said, trying to keep his voice reasonable. A few millimeters under six feet tall, thin but athletic, he ran a hand through his red hair, struggling not to get mad back at his mom. "I'm trying."

"Try harder!" Elisa turned on her heel and marched out the front door, leaving Christopher alone in his empty house.

He couldn't say that he was used to his mother's temper, since she was normally far more reasonable than this, and it seemed to have come on recently, but he took it philosophically as something he couldn't do anything about. His father had asked that he be patient: Christopher would turn eighteen in three days, at which point his plan was to apply for a police officer trainee position, rather than to attend Dickenson, even though he'd gotten in. It was freaking his mother out, and Christopher's father guessed that Elisa was hoping that if Christopher got some other kind of job he would change his mind.

Christopher was pretty sure that being a policeman—on the way to ultimately joining the FBI—was what he wanted to do, however, and he hadn't actually turned Dickenson down. He'd talked to them about the possibility of deferring for a year, the deadline for which was August 1st, and they told him to just let them know. If the admissions office wasn't complaining, he didn't see why his mother should either.

It was true that in order to be an FBI special agent he needed a bachelor's degree. He just didn't see the need to get one *now,* though, when David could come back at any time. And if Christopher was already in the work force, he could be of better use than if he was in school. Besides, if he didn't get any kind of decent work between now and August, he'd go to school. Dickenson even had a major in domestic and international security, which sounded cool.

Christopher completely understood why his mother minded. She was afraid that he would a) get a police officer position; b) like it; and c) die in the line of duty; or d) (and worst of all) take the skills he'd learned in the line of duty and go to the Middle Ages with David the next time he came back.

Meanwhile, the dad of one of his friends had refurbished an old mill on his property (he was a surgeon in his day job) and had been teaching Christopher about all sorts of ways to use a watermill to not only create electricity but to power everything from mill stones for grinding oats, to saws, drills, and the bellows for a forge (along with an occasional lecture on human anatomy and medicine). Christopher hadn't known how important a crankshaft and flywheel could be, and he'd learned more cool things in the last six months since they'd gotten back from Wales than in his entire high school career.

He'd also gained ten pounds of muscle in his upper body working with Jon's dad, and he'd started doing a hundred push-ups and a hundred sit-ups every day to augment the process. He'd need the strength for the police academy when he went. For whatever reason, his mother didn't approve of Jon's dad either, so Christopher didn't bother to tell her that he was going to Jon's house this morning, rather than continuing his quest for a job.

He settled into his 1998 Honda Prelude, which his father called his *chick magnet*, though only under his breath so Christopher's mom couldn't hear. On the Main Line, where every other kid Christopher knew drove a hand-me-down (or new!) BMW, Mercedes, or Lexus, the little Honda stood out. It had even been stolen once, since old Hondas made great street racers. The thieves had painted it matte black, put on three thousand dollar tires, and made a giant hole in the dashboard when they'd taken out the stereo. What's more, even after two hundred thousand miles, the sunroof didn't leak, and whatever the thieves had done to the engine had made it one of the fastest cars at his high school.

Not that he was supposed to know that.

The cops had recovered it because the guy who'd stolen it had been driving around suburban Bryn Mawr at midnight without headlights or a muffler. Once pulled over, the driver had proved to have a gun in the driver's side door, one on the passenger seat, and a military knife in his boot. The cop's comment to Christopher's father had been, "Stealing your car is the least of his problems."

Christopher really wanted to be a cop.

That wasn't going to happen today, however, so rather than stew any more about his mother's attitude, Christopher headed to his friend's house. Jon lived southeast of Radnor, and the best way to get there was to drive the back road past Bryn Mawr College, swing around the train station, and then cut across Lancaster Avenue heading south. Halfway there, however, he heard a rattling from the front right fender and realized that the driving light had come out of its socket again. When the police had recovered the car, it had still been a work-in-progress for the thieves. In the process of turning it into a street car, they'd stripped the screws on some of the lights. Christopher was responsible for paying for his own car, so he'd replaced this particular screw three times himself, rather than take it to a shop. It was probably time to let a professional handle it.

For the moment, however, he pulled across the cobbles in front of the train station and stopped in a parking spot for taxis. A train wasn't due for another twenty minutes, and he figured he'd be long gone by then. He got out of the car and walked around to the front to squat by the light. Sure enough, the screw had worked loose again. It was clear that the issue was the stripped threads in the fixture itself, not the screw, which appeared to be intact. He stuffed it back into place anyway, and then popped the trunk. Duct tape was the logical solution until he could get it fixed properly.

It was only after he closed the trunk and was holding the duct tape in his hand that he noticed the girl and boy sitting on the bench as if they were waiting for a taxi. The little boy was crying, and the girl had her arm around his shoulders and was whispering into his ear. She looked Amish in her long dress and braids down her back, and the boy was wearing a dress-like garment too, though on closer inspection it was more like an oversized shirt belted at the waist.

At the thud of the closing trunk lid, the girl looked over at Christopher, and he realized that she was closer to twelve than the fifteen he'd first thought. Though she was blonde and tall—maybe as tall as his mom (without heels)—her face was really young. He didn't think intervening in an Amish family issue, which he figured this had to be, was the best idea on the planet. Plus, he was about to be later than he'd told Jon and Paul he'd be there. But the girl was so close in age to his little sister that he couldn't just drive away and leave them crying on the bench.

"Are you guys okay?" he said from where he was standing beside his car. He thought it would be better not to actually go over to them yet. They might be afraid of a stranger.

The girl's eyes widened. "What did you say?" She spoke with a bit of an accent, which he couldn't place.

"I asked if you guys were okay," he said.

The girl looked at him warily for a second, and the boy stopped crying enough to look at him too. Christopher risked stepping closer. "Are you waiting for someone?" When they didn't answer that question either, he added, "I'm Christopher."

"I'm Ar-ar-arthur. I'm four, and this is Gwenllian. She's almost eleven." Arthur said the girl's name with that spitting *sh* sound Christopher had heard in Wales.

Christopher swallowed hard and moved onto the sidewalk. "Did-did you say your names were Arthur and Gwenllian?" He knew he wasn't pronouncing the girl's name right, but he thought he might be close.

The girl nodded.

Christopher's heart started pounding hard. With some more tentative steps, he crossed the sidewalk and crouched in front of them, one hand on the arm of the park bench they were sitting on. "Um ... I'm David's cousin."

Gwenllian and Arthur both looked stricken rather than overjoyed at this news, which wasn't the reaction he was hoping for.

"David's the King of England, right?" Christopher tried again. "You've come here from the Middle Ages. He isn't with you?"

Gwenllian nodded and shook her head at the same time. "Dafydd isn't here."

"Then how did you get here?"

"Arthur and I jumped out of a window at Westminster Castle."

"Why?"

"Because Gilbert de Clare says that Dafydd is dead!" At her own words, Gwenllian burst into tears.

A giant lump formed in Christopher's throat, and tears pricked at the corners of his eyes, but he fought them back. It couldn't be true. David couldn't be dead.

Gwenllian hiccupped. "Lili says he isn't though. She had a vision of one of Clare's men trying to kill him, but he fell from the battlement into a river."

"What river?" Christopher said.

"It's in Aquitaine."

"Why was David in Aquitaine?"

"He was meeting with the French king."

Christopher pressed his lips together, uncertain what to make of the vision thing, but he desperately wanted to believe in it. "Why didn't David come here?"

"I don't know. He always travels to Avalon when he's in a lot of danger. Maybe it wasn't enough danger."

David had talked to Christopher about dying when they were at Aber together. He'd explained that the time traveling only worked when he was in danger and in motion. If someone shot him or chopped off his head, he'd be just as dead as everyone else, and that meant Clare could be right. Still, David wore armor all the time and, last Christopher had heard, MI-5 was getting him more Kevlar too.

Christopher eyed Arthur, who was listening with rapt attention but not crying anymore. This was his father they were talking about, but Christopher didn't see any way around asking more questions. "I'm sorry to ask you this, but have any of you seen the body?"

"No." Gwenllian gave a little shake of her head. "Clare hasn't seen him either."

"Okay." Christopher straightened up. Crouching for so long made his thighs hurt, and he made a mental note to add deep knee bends to his exercise regime. "We'll put that aside for now." He knew he sounded like David, and part of him felt that if David really was dead, then it was up to him to help Gwenllian and Arthur—just like David would. David had been only fourteen when he'd gone to Wales for the first time. Christopher was essentially eighteen. It was time to be a man. "You left Westminster by jumping out a window and then you *traveled* here. Did this just happen?"

"Yes. We landed over there." Gwenllian pointed to a spot of grass on the other side of the train tracks.

Christopher thought she was lucky to have survived crossing the tracks to reach this bench, but he was a believer in David and always had been. The coincidence of Christopher meeting Gwenllian and Arthur here within a few minutes of their arrival felt like it was exactly how things were supposed to go.

Except for David being dead, of course. Tears formed in the corners of his eyes again, and Christopher gave a little shake of his head. He didn't have time for them.

"Where's mama?" Arthur stuck his forefinger into his mouth.

Gwenllian hugged him. "We'll get back to her soon."

"Is Lili still at Westminster Castle?" Christopher said.

Gwenllian nodded. "With Alexander, the new baby."

Christopher had forgotten about the baby, another cousin. That meant, if David really was dead, Christopher had even more people to protect and worry about. "Do you know anything more about Clare's plan?" He was trying to think like David would, and that meant figuring out what the opposition was doing.

"He says he doesn't want to be king, but we don't believe him." Gwenllian shot a swift look at Arthur before leaning towards Christopher. "I jumped because I was thinking that if I could keep Arthur safe in Avalon, and Clare knew that he was here, he would be less likely to hurt Lili and Alexander."

What Gwenllian meant but didn't say was that Clare might *kill* Lili and Alexander, but there was no way either of them was going to say that in front of Arthur.

"That was good thinking, especially since the time traveling put you where you were supposed to be, which is with me," Christopher said. "We have to trust that you'll end up where you're supposed to be when you go back too. Until then, I'll keep you safe."

Gwenllian nodded and seemed reassured, but Christopher's stomach clenched. He'd just made a promise he had no idea how he was going to keep.

20

16 June 2021

Christopher

"Talk to me," Christopher said, once he'd settled Gwenllian and Arthur in the car and started driving. He knew things had to be really unfamiliar to them but, if he remembered correctly, his car was a lot like Bronwen's, even if it was lower to the ground and a little louder. It was even a Honda.

"You're going really fast."

Though he hadn't been going over the speed limit, immediately Christopher eased off the gas pedal. He glanced in the rearview mirror at Arthur, who sat strapped into the back seat. He was too short to see out the side windows, so he just stared through the front with wide eyes and sucked on his forefinger in a way that told Christopher he was nervous. At least he wasn't crying anymore. Legally, he should have been in a car seat.

"All right, I slowed down. What else?"

"Nothing looks like I expected. It looks kind of like Gwynedd, and the roads and the cars look exactly like David said they would." She paused, and then said in a softer voice, "Except everything is completely different too."

"Sorry," Christopher said, which sounded lame, but he couldn't think of anything else to say or how to make Gwenllian feel better. She'd just learned that David might be dead and had herself jumped out of a castle to time travel to the modern world, though she called it Avalon. He didn't think there was any way to make that better.

They drove for a little while longer, Christopher concentrating on the road, before she said, "Where are we going?"

"To my friend Jon's house. His dad's a surgeon. He's good in a crisis." Christopher took his eyes off the road for a second to look at her. "At least that's what my dad says."

"Where are your parents?"

"My dad left this morning on a business trip to L.A.— that's Los Angeles. It's a city three thousand miles from here and three hours behind us in time. I tried calling, but he might still be in the air. I left a message."

"What-what do you mean it's three hours behind in time? He time traveled there like I did?"

"Oh, no, no—" Christopher took his hand off the stick shift for a second to reach out to her. "Um—I don't know how to explain this exactly, but the earth is really big."

"It's a ball hanging in space that rotates around the sun," Gwenllian said. "The sun looks like it rises in the east, but that's because the earth is really turning on its axis."

"Right," Christopher said, a little nonplussed that she should have that information on the tip of her tongue and state it so matter-of-factly. He soldiered on, "And in order to keep track of the time and have the morning by the clock be a time when the sun is up everywhere, the earth is divided longways into twenty-four sections."

He knew he wasn't explaining this right. His dad would have done better. David probably had done better, but since Gwenllian had never left Wales before, she wouldn't have seen for herself how it worked.

"Anyway, Los Angeles is three thousand miles to the west, so when the sun is coming up here it's still dark there, so if it's nine in morning here, it's only six in the morning there. They're called time zones. Do you see?"

"I guess," Gwenllian said in a way that Christopher was pretty sure meant she had no clue what he was talking about.

He cleared his throat and was saved from having to explain further by their arrival at Jon's driveway. "This is it." He turned onto it. They were kind of out in the country here, and the road was dirt. The bumpy ride made Gwenllian sit straighter in her seat and look out the window with interest. When he put on the brake, she opened the door as if she'd done it a million times before and stood up.

"Chickens!" She left the door open and ran forward.

Christopher laughed and pressed the button that moved his seat forward so he could get Arthur out of the back. It was hard to believe that this little boy was David's son, that he was a prince of England, and that he would one day be king. It wasn't because there was anything odd or unusual about Arthur. That was just it—he was a normal looking kid.

If David is dead, then it's my *job to keep Arthur safe from Gilbert de Clare until he can grow up and return to overthrow him—just like in the stories!*

Then Christopher mentally shook himself and returned to reality. He didn't think his mom and dad were going to want to raise Gwenllian and Arthur for the next fifteen years. They didn't even have birth certificates. Besides, if David was dead, they needed their real mother. Sooner or later, Anna or Meg was bound to show up and retrieve them.

Unless Gilbert de Clare had gotten to them too.

It was hard to think about his Aunt Meg time traveling to the modern world because David was dead. On top of which, were she to come, she might appear in Wales, not Pennsylvania. She'd have no idea where to start looking for Arthur and

Gwenllian and could be picked up by MI-5 and put in prison before she had a chance to find out. David hadn't even been allowed a phone call after he'd been arrested.

Then an even worse thought struck Christopher: the authorities would have noticed the *flash* as Arthur and Gwenllian arrived and even now they could be racing towards Radnor. That meant he couldn't return to his house. That meant he shouldn't have left that message on his dad's phone or the texts on his mom's. He thought back to what he'd told them. He hadn't actually said Arthur's or Gwenllian's name, only that something important had happened and that they should call him. His mom was still mad at him, so maybe she wouldn't, but his dad was always good about getting back to him quickly.

He closed the car door and walked Arthur over to where Gwenllian was crouched in front of a chicken, perhaps inspecting it for similarities with medieval chickens. Radnor wasn't exactly cowboy country, but Jon's family had horses and a dairy cow too. It was more like an estate—or better yet, a hobby farm.

Jon's father, Paul, came out of the barn, which was adjacent to the mill. "Hey, Christopher, I expected you a half-hour ago."

"I know, Paul." Christopher straightened. "I ran into my cousins. This is Arthur and Gwenllian."

Paul scratched his head, frowning. "Uh-what—"

Christopher decided he was better off not shouting across the yard. In a weak moment, he'd told Paul and Jon about his cousins and aunt who'd disappeared. After last Christmas, he'd been dying to talk about meeting David again, but ended up passing off the whole thing as an elaborate dream. He jerked his head towards the barn, and with a puzzled expression, Paul followed him into it.

"I thought your cousins disappeared when you were seven and that your dad was an only child."

Arthur followed them to the barn too, but Christopher shooed him back towards Gwenllian, not wanting him to hear another conversation about his dead father. So far, Arthur had said almost nothing, which Christopher thought was worrisome in a four-year-old boy. The chicken had run off and been replaced by the family's golden retriever and two cats, so when Gwenllian saw Arthur coming, she gestured him closer. She seemed used to caring for him, and he trusted her, so Christopher wasn't worried about either of them getting into trouble among the pets.

He turned back to Paul. "You know that dream I had about David being the King of England in an alternate universe?"

"Yes."

"It wasn't a dream. He really is the King of England in an alternate universe. Arthur is his son, and Gwenllian is his half-sister."

The 'v' of concern between Paul's brows deepened as he looked at Christopher.

"You don't have to believe me. Just ask them. It's all real, including the times they've been chased across the planet by MI-5 or the CIA." Christopher bit his lip.

Paul barked a laugh. "Just ask them, huh?"

"I really shouldn't have brought them here at all, but my parents aren't answering their phones, and I didn't have anyone else I could trust. My dad says you're good in a crisis."

Paul didn't respond to that. Though in a way Christopher couldn't blame him for being skeptical, he found himself growing impatient. Before Paul could answer, Christopher put up both hands. "You know what? It's okay. I should have known that coming here was a bad idea." He turned on his heel and strode back outside, bending to scoop up Arthur on his way towards the car.

"Wait! Christopher, wait." Paul took a few steps after him. "It's just a lot to take in at once."

With Arthur clutched awkwardly in his arms, Christopher turned around to face Paul, though he kept walking backwards to his car. "I know it's too much, but I don't have time for you to process it. I need help now, and not the kind that ends me up in a mental institution."

"You have to admit it sounds crazy."

Christopher shrugged. "I'll figure it out. Come on, Gwenllian."

"We're going?" Gwenllian had looked up when he'd picked up Arthur, and now she hustled after him.

He motioned that she should go around to her side of the car. "Yeah."

He plopped Arthur into the backseat again before sitting himself and starting the car. Before he could back down the driveway, however, his friend Jon ran out of the barn, past his dad, and skidded to a stop by the passenger door of the car. He pulled it open and made a shooing motion to Gwenllian that she should scoot over.

"What are you doing?" Christopher said.

"I heard what you said to my dad. I'm coming with you." Jon managed to squash himself into the bucket seat to the point that he could pull the door closed, even though he was pressed up hard against it.

Christopher gave his friend a long look, and then he motioned with his head to Gwenllian. "Get in the back with Arthur. I can't drive with you sitting on the gearshift."

"Okay." Gwenllian scrunched up her dress to her knees, revealing skin-covering green leggings, and scrambled between the seats in order to sit beside Arthur. She buckled the seatbelt as if she'd been doing it her whole life.

"You're sure?" Christopher said to Jon. "This isn't a game. Time travel is real."

"I know. I heard you the first time."

Shaking his head but happy for the company and glad to know he could count on someone, Christopher shifted into reverse and backed his car down the driveway. At the mailbox, he glanced once more to where Paul stood, watching them. During Christopher's conversation with Jon, Paul hadn't tried to talk to them, stop them, or interfere with what they were doing in any way. He just stood there, and the way he was standing made Christopher think he was feeling as helpless as Christopher himself.

Paul lifted a hand, which Christopher took as a good sign. But as the car backed onto the main road, Paul pulled his phone from his pocket and put it to his ear.

Christopher felt sick to his stomach. He wasn't as smart as David and was totally unprepared to have two medieval kids depending on him. He needed a plan—and he needed it now.

21

16 June 1293

Carew

"Gwenllian!"

Carew threw himself the last few feet to the windowsill. He then immediately cursed himself for his stupidity. If he'd kept quiet, she and Arthur might have been given more than a few moments before they were missed—and maybe they would have had a chance to escape detection long enough to float downstream or reach the opposite shore. That is, if either could swim, which Carew didn't know.

At first, when Gwenllian had hidden herself and Arthur behind the window curtain, he'd made sure to avert his eyes. But while Clare had been talking to Lili, Carew had edged his way across the room so he was within a few feet of the window and was even blocking it from general view.

He'd thought initially that the girl meant merely to hide, as she'd been hiding two days ago under Lili's throne in the audience room. When she'd crouched on the sill, Arthur clutched to her chest, however, there was a moment in which time had stood still and both she and he had been suspended— Gwenllian in the act of pushing off from the stones and Carew about to shout and make a grab for her arm. Even as he'd done so, he'd known that he would be too late to stop her fall.

When he flung himself onto the window seat and looked down, he still expected to see the pair fall into the water, but they hadn't. He blinked and then blinked again, staring hard and willing them to come up for air. The Thames was hardly a torrent this time of year, and he couldn't understand how he could have missed their entry.

He continued to stare down at the river below the window, his mind refusing to process what he was seeing—or rather, not seeing. Gwenllian and Arthur weren't struggling in the water. They hadn't swum to the opposite shore nor instantly been picked up by a fishing boat. They had vanished.

Carew pulled out of the window. "They're gone." He breathed deeply in and out lest the magnitude of their loss render him incapable of thought.

"Don't be absurd." For a single moment, Clare's façade was shaken, and he spoke as if Carew, with whom he'd worked closely for five years and even conspired with at times, had suddenly become the village idiot. It indicated what he'd thought of Carew all along.

Clare brushed past Lili, who was staring at Carew rather than Clare, and thrust his head out the window. After a moment, he straightened, spinning on his heel in order to point at the two men who guarded their room, who'd been standing in the doorway behind Geoffrey. "Don't just stand there! Roust the river watch! If you hurry, you might be able to grab them from the dock. They could drown!"

"Yes, my lord." The men bowed together and hastened from the room.

The dock to which Clare was referring extended out from the ground floor of the King's Tower and was accessed by a narrow doorway a few yards upstream from the window. It had been intended as a means to provision the castle from the river or as an escape route for the defenders. The Tower of London, which protected the eastern edge of the city, had a similar arrangement.

With Clare no longer looking out the window, Lili moved past him and climbed into the window seat in order to better look straight down. With one hand on the window frame to support her weight, she stared at the water.

Clare put a hand on her shoulder. "We'll find them. Don't worry." Even though his primary prize—Arthur, rather than Lili—had escaped his clutches, he was back in character. Motioning that Geoffrey de Geneville should come with him, he strode out the door after the guards and gradually his footsteps faded down the corridor.

Lili pulled back from the open window, sat on the edge with her feet dangling to the floor, and burst into tears. Her arms wrapped around her waist, she curled into a ball, sobbing. Carew reached her in one stride and pulled her off the seat and into the comforting circle of his arms. He might be only fifteen years older than she, but he held her as if she were his own daughter. And since he loved David as a son, or perhaps a beloved nephew, that wasn't far off. David was King of England and Prince of Wales, and Carew just a courtier, but David had never been one to emphasize rank, and he had entrusted Carew with his family for a reason.

Finally, her tears abating, she said into his chest, "What did you see?"

"Gwenllian jumped and then—" He broke off, finding himself unable to continue.

Lili gripped his arm tighter, "And then what?"

"They were gone. I know I reached the window in time to see them fall into the water, but I didn't."

Lili blew out a breath and sat abruptly on the edge of the bed. Alexander lay under a blanket in the middle of the bed, fast asleep. Carew had children of his own, and he knew babies sometimes fell asleep when they were scared. He thanked God that his own wife and children were safe in Wales at his seat at Carew Castle near Pembroke.

Eight summers ago, Carew had made a fateful choice. He had abandoned his previous allegiance to the English crown and thrown in his lot with King Llywelyn and Prince David. Nothing that had come afterwards—good or bad—had ever shaken his faith in that decision. He'd seen the irony in it too. When David had eventually become King David of England, he'd effectively renewed Carew's loyalty to the English crown.

Strangely enough, the news of David's death—if Clare was right and Lili wrong—hadn't changed that certainty. Men died. Even great men died, and while Carew thought the age of twenty-four was far too soon to have lost David, that didn't change Carew's responsibilities to him or to his legacy, which devolved upon Lili, Arthur, and Alexander.

Truth be told, the fact that Gwenllian and Arthur had not, in fact, fallen into the Thames River and drowned but had *traveled* to Avalon only confirmed him in his faith—like almost nothing else could have done. The miracle that was David's reign hadn't died with him. God had arranged for David to save Llywelyn at Cilmeri, and He was still looking after David's family. Who was Carew to question the Will of God?

He sat beside Lili on the bed and put an arm around her shoulders. After a moment's hesitation, she leaned into him again, no longer sobbing but just letting the tears flow silently down her cheeks. When Clare had told her about David's death in the receiving room, she'd barely had time to absorb the fact that her vision had been real before Gwenllian and Arthur had run away. The subsequent chase and recapture had aroused her maternal instincts. She had been the one to come to him in the first place with the news of the attack on David, but he could feel doubt in her now, with Clare's certainty before her. She had to be feeling that she had lost everything.

Whereas Carew was beginning to feel a little more positive about the possibility that David really could be alive. The man had proved himself impervious to death a dozen times before. "Arthur is safe in Avalon, Lili."

"I'm so scared that he isn't." She looked up at him.

He smiled down at her. "David's alive as well, Lili."

She wiped at her eyes with the tips of her fingers. "I want you to be right."

"It's you who were right all along. Two days ago, Clare stood before us, telling us the outlines of what you saw in your vision. It stands to reason that if your *seeing* could show you what he told us, it showed you the rest as well."

"I was dreaming. I could have turned a *seeing* into a wishful dream because I didn't want to know the truth."

This wasn't the time for doubt. The disappearance of Gwenllian and Arthur had laid out what had to come next for them as nothing else could have. Carew should have acted sooner but hadn't seen a way forward. Now, regardless of how difficult it appeared or what the cost, he had to get Lili and Alexander out of Westminster Castle. In order to do that, he needed Lili strong and sure. How he was actually going to achieve freedom, Carew didn't yet know, but accomplish it he would—or die trying.

Lili put a hand on Alexander's belly, rocking him gently to keep him asleep. "What exactly do we know?"

Carew was glad to see her returning to her usual sensible self. "Not much beyond the fact that Clare says David is dead. He has so far refused to tell us more."

Leaving Lili with Alexander, Carew went to the window and looked down one more time. Clare himself was now standing on the dock below, his hands on his hips. Though Carew couldn't make out exactly what he was saying, his gestures were full of rage.

Clare had been right to think that he could safely incarcerate them in this tower. There shouldn't have been any escape out the window, except he hadn't counted on the fact that Arthur could travel to Avalon like his father. It could be that, all these years, Clare hadn't believed in the legend that had grown up around David. His admiration had been for show, starting with that first moment when he found himself unexpectedly rescued by David, Lili, and William de Bohun. He'd ridden in David's train all these years, waiting for the moment to strike out on his own. The extent of the betrayal and Clare's duplicity boggled Carew's mind.

Carew wished the three of them could follow Gwenllian and Arthur. But they couldn't, not with Alexander still a babe in arms. There was a good chance the little boy did have the same ability to *travel* as his father and brother, but Carew couldn't risk it. They would simply have to think of something else.

22

Once it became clear that Gwenllian and Arthur weren't to be found, Clare had returned to the room and apologized to Lili, his tone sincere, to the point that she could almost believe that he hadn't plotted against them. Then, because she wanted to see his reaction, she took a chance and told him that she believed Gwenllian and Arthur to be in Avalon.

In the instant after she told him, just as when the pair had jumped, there was a moment where Clare didn't have complete control over himself. He didn't do anything overt—curse or sneer at her—but she saw anger and also a frisson of fear crossed his face.

It wasn't because Arthur had escaped. That loss was a setback, but not a vital one. No—Clare suddenly feared that the news of Dafydd's death was false and that, instead of dying, Dafydd had traveled to Avalon, just as Gwenllian and Arthur had done. They all had witnessed men writing Dafydd off only to be foiled in their moment of triumph by Dafydd's return. In that moment, Lili saw Clare wondering if their fate would be his and if the grand destiny he'd plotted out for himself was not his for the taking after all.

Now, with Clare gone again, Nicholas paced about the room, occasionally looking out the window as if the children might appear at any moment in the water below. Lili rocked in the chair, nursing Alexander and trying to keep her spirits up. She wasn't the same girl she'd been when she'd run from her love for Dafydd. And while she'd turned down his proposal of marriage twice, she'd learned in the intervening years that love wasn't something to run from, even as it made a person vulnerable to heartache. Her heart was breaking now with Arthur gone and Dafydd missing, but love gave her a reason to keep on living too.

Finally, with Alexander asleep again, she stood and laid him on the bed. Straightening, she walked to the window to look out it with Nicholas. Arthur and Gwenllian did not appear. "We cannot stay here, Nicholas, not even for another hour. Clare is still marshalling his allies, but losing the children has thrown him. He won't be thinking as clearly in this moment as he will another hour from now."

Nicholas shook his head. "I know. I have thought the same thing, but I'm struggling with the idea of risking you."

"But you have to," Lili said. "Every choice we make involves risk—and I say that sitting here is far more dangerous than trying to leave."

"Do you think to distract the guards with a request for the toilet?" Nicholas gestured to the door. "They might let you out, but like as not they'd simply tell you to use the chamber pot in the next room as we've been doing. We are in the most heavily fortified castle in London. I can't overcome a dozen men by myself with just my sword."

Then he frowned as men shouted and footfalls rang in the corridor outside their room. Two heartbeats later, the door opened and Geoffrey de Geneville walked in. Lili would have spat at his feet if it didn't mean befouling her own room.

"Come with me." It wasn't a request.

"Why?" Lili said.

"There will never be a better time to escape than now."

Lili gaped at him. "You're defying Clare? You're letting us out?"

Geoffrey pressed his lips together for a moment, his eyes narrowing. "I don't know what's going on. With David dead, the world is uncertain, but Clare has gone to the hall to meet with Parliament, and I no longer feel comfortable leaving you in this tower, under his so-called protection. I think you need to leave, and I have made arrangements for it."

Bong, bong, bong. Since Parliament met inside Westminster Castle itself, a stone's throw from where they now stood, the bells calling the representatives to meet reverberated throughout the castle. Lili had been far too occupied with what was going on inside the room to worry about what was happening outside it, but now she shivered at the thought of what might transpire this day within the parliamentary hall.

"We must hurry," Geoffrey said. "Clare intends to declare war on France and is asking for the power to do exactly that. News of David's death has been all over London for two days, and Clare claims the French are responsible. He says a French fleet is even now sailing for our shores."

"I know he told us that, but he knows this for certain?" Lili said.

"I know only what Clare says." Geoffrey grimaced. "The printers have filled the streets with broadsheets, and the radio speaks of nothing else. You know how newsmen are: they make up the news if they don't have something true to say. We expect to see white sails on the horizon at any moment. Parliament will give Clare what he needs to act—maybe even the throne."

Nicholas moved to stand protectively beside Lili. "We believe Clare arranged for David's death."

Geoffrey's expression didn't change. "How could you know that?"

"We had indications months ago, before the Christmas incident, about an alliance between Clare and France. How is it that David is dead and Clare on hand to take his place? Why wasn't Clare in Aquitaine with David participating in the very meeting where he met his death?" Nicholas canted his head. "Why weren't you?"

"I received a message from the king that I wasn't needed," Geoffrey said.

Lili scoffed. "That message wasn't from Dafydd."

"It bore the royal seal!"

"I imagine it did," Nicholas said. "What is Clare's excuse?"

"The same—a message from the king. But the missive to Clare told him that the meeting with King Philip had been delayed and that he didn't need to arrive at Chateau Niort for another fortnight. Clare was in London taking care of some business affairs."

Geoffrey opened the door, looked into the corridor, and then looked back at Lili and Nicholas. "We are wasting time. Everyone knows that from the very beginning of David's reign Clare was one of his staunchest supporters. Nobody will question his fitness to lead us. He probably won't even need to ask."

"Where are our guards?" Nicholas stepped into the doorway with Geoffrey.

"Seeing to the safety of the arriving members of Parliament. The guards who aren't guarding the gates and wall-walks are preoccupied with the city. London is full of unrest. It seems that not everyone accepts David's death or agrees that they should support Clare. Still, we can't count on more than a quarter-hour's grace. We should hurry."

"If you do this—help us—and Clare wins out, your life will be forfeit," Nicholas said.

Geoffrey smiled wryly. "We all die a little bit every day, Carew. The key is to make each day worth living."

Lili had a thought to grab her bow and quiver from where they hung on the wall, but as she took a few steps in that direction, Geoffrey motioned to her. "I'm sorry, my queen, but we want to look ordinary. If you have your weapon, it will draw attention and questions will be asked. You are grieving the loss of your husband. Why would you need your bow inside the castle?"

Irked but knowing Geoffrey was right, Lili gathered up Alexander, who was still asleep, and left the room with the men. Geoffrey led them south along the corridor to the tower stairs, which they followed down to the ground floor and then turned north again, heading for the dock entrance. Earlier, Clare had taken that avenue to the dock to look for Gwenllian and Arthur.

No men guarded the door. They hadn't encountered any in the corridor or on the stairs either. A rowboat was pulled up alongside the dock with two men waiting—one at the oars and another on the dock, holding the mooring line to keep the boat from floating free.

The nearer man wore a felted hat pulled down low over his eyes, so it wasn't until he held out a hand to Lili and she took it that she saw that it was Huw, Dafydd's ever faithful follower and a member of the Order of the Pendragon. When Dafydd was sixteen, Huw and his father had walked him across Gwynedd after men tried to assassinate him. Here was Huw, eight years later, providing a similar service to Dafydd's wife and son.

Lili clutched his hand. "Thank you."

Nicholas stepped into the boat behind her, nodding his head to Huw in acknowledgement of the great service he was rendering. Geoffrey, however, did not follow.

"Aren't you coming with us?" Lili motioned with her hand that he should hurry.

"We don't have much time. Someone will see!" Nicholas pointed to the battlements, though there was no one was looking down on them at the moment. Even if someone had been, he wouldn't have been able to make out Geoffrey from that angle.

Geoffrey shook his head and stayed where he was in the doorway to the castle. "I can do more good for Arthur if I stay here."

"Clare will know it was you who released us," Nicholas said.

"How? My clerk will claim that I was in my office all this time. I am not even a member of the Order." Geoffrey gave them a small smile. "Pray for me."

He closed the door, and Huw climbed into the boat and released it from the dock. He made a move as if to sit beside his friend, a man Lili didn't know, but Nicholas had already sat in the second seat and grabbed an oar for himself. The two men started rowing, making for the far shore rather than turning the boat into the middle of the stream.

"Where are we going?" Lili said.

"Home," Huw said, "where we should have stayed all along."

Lili understood why Huw would say such a thing. It was easy to think that all Dafydd had achieved in becoming King of England was danger to his family and death for himself. But as Geoffrey had said, everyone died a little bit every day. Far better to strive for more than the ordinary. From the way it looked today, Dafydd had risked everything and lost. And yet, he had made a difference to millions of people in the five years of his reign. Even now, no matter how lost or hunted he might be, Lili thought that he would consider it a fair trade.

23

16 June 1293

David

At least he wasn't cold.

Or as injured as Philip.

Or dead.

As David thought about it, things could have been a lot worse. It had taken only two days to reach Le Havre, which was a Herculean feat that one of his Welsh bards might sing about if David lived to tell the tale to him. Three hundred and twenty miles in forty-eight hours by horseback wasn't a world record, but it was coming close, and he would have been proud of himself and Henri if both of them weren't nearly falling off their horses in exhaustion.

They'd been delayed by thrown horseshoes, by the weather, by a desperate need for sleep that had both of them lying down at the Templar station last night at their twenty-second change of horse and mistakenly sleeping for a full seven hours. The Templar sergeant who manned the stable had been asked to wake them after four hours of sleep, and he hadn't done it—not without an apology, admittedly. He'd told them he felt it a shame to wake them, given how far they'd come—and he'd sat watch over them the whole night.

As the King of England, David hadn't ever slept with only one guard, in a barn or otherwise. Of course, the man hadn't known David's identity, as Henri still did not, and the Templars were so renowned throughout France for their fighting skills that only a lunatic would think to attack them, even in an unfortified stable.

But sleeping had delayed their arrival at Le Havre from the morning to early afternoon. David took the lead, allowing the horse to pick his way the last hundred yards to the town. Every motion of the horse had David's muscles screaming at high volume. If he never sat on a horse again it would be too soon.

"Perhaps a boat is sailing with the evening tide," Henri said. While with the loss of the Holy Land, many Templar ships had docked in Cyprus and La Rochelle, some were stationed here, at Le Havre in Normandy.

David could see the fleet in question, and he prayed that the pass from Pierre de Villiers, which had stood them in good stead for two days, would do its job one more time.

"The commanderie is there." Henri gestured to a complex of buildings along the Seine River, which flowed to the south of the town into the English Channel.

David had learned a single factoid about Le Havre from his middle school history textbook, which, though woefully incomplete, had spent a lot of time on World War II. It had told him that Le Havre had been entirely destroyed by the British during the war. This Le Havre had an expansive port on the mouth of the Seine. It hadn't been built with United States reconstruction dollars but by the Templars, who, from the looks, basically claimed all of it. Their commanderie took up a football field of space, with a high stone wall around the whole of it, just as at La Rochelle.

"Come, Henri." David directed his horse towards the front gate. "God shall be my hope, my stay, my guide and lantern to my feet." Now that he was in France, he was feeling something of an affinity for Henry V.

In that instant, however, a rider dressed as a Templar sergeant raced past them heading for the commanderie too. He threw himself from his horse and began beating on the door. "I bring news that is urgent! Open!"

"I have a bad feeling about this," Henri said, inadvertently coming up with a famous quote of his own. "Somehow, I think we know what his news is."

By the time they arrived at the door and dismounted, the rider was leading his horse inside. David held up his pass and, as had been the case thirty times before, he and Henri were admitted too.

This gatekeeper was younger than twenty, tall and thin, wearing sergeant's colors. Though the rider who'd come was practically dancing with impatience to speak to someone in authority, David and Henri, in their white garb, outranked him, and the gatekeeper turned to David first.

"How may this commanderie be of service to La Rochelle?"

David gestured to the rider. "I defer my business to the boy, provided I may witness his speech to your master." He really shouldn't be calling the young sergeant a boy, since David was hardly older himself at twenty-four, but he felt he'd aged twenty years in the last two days. His entire body felt drawn and gray from too much riding and too little food and rest. And then there was his wounded ribs, which at times during the ride had pained him so much he could hardly breathe.

The rider frowned. "Why?" And then he swallowed hard and ducked his head. "Why would you ask for that, sir knight?"

"Because your news is obviously of the highest importance, and I want to know what it is," David said. "I have news of my own that will interest your master, and I suspect that it is related to yours."

The gatekeeper bowed and gestured that they should enter the inner recesses of the commanderie. "If you will follow me."

The master of Le Havre was a middle-aged man by the name of Hugh de Lusignan. Unlike Pierre, Hugh did not receive them in his office but in the center of a sandy ring where a dozen men, stripped to the waist, were fighting each other in mock battles. It was a good reminder: these men were monks, but they were warriors too.

Hugh finished his fight by upending his opponent and fake jabbing a blunt sword into his throat. Then he straightened and spied the gatekeeper, who gestured that he should come over.

"What is it?" He looked the four of them up and down, eyebrows raised at the sight they presented. Henri and David, while dressed as knights, were three hundred and twenty miles worse for wear, mud-spattered, sweaty, and exhausted. The sergeant, who'd ridden in before them, didn't look much better. For his part, Hugh's muscled torso glistened with sweat and would have done a Greek god proud.

"Sergeant Jean has come with grave news that cannot wait." The gatekeeper pointed with his chin to the young rider.

"The King of France is dead!" Jean had been dying to share his news, and he couldn't wait a moment longer. "The

Duke of Aquitaine is dead too, ambushed by men serving Gilbert de Clare."

Henri and David exchanged a significant glance. It was as David had guessed: the people of France were to be told that Clare had arranged for the assassination, while the people of England and Aquitaine would be told that the culprit was Charles, Philip's brother. Clare and Charles would cover themselves in patriotic glory and go to war against each other, sacrificing men in a few battles or skirmishes before arranging a truce.

Hugh's hair was receding from his forehead, and he wiped at the shiny pate with a cloth. "You say truly? How is it you learned of this?"

"Word reached Paris two days ago, and I set out immediately to inform our commanderies throughout France."

"Where is Clare now?" Hugh said.

"We don't know. Our master was hoping that you might have received word of him from Temple Church in London."

Hugh gave a noncommittal grunt and rubbed his chin without answering. As the crow flies, Temple Church in London was one hundred and thirty-five miles from Le Havre. A homing pigeon could easily fly forty to fifty miles in an hour, so if there was something happening in London, Hugh really might have heard about it by now. Unfortunately, that meant Clare might have too, but the thought was so sickening to David that he immediately put it aside. It wouldn't do to dwell on or worry about things that he couldn't change.

David felt it was time to speak. "The sergeant's news is not entirely accurate."

Hugh looked at him. "And you are?"

"My name is not important." David showed Hugh the pass Pierre had given him. "Pierre de Villiers has sent us to say that neither King Philip nor King David is dead. We ask your assistance in bringing this news to London."

Jean was looking extremely put out that his news had been trumped by David's. "But—"

Hugh cut him off. "How do you come by this information?"

"I have seen both men alive with my own eyes, well after their reported deaths. King Philip was wounded in the assassination attempt and has found sanctuary in a place he can heal. Even now, King David makes for England under duress."

Henri stirred beside David, but he didn't speak. He was a smart man and even now might be reconsidering his assumptions about David's identity. David had arrived at the commanderie at La Rochelle with a wounded man who was indeed now in a place of sanctuary. Another minute and Henri was going to put two and two together. Truthfully, it would be a relief if he did.

"I have heard similar news, sent from our Templar brethren in London."

David stared at him, astonished. "How could they possibly know?"

"Master Windsor did not choose to impart that information. Suffice to say, I was asked to offer every courtesy to King David, were he to cross my path."

Henri took a step forward. "Master, King David stands before you. We apologize for the deception, but it was necessary to ensure the king's safety." He had figured it out, but he had such control, as befitted a Templar knight, that nothing about his stance or expression showed surprise or anger, and he spoke matter-of-factly.

For his part, David gazed steadily at Hugh, trying to be as unemotional as Henri. His identity hadn't been Henri's secret to tell, but presumably now he and Henri would, in fact, receive every courtesy.

"You are dressed as a Templar," Hugh said.

David almost laughed, totally unsurprised that Hugh's objection to the deception was his use of Templar clothing and gear. Instead of laughing, however, he answered Hugh in a grave voice. "I am King of England, anointed by God to rule. I have sworn oaths, just as binding and sacred as yours. Thus, Pierre de Villiers deemed me worthy of wearing your colors."

Hugh gave a little *huh* sound. "He knew who you are, my lord?"

"Of course."

"Why did he send you to Le Havre?"

"We hoped by riding I could make London more quickly than by sailing directly from La Rochelle."

Hugh looked at him warily. "When did you leave La Rochelle?"

"The afternoon of the fourteenth," Henri said—and then he grinned at Hugh's astonished look.

Hugh barked a laugh. "Master Villiers wasn't wrong. The winds turned favorable this morning. If you'd sailed from La Rochelle, it would have taken you at least five days to reach England. I have a ship sailing for Portsmouth within the hour. It's far closer than Dover, and the Portsmouth master, a man named John Fitztosny, can see you safely to Temple Church in London."

David really wanted to go to Hythe—though he would have taken Dover in a pinch. He knew people in those places. Perhaps some of his men had recovered from their sickness by now and could aid him. By contrast, even having reached England, from Portsmouth he would have to continue to pretend to be a Templar.

"That would please my lord." Henri put his heels together and bowed. "Thank you."

"My men will see to your preparations." Hugh snapped his fingers at several of the battling sergeants, who ceased fighting and came over. They nodded at the instructions Hugh gave them about arranging an escort for David and Henri to the ship. Then he turned back to David. "Have you dined?"

David gestured to indicate himself and Henri. "We have ridden nonstop for two days. I reek of horse and sweat and am covered in mud. I wouldn't want to disgrace your table."

"Such is the life of a warrior—and a king," Hugh said. "It would be no disgrace, my lord. Still, we have little time and perhaps it is best to supply you with provisions, and you can eat at your leisure on the ship."

That sounded like a better plan to David too. Within fifteen minutes, he and Henri were mounted again. They were about to ride out of the castle amidst three Templar sergeants, having said goodbye and thanks to Hugh, when a messenger came racing out of the main hall. "A pigeon has brought more news!"

Hugh held out his hand for the tiny piece of paper, unrolled it to read briefly, and then passed it to David, who leaned down to take it. The message consisted of fourteen words: *War with France imminent. Clare seeks throne. If news from King David, please advise.*

"So it begins." Hugh took back the paper from David. "I will send a pigeon to Master Windsor to tell him that you are alive and pray for a swift journey for you." And then he actually smiled. "By God, I wish I could come with you just to see Clare's face when you stand before him, alive and whole."

David found himself unbearably angry to be so far behind Clare still, even with all the work to reach this point, but he managed a smile and a question, "Do you and Clare have a history?"

"I knew his first wife well. I crusaded with her brother."

Clare and his first wife, Alice de Lusignan, had separated many years ago. She was rumored to have been King Edward's mistress, and there was a great deal of controversy about their divorce and talk about how badly she'd been treated by Clare. In his defense, he'd been only ten years old when they'd married.

David gathered the reins. "We reap what we sow, Hugh. I will attend to him."

Hugh stepped back. "Godspeed."

Once they reached the dock, David headed up the gangplank to board the ship, which was terrifyingly small by modern standards. He turned back, however, when he realized Henri hadn't followed and was hesitating at the far end of the gangway.

David walked back down to stand in front of him. "You don't have to come with me. If you owed your master anything, that debt was fulfilled by accompanying me to Le Havre. Your place is in France. I understand if you feel betrayed by my deception."

Henri scoffed. "Betrayed? I was a fool for not seeing sooner." He shook his head. "I understand the deception."

"Then what is wrong?"

"I am seeing the journey through new eyes." He gestured helplessly to the ship. "You have suffered here in Aquitaine. Nothing that has passed has been fit for a king. And yet, you have accepted all without complaint or remark."

It wasn't really a question, but David answered as if it had been. "I've found some freedom in anonymity. You and I became friends, if you don't mind me saying so, without having my title come between us."

"*Oui*. It has been an honor." Henri seemed to have decided something because he started up the gangway with determination. "My place is at your side, and I desire to see how this ends."

"Hopefully not in our deaths," David said. "It may be that every port and castle in England is now held against me."

"Surely you don't believe all your barons to be as fickle as Clare?"

David looked down at his feet for a moment. "I honestly don't know."

"I do not know England as well as you do," Henri said, "but we have heard things in La Rochelle. You have brought order and prosperity to your country. You have quelled the bickering among your barons. You are King Arthur returned. It seems to me that if your people knew how little faith you had in them, they would be most disappointed in you rather than the other way around."

David smiled to himself at being chastised by the Frenchman and followed Henri onto the ship. Speaking truth like this was the Templar way. "You are right that one betrayer does not an insurrection make, and if Clare is telling everyone that I am dead, as it seems he is, then my sudden resurrection will be welcomed by many. At the same time, we shouldn't underestimate Clare's power and reach. To pull this off, he will have been bribing men for months, if not years. He also knows the names of many members of the Order of the Pendragon, and thus the lives of every one of them could be forfeit."

Henri's mouth turned down. "This *Order of the Pendragon*, I have heard of them too—they are crusaders as well?"

"No. Their goal is to protect me."

"Hmm." Henri scratched his forehead. "Perhaps I've misunderstood, but I don't think they've been doing a very good job."

24

16 June 2021

Christopher

Jon was one of those friends who couldn't think on an empty stomach. Christopher had to feed him every two hours or he started getting grumpy. Thus, since he hadn't yet come up with a viable plan of what to do next, Christopher took everyone to Aristotle's Diner. He figured it would be what his mom called a *cultural experience* for Gwenllian and Arthur and would have the added benefit of feeding everyone because the menu was huge and varied.

"Start at the beginning," Jon said. "I need to hear it again."

So Christopher told him—all about Meg disappearing long before he was born; and then about David and Anna; the visit from David when Christopher was ten; and then what happened last Christmas when he and his family had met David's family in Wales. All the while, Gwenllian and Jon ate like they were never going to have another meal. Arthur still wasn't talking, but he laid into his chocolate-chip whipped-cream-covered pancakes anyway.

Christopher himself was having a hard time eating anything. His bacon omelet suddenly looked unappetizing, and he pushed it towards Jon, who'd been eyeing it for the last five minutes, having finished up his own plate. Christopher's throat was dry from all the talking, so he took a sip of milk. Then his phone rang.

Hoping it was his dad, he pulled it from his pocket, only to find that the call was from a number he didn't recognize. He stared at it, hesitating.

"Aren't you going to answer it?" Jon said.

"It's probably a telemarketer."

Jon nodded, but then his jaw dropped as another thought struck him. "What if it's the CIA? Dude, you should have ditched the phone first thing. You're on the grid!"

"If I did that, my parents couldn't call me back." Deciding he might as well answer and find out how badly he'd screwed up, Christopher pressed talk and put the phone to his ear. "Hello?"

"Is this Christopher Shepherd?"

The man spoke with an English accent, which at least suggested he wasn't CIA. "Yes." Christopher didn't see any point in denying it.

"This is Mark Jones, MI-5. We met last year in Caernarfon."

"Hi." It was a lame response, but he couldn't think of anything else to say.

"Your GPS says you're at something called *Aristotle's Diner* in Radnor, Pennsylvania. Is that accurate?"

"Wha—how did you know?"

Mark tsked through his teeth, and in retrospect Christopher shouldn't even have asked the question because the answer was obvious. Mark was MI-5, and in keeping his phone, Christopher had ensured that he remained on the grid.

"Is-is-are we—" Christopher stuttered, "—how much trouble are we in?"

"Thank God you said *we*." Mark blew out a breath on the other end of the line. "This is a secure connection, if you're worried. Tell me—there was a flash not far from where you are. Who is *we*—did someone come—who are you with?" Mark also seemed to be stumbling over his words in his need to get them out.

"It's Arthur and Gwenllian," Christopher said, knowing he wouldn't have to explain to Mark who they were.

There was a pause before Mark spoke again, and now his voice sounded wary. "Just Arthur and Gwenllian?"

"Yeah. They jumped out of a window at Westminster Castle because Gilbert de Clare told them that David was murdered during a meeting with the King of France, but then Clare decided to take the throne instead of making Arthur king and—"

"Slow down; slow down. Did you say David is dead?"

"That's what Clare thinks, but it isn't true, according to Gwenllian. David escaped and is stuck wandering around Aquitaine by himself."

"Is Gwenllian there?"

"Yes."

"Can I speak with her? She knows me."

A little nonplussed, Christopher held out the phone to Gwenllian. "It's Mark Jones. He says you know him. He wants to talk to you."

Tentatively, Gwenllian took the phone and put it to her ear in imitation of Christopher—and then launched into a flurry of Welsh of which Christopher understood nothing.

He looked at Jon, who was eyeing him. "Did I hear him say he's MI-5?"

"Yeah. He's one of Callum's men."

"Whoo." Jon let out a rush of air and sat back in his seat, one of a long line of booths at the diner, which was decorated in a 1950s style and was owned by a Greek family. Apparently, when Greeks came to the United States, many bought diners, just as Italians opened pizza parlors and Vietnamese ran doughnut shops.

Gwenllian had tears streaming down her cheeks, and Christopher felt bad, because she was sitting across from him so he couldn't hug her. The tears came a little harder every time she said David's name. Arthur, who was sitting next to Christopher, had stopped eating and was staring at Gwenllian.

Christopher put his arm around him, and Arthur didn't pull away. "It's okay. It's going to be okay."

Any fool could see that it wasn't, but before Arthur started crying too and Christopher had to figure out a way to calm him down, Gwenllian wiped at the tears on her cheeks and handed the phone back to Christopher. "He says David is alive."

Mark was still on the line, so Christopher put the phone up to his ear. "How could you possibly know that? Did you see a flash? Is he here too?" That would solve all of Christopher's problems at once.

"No, but I don't think the time traveling would be working if he were dead."

"What do you mean?"

"Because it's about David. It's always been about David. Every single time someone has time traveled, it's been because either David needed to or needed them to," Mark said. "Does David need his son alive? Yes, he does. It's that simple."

Gwenllian was looking a little better since Mark had talked to her, though Christopher thought Mark's idea was wishful thinking. Anna and Aunt Meg had traveled on their own enough times that he didn't see how Mark could be right. But if it got them all through the next few days, he wasn't going to argue with him. And honestly, believing David was alive didn't change anything. Christopher still had to get Gwenllian and Arthur back to the Middle Ages in one piece.

He made a sweeping gesture with one hand, though Mark couldn't see it. "Whatever. What do I do now?"

"Where are your parents?"

"Dad's in California, and Mom's mad at me. I haven't been able to reach either of them."

Mark made a *gah* sound in the back of his throat. "Let me liaise with a friend of mine in the FBI."

"How do you know we can trust him?" Christopher said.

"We can trust him," Mark said, without answering Christopher's question. "His name is Jim Jenson, and you'll know he's the right bloke because he looks like Bruce Banner. Actually, on second thought, text me his picture when you meet him, just to make sure."

"Why do we need him?"

"Because I'm worried about who else picked up the flash, and you're an ocean away. I'm pretty sure CMI—that's the private security company that's been chasing David for years—hasn't given up, and there might be other interests, governmental or otherwise, who look at the possibility of traveling to the Middle Ages as an opportunity to make a fortune."

"Oh."

"Can you stay where you are for a while?"

"If we order more food," Christopher said.

"Order more food. Let me make some arrangements and get back to you."

"Why don't I just take them back to the Middle Ages now?"

Another pause. "You're sure you want to do that? You're sure David would want you to do that? They're here because it's safer here."

"They always arrive back where they're supposed to," Christopher said. "David said so."

"Yeah, but even if David is alive, he's still in France. Give him some time to straighten things out there before you put his kid back into the middle of it."

"Okay," Christopher said. "But hurry."

"Before I go, does your friend have a phone?"

"Yes."

"I want you to take apart your phone and bin the pieces. What's his number?"

Christopher told him, hung up, and then related the gist of his conversation to the others.

"Waiting to go back sounds like good advice, actually." Jon held out his phone to Christopher and made a *gimme* motion with his fingers for Christopher's. Silently, Christopher handed it to him. He had forgotten to tell Mark that the case for his phone was solid and wouldn't open. Jon would have to pry it apart if he was going to take out the battery.

"I have an idea." Jon turned slightly in his seat. The people in the booth behind them were just getting up, and one of the men had hung a raincoat over the wooden partition between the booths. Jon slipped the phone into the outside pocket, seconds before the man's wife scooped it up and hung it over her arm as she walked away.

Christopher laughed softly and looked at the other three. Gwenllian seemed to be feeling much better, and Jon was grinning, engaged in the adventure and pleased with himself for his quick thinking.

Arthur turned his bright eyes on Christopher, and it wasn't just their piercing blueness that reminded him of David. "Can I have some ice cream now?"

25

16 June 1293

Lili

As soon as they reached an accessible spot along the riverbank, Huw moored the boat and leapt out. He held out his hand to Lili, even as his eyes went past her to Westminster's battlements, still visible in the distance.

"Do you see anyone?" Carew said.

Huw shook his head. "There's no alarm yet, and with all the traffic on the river, we should be hard to spot."

Here in the late afternoon, the Thames was almost as busy as a city street. In fact, the people of London used the Thames as a street, hauling goods from one side of the city to another more easily than by cart. The southern side of the Thames wasn't normally a place to stop, however, since it wasn't really part of the city. As Lili's soft leather boots squished into the mud, she remembered that it was essentially a marsh. At times, in the never-ending quest for land to expand the city, parts of it had been filled in, but most of it was wet and difficult to traverse due to the narrow paths and the forests of reeds, which, of course, made this area all the better to hide in and was the reason Huw had taken them here in the first place.

Fortunately, they didn't have to stay. Huw led them unerringly down a narrow path through reeds that grew higher than Lili's head and everything she could see was green and wet. After a quarter-mile of travel, they came to a place where the reeds were replaced by trees, and they could stand on more solid ground. Huw found a spot where they were hidden on all sides from the eyes of any passer-by—were one to brave the marsh at all—and shrugged his satchel off his shoulder.

"I have a change of garments for you, my lady." He looked apologetic for even mentioning it. "It won't do for you to go about in those clothes."

"I am in no way offended, old friend." Lili took the plain blue overdress he offered. "You saved us, and you know as well as I that I have spent far more of my life wearing clothing like this than the gowns of a queen."

"I'll stand guard, Huw." Raff, the second man, who'd shared the rowing with Nicholas, paced away from them back towards the river, his boots leaving clear prints in the soft ground. Other than ducking his head when they'd been introduced, these were the only words he'd said.

Nicholas looked intently at Huw. "Who is he and why do you think we can trust him?"

"He thinks more than he says. He's a good man, despite being from Yorkshire," Huw said, as if it was obvious that being from Yorkshire was something to apologize for.

"He's willing to come with us to Wales?" Lili gently laid Alexander down on the ground, still asleep in his wrappings. He had a tendency to take one four-hour nap in the afternoon, and they were fortunate that he could sleep—and maybe sleep a little harder and longer—through the upheaval of the day.

"To the ends of the earth," Huw said.

"Why?" Nicholas's tone was just short of demanding.

"His father stood for Parliament this last election and won; his sister was allowed to divorce an abusive husband, thanks to Dafydd's reforms," Huw said. "Raff himself is a bastard, now allowed to inherit because of that law Dafydd pushed through in April. Some in the Church hate these changes, but the result has been an unswerving loyalty in those whose lives have been transformed."

Nicholas subsided at this rather eloquent speech, nodding, and took off his own ornate tunic in favor of a leather jacket and mail vest that Huw pulled from his bag. Without concern for propriety, Lili untied the strings on her dress and shoved it down to her hips. She wore a linen shift underneath, which covered her completely, but Huw and Nicholas swiftly turned their backs anyway.

Laughing at their embarrassment, especially since she'd been nursing Alexander in front of them, Lili tugged on the coarse dress of a peasant woman, thankful it wasn't itchy and that she didn't have to give up her linen shift, which was softer against her skin. While it was true that she'd worn dresses like this one before—and more often simple breeches—the roughness of the fabric wasn't as familiar to her as it once had been. She then wrapped her hair in a headscarf and tucked in the strands. She was now transformed into Huw's wife or sister.

She tapped Nicholas on the shoulder, and he turned back. "What about your sword?"

"Keep it," Huw said. "Queen Lili and I shall act as your servants, and Raff as your man-at-arms. Nobody will look twice at us, especially when the queen carries a baby in her arms."

"You'd better start, both of you, by calling me Lili."

Huw looked unhappy, but Nicholas smiled gently. "I will go down on bended knee before David when he—" His face paled.

"None of us believe he's dead, Nicholas—I mean, *my lord*. My heart beats constantly—against all expectation—that I will see him coming around a bend," she gestured back the way they'd come, "or sailing down the Thames, as he did when he defeated William de Valence."

Huw bent to pick up the baby, who'd opened his eyes. "I'll carry him for now." He whistled like a bird through his teeth.

Raff came hustling back, sweeping a stick behind him to scatter dirt, grass, and leaves. He'd noted the footprints too and was doing his best to disguise them. "Men patrol the walls of Westminster. Chances are they know by now that you've escaped. We should hurry."

The little group started walking with long strides, led by Nicholas, the group's natural leader. As they headed southwest from the river towards the main road out of London, leaving the life Lili had led for five years behind her, tears fell silently down her cheeks. She had never wanted to be queen, but she'd accepted it because Dafydd had needed to be king—not for his sake, but for Wales and ultimately for the people of England.

She kicked at a rock in her path, suddenly angry at Dafydd for going off to Aquitaine when she and the boys still needed him. Never mind England and Wales, which would fall into iniquity under Clare's rule.

In between alternating bouts of gut-wrenching fear and boredom of the last few days, Lili had been spending quite a lot of time thinking about the Order of the Pendragon—even more now as she had her friends in it to thank for her and Alexander's survival. For all that they'd—she'd—been completely taken in by Clare, it wasn't for a lack of information or because any one of them had been asleep at the wheel, as one of the twenty-firsters who'd gone back to Avalon had liked to say.

Their mistake had been in not putting the pieces together from the bits of information and rumors they'd heard, starting last autumn, and they'd allowed Clare's own reassurances to lull them into a false sense of security. Clare was a charmer. She'd seen him work his way through a room and been the recipient of his charms more than once. Because Clare had no royal blood, he'd settled for less than the crown time and again. His new French wife had died in childbirth shortly after the Christmas feast, and Lili wondered if it had been her death that had made him choose this moment for his ultimate betrayal. Maybe it had been the final push to make him decide that he should—as Lili had heard Cassie say more than once—*go big or go home.*

Last January, after Clare's wife had died at his estates in Ireland, he'd risked a winter voyage across the Irish Sea, landing in Wales at Rhuddlan. He'd ridden to Llangollen, where Dafydd and she had remained for a month after Alexander's birth, since it would have been unhealthy for her or the baby to travel far, and Dafydd had been reluctant to leave them.

She'd been present when Clare had strolled into the reception room at Dinas Bran and drawled in that casual way he had, "I hear someone has been impugning my name."

Dafydd had reassured him of his continued trust, since he had every reason to believe that the plot that had been uncovered was not between Clare and the King of France, as rumors had told it, but between Aymer de Valence and the Red Comyn.

That all seemed foolish and naïve now. Clare had probably encouraged Valence in his mischief and treason, at no cost to himself, knowing that he was far away in Ireland, awaiting the birth of his child, and wouldn't be implicated in the plot, no matter how it ended.

It hadn't ended well for Aymer de Valence, though Dafydd had intended to let him out of the Tower of London once the treaty with Philip was signed. Releasing Valence was probably the first thing Clare had done after capturing Lili and the boys, accompanied by a speech about how now was the time for reconciliation and forgiveness.

After another half-mile, they reached the Portsmouth road and fell in behind a merchant traveling south with a wagon full of spinning wheels, which had been invented in the east and arrived in Europe a few years ago. Dafydd had immediately encouraged the spread of the technology—adding the treadle and the flyer—and thus energized the wool industry, which had been further transformed by Bridget's introduction of knitting.

"The day wanes, Huw," Nicholas said. "I hope you have a plan?"

"We will stay in Kingston tonight." Huw glanced back at Nicholas and Lili. "We have friends at the Church of St. Mary." Kingston was a market town, established during Saxon times.

"How many miles?" Nicholas said.

Lili was glad he'd been the one to ask, because she was afraid to.

"Five miles—no more than that," Huw said.

Lili could walk fifty miles if she had to, and she was glad now of her simple garb. She wasn't a queen any longer. All that mattered was the safety of the children. She prayed that when Gwenllian and Arthur returned, they would arrive in the right place at the right time. She prayed too that they were safer in Avalon than they would have been if they'd stayed with her.

26

Gwenllian

After a while, even with their orders of ice cream, which Gwenllian enjoyed very much, they couldn't stay at the diner anymore. They were just getting ready to leave when Mark called back to say that the FBI man needed a place to meet, and Christopher should choose one quickly. Since it had started to rain, Christopher didn't want to go to a park or some place outside, and he didn't think they should go to either his house or Jon's, so he settled on a place he called *Bryn Mawr College,* which was where his mother had gone to university. Gwenllian had traveled once with Dafydd to Cambridge, where he had met with scholars from all over the world, so she knew what a university should look like.

Or so she'd thought.

Bryn Mawr, she decided instantly, was where she would choose to go if she was allowed to attend university. It might be that men and women were equal in Avalon (according to Mom and Anna and Bronwen and Cassie), but it looked to Gwenllian like women who attended this school had the better end of the deal. Huge stone buildings, almost as impressive as Dafydd's castles, loomed over her, and the great hall was more magnificent than any hall she'd ever been in—not so much in size but in decorations.

"Wow." She spun slowly on one heel as she studied the images in the stained glass windows. Then she frowned and pointed at a red and yellow banner that hung on the far wall. It showed Gwynedd's three lions. "That's Papa's banner!"

Christopher laughed. "This is *Bryn Mawr*, Gwenllian. The people who settled here, and who founded the college, were Welsh. Didn't you realize?"

Gwenllian shook her head. She hadn't given any thought to the Welsh name, since most names in her experience were Welsh.

"They remember that your dad was the last Prince of Wales—in this world anyway," Christopher said.

Jon had come into the hall with them, slouching with his hands deep in his pockets. "I don't know about this, Chris. Why are we meeting the FBI guy here?"

"Because it's private, but it's also public. I suppose I could have chosen the mall."

Gwenllian didn't know what a *mall* was, but she was glad Christopher had come here, even if Jon wasn't. Arthur was back to sucking on his finger, which Gwenllian didn't take as a good sign, though he wasn't crying and held her hand willingly enough. She wished she could wrap him up in her arms and protect him from all of this. That's what she'd thought she was doing when she'd jumped out of that window. Now, she hoped she'd made the right choice. She had been thinking only of escaping and hadn't given any thought to what they were going to have to do to return. It would have to be something spectacular and terrifying.

Honestly, she hadn't really believed they would *travel* to Avalon when she'd jumped. She'd hoped for it—or at least part of her had done so—but she'd really been thinking about swimming. Both she and Arthur were good swimmers, Arthur having learned last summer from Huw, and there were worse things than falling into the Thames. Because Westminster was on the western side of the city, and thus upstream from London proper, the river wasn't even that dirty.

She'd planned to swim with him to the Lambeth Palace shore and get away that way. She hadn't been allowed to spend very much time on her own outside castle walls—okay, no time—but she wasn't completely stupid, and she'd had a tiny bit of a plan. People were often nicer than you thought they might be, and when she was with Arthur, they tended to treat her well because of him. Four-year-olds, especially cute ones, drew adult sympathy.

It wasn't as if she thought she could walk all the way to Wales or anything, but getting out of the castle with Arthur had seemed a better idea than staying in it. The black abyss had swallowed them whole, so she'd known when they'd landed in a heap on the grass beside the train station instead of in the river that she'd *traveled*. She'd thought the stories David had told her had prepared her for Avalon, but they hadn't—hardly at all. Those first minutes with Arthur had completely overwhelmed her, and she'd sat on the bench to think because she'd had no idea at all what to do.

And then Christopher had come, and whatever faith she'd lost after learning of Dafydd's possible death had been renewed. She really did think that Mark was right and whatever magic was inside Dafydd was still working in her favor. As she stared at the rows of Welsh banners, she took their existence as a sign that it would continue to do so.

"Can I help you?"

They all spun around to look at the young woman who'd appeared in the doorway. She had dark skin like Darren Jeffries and was dressed almost identically to Christopher in brown pants and a blue shirt.

"We're waiting for someone," Christopher said.

The woman shrugged. "It's almost five o'clock, so we'll be locking the doors in a few minutes."

Christopher pulled out Jon's phone and looked at it. "We'll be out of here by then."

"Okay. Thanks." She left.

Keeping the phone in his hand, Christopher looked at the others. "We'd better wait outside." He led the way out of the hall and started down the steps, but before he reached the bottom, one of the heavy double doors opened, and a man entered.

They all pulled up in response, including the man, who said, "Christopher Shepherd?"

Christopher identified himself with a nod.

"Mark Jones sent me. I'm Jim Jenson."

Beside her, Jon gave a visible sigh of relief. Gwenllian didn't know who Bruce Banner was, but the man was dressed in what Gwenllian understood to be a suit and tie (she'd only ever seen Callum and Darren Jeffries wearing that kind of clothing), albeit somewhat rumpled, as if he'd wadded his clothing into a ball before putting it on. Water glistened on his shoulders, and Gwenllian could see past him through the open door to the rain puddling on the ground behind him.

The man held the door wide and gestured them through it. "Come with me."

Christopher hesitated. "Where are we going?"

"Somewhere safe. I've made reservations at a hotel. We'll be completely anonymous."

"Okay. Lead the way."

They hustled through the rain after the man, following him to where he'd parked his car, one twice as big as Christopher's. Christopher kept moving, however, heading towards his small vehicle, which was parked farther down the street. It was raining hard, so Gwenllian didn't stop until she reached the passenger side door.

The man, however, came to a halt by his vehicle and called after them. "It would be easier to go in my car."

"I don't want to leave mine here because it will get towed," Christopher said. "Just tell me the name of the hotel in case we get separated in traffic."

"The Hilton in Valley Forge." The man didn't argue further, and entered his vehicle.

Christopher then waited for the man to leave his parking space and pull past them so he could follow him. Meanwhile, however, Christopher pressed on his phone with one finger and then gave it to Jon. "We're on our way in my car. He's leading."

"Okay, Christopher," Mark's voice bellowed out of the speaker, far louder than before in the diner. "You need to stay smart and loose."

Gwenllian leaned forward from her place in the back seat. "What's going on?"

"That's not Jim," Christopher said. "Mark doesn't know where Jim is. This guy knew where we were, and he looks a bit like Jim, but it isn't him."

Jon looked skeptical. "How do you know?"

"Dude, I took a picture and texted it to Mark!" Christopher said.

"Oh," Jon said. "What happened to the real Jim Jenson?"

"You let me worry about that," Mark said. "I need you to get yourself someplace safe."

Arthur tugged on Gwenllian's arm, and she bent to him so he could whisper to her. "He had a thing in his ear." To Arthur, everything he didn't know the name for became a *thing*, which in his lisp came out usually as more like *fing*.

Gwenllian straightened. "Christopher, Arthur says Jim has a thing in his ear."

Christopher looked at Gwenllian through the mirror that hung from the front window glass. "What kind of thing?"

This time Arthur spoke for himself. "It was inside." He stuck his finger in his ear and swiveled it. "It was the same color as his skin."

Jon turned around to look at Arthur. "Like a hearing aid?"

Arthur looked blank, and Gwenllian spoke for him. "What's a hearing aid?"

"They don't know, Jon. They don't have those," Christopher said. "It could be a hearing aid. Did it have a wire sticking out of it, Arthur?"

Arthur shook his head.

Mark was still on the phone. "What are you talking about?"

Jon brought the phone closer to his mouth. "Arthur saw something in the man's ear. We're wondering if it's a communication device."

"Depends on who he's working for or if he's freelance," Mark said. "Christopher, are you being tailed?"

Christopher jerked his chin to look in the front mirror, though this time he was looking past Gwenllian out the back window. "I don't know."

Gwenllian and Arthur turned at the same time, Arthur standing on the seat so he could see better.

"Arthur should be buckled, Gwenllian. It's too dangerous to ride like that." Christopher stopped the car.

At first Gwenllian thought he'd stopped so she could fix Arthur's seat belt, but then he started going again before she'd finished. The cars in front and behind them went at the same time.

"Coming up in about a quarter-mile," Mark said from the phone, "you need to do exactly as I say."

"Okay," Christopher said.

"You're going to take a right, go until you can take another right, speed as quickly as you can until you hit a *T*, take a left, drive a thousand meters and pull into Bernie's Car Wash on the left, which currently has no clients. It's the kind where you drive straight in. Can you do that?"

"Right, right, hit the *t*, left, left into car wash. Got it," Christopher said.

"I'm tracking you, but there might be some delay in the GPS. You just passed Henderson, correct?"

"Yes." Jon answered for Christopher.

Gwenllian had no idea who Henderson was, presumably the son of Hender, but she was glad that Jon and Christopher did.

"How far ahead of you is the fake Jim?"

"Two cars," Christopher said.

"Slow a little until just before your turn and then speed up and take it. Your car is fast, isn't it?"

Christopher laughed. "Oh yeah. Hang on, guys."

Gwenllian was thrown into the door as Christopher took the turn and sped to the next corner. She tried not to scream as she gripped the door handle and was thrown against the door again for the next turn. She glanced at Arthur, afraid for him, but his eyes were open, and he had a huge smile on his face.

"You okay back there, Arthur?" Christopher asked.

"Yes!" Arthur said.

In hardly any time, they turned into a large empty space that Jon called a *parking lot*. Christopher gave the attendant a white and green piece of paper that he took from his pocket, and they drove into the darkness of what Gwenllian had to conclude was the car wash.

"Make sure the windows are up," Jon said, and without Gwenllian doing anything, her window went up the last inch.

Water began to spray all around the car so Gwenllian could no longer see through the windows. It was as if a giant monster was attacking the vehicle. Christopher and Jon—and even Arthur—appeared unworried, so Gwenllian tried to pretend that she wasn't frightened either.

Mark spoke from the phone, "Did you lose them?"

"No idea," Christopher said. "But I've pretty much given Gwenllian and Arthur the grand tour of the twenty-first century, haven't I?"

"How's that?" Mark said.

"Chocolate chip pancakes and a visit to a car wash."

27

16 June 2021

Christopher

As Christopher made the offhand comment to Mark, he thought he sounded calm and mature, disguising the fact that his heart was beating a million miles an hour. Back at Bryn Mawr, he'd palmed his phone, surreptitiously taken a picture of the fake Jim, and then texted it to Mark. He'd done it as a precaution and honestly been shocked when Mark texted back that the guy was an imposter.

The car worked its way through the car wash, its wheels locked into the conveyer belt, and Christopher sank deeper into his seat. He felt a little bit safer, just for a second, but the burden of Gwenllian's and Arthur's lives had never felt heavier. If not for his pounding heart, Christopher might have thought he was dreaming. He'd been excited to meet a real FBI agent, and now he was running from a fake one. Stuff like this didn't happen to regular people.

"What am I supposed to do when the wash finishes?" Christopher said.

"I'm working on it," Mark said.

Jon held up one finger in imitation of their high school calculus teacher. "I know where we can go."

"Where?" Everyone spoke together, including Gwenllian from the back seat.

"My friend Gary and his family are out of town for the week," Jon said. "Christopher can park his car in the back of their property, and everyone can stay in their guesthouse."

"A guesthouse, eh?" Mark said.

"Lots of people have them out here," Jon said.

Christopher had grown up on the Main Line, so he knew that anyone who could afford property anywhere in the area had serious juice behind them. Christopher's family was rich compared to 99% of the country, but they were in the bottom quarter for Radnor, so he didn't usually feel very rich when most of the other kids around him were taking annual trips to Europe.

He'd been to Wales, it was true, but they hadn't stayed at a castle, and it was only on the way home, after what his dad called *their traumatic week*, that he'd upgraded their flights to first class. The Black Boar Inn had been the most exciting place they could possibly have stayed, but it wasn't luxurious. His parents didn't believe in showering their kids with stuff. At the moment, Christopher was appreciative of their thriftiness, since he really did have the fastest car in the school, even if it was over twenty years old.

"We're coming out of the car wash," Christopher said to Mark.

"Be ready to drive," Mark said.

It was as if they were held in suspended animation, all praying that the fake Jim hadn't figured out what they'd done and wouldn't be parked in front of the car wash when they came out. Christopher hadn't spotted a tail, but that didn't mean a) there hadn't been one; or b) that if they'd had one, they'd lost it. Or, now that he thought about it, c) Jim hadn't put a tracking device on one of them or the car.

It was still raining, which was probably why the car wash had been empty. It was kind of stupid to wash your car in the middle of a rainstorm. The second he passed a truck, the mud spit out from its wheels would get his car dirty again.

"Can you see Jim?" Mark said.

"No," Christopher and Jon said together, and then Christopher hit the gas.

The little car zoomed out of the parking lot. Last winter, when David had told Christopher the whole story about the aborted attempt by David and Anna to pick him up at his friend's house all those years ago, David had vividly described the winding roads and lanes that made up the Main Line. The way the streets wandered had confused Anna and David, but Christopher had grown up here and, more importantly, had been driving these same roads for two years now. Mark was trying to give Christopher directions, but Christopher knew where he was and where he was going. He also knew where the cops liked to hide out, and for all that he aspired to be one, he would be delighted to avoid a speed trap today.

"Anyone following, Jon?" Mark must have given up on talking to Christopher, which was probably for the best since he was too focused on his driving to answer.

"Not the way Christopher is driving." Jon clutched the door handle. "We may not survive this."

"I don't see the downside of crashing," Christopher said—and meant it. He checked behind him to change lanes and caught another glimpse of Arthur's face. He was still wide-eyed and smiling. Gwenllian wasn't quite as cheerful, but she wasn't as close to screaming as Jon.

Christopher hit a straight-away that he wouldn't normally have driven down this fast. Gary's house was off to the south, but he was wary of going directly there and wanted one more chance to shake off any pursuer. He blew by the Radnor Country Club and the Overbrook Golf Club and, at the last minute, took a right, circling through some housing tracts— what his dad called *strip mine developments*—and then back onto a larger road.

He pulled off to the side for a second to allow two cars to pass him. Once they disappeared around the curve ahead, he pulled back onto the road and then almost immediately turned into Gary's place. He sped down the paved driveway, canopied this time of year in leafy branches. In another ten seconds, his car was invisible from the road.

He reached the back of the property and stopped, making sure the hedge that surrounded the main house screened them from anyone entering the front door. "We're here, Mark."

"You're sure about this, Jon?" Mark said. "Don't they have a caretaker?"

"Yeah, me," Jon said. "Taking care of all these mini-farms while their owners are on vacation is my job for the summer."

Christopher looked at his friend. "You didn't tell me that. That's cool."

"Really cool," Jon said, showing more enthusiasm. "It's a lot of work, but it pays really well."

They closed the connection with Mark and got out of the car. His phone to his ear, now talking to his father, Jon led them to the back door of the guesthouse. He moved aside a potted plant on the top step, bent for the key, and used it to unlock the kitchen door. He then ushered everyone inside.

Christopher found the light switch, and the blue and white open plan kitchen lit up as if it was welcoming them. When he turned to look at Jon, however, his friend was looking worried.

"I should go home. I put off my parents by saying that we've been at a movie, which is why I didn't answer their texts for a while, but Dad wants me home. If I don't go, he might find a way to track where we are through the GPS."

"When we drove away, your dad was talking to someone on his phone—did anything come of that?" A now familiar rocky feeling took over Christopher's stomach.

"He didn't say directly, but I don't think so. Just now he complained about dealing with a patient all day who isn't recovering from surgery as well as my Dad would like. He'd almost forgotten what happened with you."

Christopher gave a low laugh. "All this time I've been worried. Just tell him I dropped you off so you could take care of Gary's place, and then you walked home."

"You'll be back?" Gwenllian said to Jon.

"In the morning," Jon said. "They want me here at six to feed the animals again, and my parents know it."

"What if you're late?" Gwenllian said.

"Just stay put until morning. I'll be here. I promise."

The boys looked at each other for a second, and then Christopher surprised himself and Jon by sticking out his hand. "Thanks."

"You bet." The boys shook. "What kind of friend would I be if I let you take care of your time traveling cousins from the Middle Ages all by yourself?"

Christopher spent the next hour getting Gwenllian and Arthur fed, bathed—because they couldn't come to the modern world without getting the full bathing experience—and then settled in twin beds in one of the rooms off the kitchen. As a final touch, he put on an old Star Wars DVD. He figured a galaxy far, far away was about as preposterous and impossible to believe as the fact that they'd time traveled, so why not blow their minds completely?

He was pretty sure that he wasn't going to sleep at all. He wanted to talk to his dad, and he felt lost without his phone. The guesthouse had WiFi and a tablet for guests to check their email. While he was wary about doing anything online, in the end he decided that anonymous web surfing wouldn't be traceable to him and fired up the tablet. Then it occurred to him that he had an online phone account, and his dad did too. He didn't have skills like Mark, but he knew a thing or two about disguising his IP address. After some finagling on the internet, he finally called his father.

"Hello? Christopher?" To have answered that quickly, his father must have been holding the phone in his hand. Christopher felt bad that he'd been waiting all day for Christopher to call him.

"Hi Dad!"

"Your mom and I have been worried sick. Both of us have been calling and calling."

"I know. I'm sorry. Things have been kind of crazy." Christopher was wary of saying anything specific to his father, and things *had* been crazy, so it wasn't a lie.

"Where are you?"

"Did you call the police on me?" Christopher said.

There was a pause. "No."

"Are you alone?"

"You're really lucky that you caught me when you did." His dad let out of a burst of air. "I'm alone in a bathroom right now, but I just had a visit from the FBI."

"They came because of me," Christopher said, not as a question. "They know, don't they?"

"More than I do, obviously," Christopher's dad said. "One of their agents, Jim Jenson, was the victim of a home invasion. Someone knocked him out and took his phone and computer."

"Is he okay?"

"He's concussed and doesn't remember anything from the hours before the attack. But he'd scribbled down your name and cell phone number on a piece of paper—apparently he's somewhat old school—and his cell phone records show that his last call was to an agent at MI-5, who we met last year—"

Christopher was feeling sick to his stomach. *Again.* "I was afraid something like this had happened. Mark Jones arranged for Jenson to meet with us, but then some other guy showed up instead. We got away."

"Holy sh—" his father cut himself off.

"It's okay, Dad. I'll be eighteen in a few days. You can say it."

"I don't need to," he said. "So that's what has them all excited. They wouldn't tell me what was going on, just kept asking me why Mark Jones would be interested in you. Christopher, you shouldn't be having to deal with this by yourself."

"Nobody else can."

His father paused. "Am I to understand that someone's come home?"

"Arthur and Gwenllian—all by themselves."

His father swore for real this time. "Are they okay?"

"No." Christopher decided not to beat around the bush and told his father everything Gwenllian had told him.

"Aw, David—" his dad was silent for a moment, and Christopher could picture him with his head bent.

"Mark says he doesn't believe he's dead, and that Lili's right, even if it makes no sense that she should know. She predicted everything that has happened, so if she's right about that, we have to believe she's right that he's alive."

His dad thought about that for a second, and Christopher could almost hear him shrug. "I want to believe David's alive, so for now I'm going with it."

"Mark thinks the time travel thing is linked to David, and if he weren't alive, it wouldn't be working."

His dad let out a disbelieving laugh. "It's a nice thought."

"Does the FBI know that someone's here? Do they have someone watching for the flash like Mark did?"

"I don't know. If they did, the two agents who came to see me didn't share that information with me."

"Dad—I may have to go with them."

His father didn't ask which *them* Christopher meant, knowing that he was talking about Gwenllian and Arthur. He let the silence drag out in another pause, this one longer than before. "I—I—"

"You could come too."

"I can't leave your mother and sister," his dad said.

"Yeah." Christopher swallowed hard. "We're safe tonight, I think. I'll call you in the morning."

"Okay. Don't use the regular phone."

"No." Another pause.

"I love you, Christopher."

"I love you too, Dad."

"I don't want you to go—" His father broke off. "Someone's coming. If this call is traceable, I've probably talked too long already." He closed the connection, leaving Christopher alone again in the dark.

28

16 June 1293

David

When the Le Havre master had told David that the winds had turned favorable for a journey to Portsmouth, which lay directly to the north of Le Havre, he hadn't been kidding. Normally, as David had witnessed nearly every day of his life, whether in Oregon or Britain, the prevailing winds blew from the southwest. Thus, when journeying from France to England, the easiest course was to follow the English Channel from southwest to northeast, landing at Hythe or Dover.

This afternoon, however, the winds were coming directly from the south—in other words, blowing directly behind the ship as it sailed from Le Havre to Portsmouth. It was a potentially dangerous situation to be in, so, of course, the captain and crew were in high spirits. David had no other task than to stand at the prow of the ship and wait for England to appear on the horizon.

"You don't have a mind to journey with us more often, do you, my lord?" the captain said from behind David. "The men are saying they've never seen such a wind. We might well break the record from Le Havre to Portsmouth. But then—"

He paused, and David glanced back to see the captain eyeing him.

"—I hear such a feat wouldn't be the first for you."

David smiled at what he assumed was a reference to his journey from La Rochelle with Henri, but didn't elaborate on his own feat. "What is the record for this trip?"

"Ten hours, accomplished with a dead downwind like today, but with less load." French wine made up almost the whole of the cargo, some of which might ultimately end up in one of David's castles, though it could equally be reserved for Templar use.

While the ship was smaller than David had expected, it had huge sails, which perhaps explained the speed. David himself wasn't any kind of sailor, and he hadn't taken the time to learn the technical terms beyond simple names like port and starboard. Sailing was such a specialized activity that it took years of practice and apprenticeship to reach the captain's position. The Templars awarded some jobs because of lineage or the wealth a man brought to the order, but sailing captain wasn't one of them.

David was pleased to see that the Templars had gone all in on the new technology for sailing he'd brought back from Avalon. He hadn't been able to bring back a working sextant, but the captain had a shiny new one, manufactured from specifications David had printed out in Avalon. The captain had set it up near the main mast, and he kept glancing lovingly at it. Still smiling, David turned away. The captain was right about the speed of the ship: a smudge that was land had appeared on the horizon.

They'd left Le Havre at approximately four in the afternoon. Ten hours would bring them into Portsmouth at two in the morning, and that initial calculation turned out to be not far off. Because of the speed and the danger in running before the wind, every member of the crew spent the entire journey awake and on alert. There was one tense moment when the captain almost turned them off course into the dead zone that could have overturned them, but he righted the ship with a few barked orders.

Thus, after a little more than nine hours, during most of which David had slept, they sailed into Portsmouth harbor. David would have bought drinks all around if he'd had any money, but he'd left Chateau Niort with nothing and, as a Templar knight, he still didn't have any coins. Both he and Henri remained dressed in the full regalia of the Templar Order, all of which they'd worn nonstop now for three days. As they docked, David put on his helmet to hide his features on the off chance, now that they'd reached England, that he'd be recognized.

With Henri in tow, David wended his way through the grinning sailors and the astounded docksmen, who were being told the story of their journey by the sailors even before the ship was securely tied. David himself was delighted to have made it so quickly. And, since he, unlike the crew, had slept for several hours on the ship, he was already focused on the next step in his journey, which was to ride to London. For that, he needed the cooperation of John Fitztosny, the Master of the Portsmouth Templar commanderie.

Unfortunately, as it was one in the morning, it wasn't an hour normally conducive to asking favors. Someone else had already run ahead, however, perhaps sent by the captain or the dock master with the news of the ship's arrival and of their special guests—namely Henri and David. They were admitted through the gatehouse and then led to the master's receiving room. The door opened before they reached it, and a tall man, a few years younger than David and dressed in the livery of a Templar knight, ushered them inside. Neither the corridor nor the room was well-lit; a lantern hung from a stand, and a few candles flickered on side tables.

Fitztosny either hadn't gone to bed yet or had hastily dressed to receive David, though he hadn't attended to his appearance beyond his tunic. His hair stood up on end, and he ran his hand through it, trying to tame it. The gesture only made it worse. From the wrinkles on his face, like all the other Templar masters David had so far encountered, Fitztosny had reached middle age. His full beard was still reddish-brown, however, like the hair on his head. David allowed himself a small sigh. He'd never met Fitztosny before, and he didn't think he needed to worry about being recognized.

"Who are you?" Fitztosny said with borderline rudeness. It *was* late.

By way of an answer, David handed the man the passes he'd accumulated so far—the first from Pierre back in La Rochelle and the second from Hugh at Le Havre. Neither mentioned that he was the King of England, and it was still David's preference that his identity remain a secret.

Fitztosny didn't even look at the passes when he took them, but handed them immediately to his attendant. "Thomas, read these for me."

David didn't think the Templar master could have come this far without being able to read, but it could be that all he needed was a pair of reading glasses. David made a mental note to send an oculist to Portsmouth to get Fitztosny fitted, and he wished he had pencil and paper in his breast pocket, like he usually carried, to start a list. Maybe it was optimistic of him to think that he would make such a present to Fitztosny, but given where he'd started and how far he'd come, it was an hour for optimism.

While Thomas studied the passes, Fitztosny poured wine into goblets, one for each of them. David's last meal had been nine hours ago on the ship, so, secure in his anonymity, he gladly removed his helmet and accepted the cup.

"We are to offer these Templars our unconditional assistance—" Having looked up from the papers, Thomas broke off, staring at David.

David cursed silently to himself for becoming complacent about his identity.

"Thomas?" Fitztosny said.

"M-m-my lord." Thomas went down on one knee with his head bent. "We were given warning days ago that you might be coming and in need of aid, but it's been all over the news that you are dead. We haven't known what to believe—"

David stared down at the back of the young man's head, shaking his own. On one hand, the odds against this meeting had to be astronomical. On the other, the world of the nobility was very small. If it hadn't been Thomas, it could easily have been someone else David knew. "Rise, Thomas."

Because, of course, this was Thomas Hartley, the boy David's mother had saved from Scottish marauders nine years ago on Hadrian's Wall, who himself eight years ago had saved David and Ieuan from his uncle's wrath (and had burned down the stables at Carlisle Castle in the process), and who was now an upstanding nobleman of twenty.

Thomas popped to his feet, his blue eyes brighter than ever, and David stepped forward to embrace him. Thomas had grown to nearly David's height, though he remained more lightly built.

"You rascal." David released him in order to take in the whole of him. "Since when did you become a Templar?"

"Since earlier this year," he said. "I finished my squireship, and my uncle knighted me. I'd always wanted to serve God as a Templar. This is my first posting."

Fitztosny had been looking uncertainly from Thomas to David and back again. Thomas turned to him, ducking his head in obeisance at the same time that he held out his hand to David. "I give you David, King of England, who is not dead as Gilbert de Clare claims." He turned back to David. "They're crowning him king at noon today at Westminster Abbey."

David raised his eyes to the ceiling. Clare was doing everything in his power to make sure his crowning was done right, since Westminster Abbey was where Norman kings were supposed to be crowned. "That gives us slightly more than ten hours to get me there."

"This is impossible," Fitztosny said, and David wasn't sure if he meant David being alive was impossible or getting him to London in ten hours.

He chose to address the latter. "In France, the Templars maintain stations every ten miles, so a rider might cross the country quickly. You're saying the Templars here do not?"

"We do. Of course we do, but—" He sputtered to a halt. "Sire." He bowed.

David spread his hands wide to encompass his appearance and presence. "I apologize for the deception. It was not my intent to offend, but I've had four days of constant travel since Clare's assassin shot two arrows into my chest, and in that time, I've learned to be warier and less trusting. Are you saying that you will not aid my quest?"

Fitztosny straightened while at the same time letting out a sharp breath. "We heard of your potential need from Temple Church and sent word on to Le Havre. The news of your death came to us several days ago, and the newsmen speak of nothing else. I must send word back to London immediately that you have arrived—not to mention stop those fools on the radio from spreading falsehoods."

"By all means send word to Master Windsor at Temple Church, but—" David put out a hand to him, "please say nothing to anyone else. I don't want Clare to know that I am alive before I arrive at Westminster." Then he hesitated. "How did Temple Church know of my potential need?"

"I do not know," Fitztosny said, "only that Master Windsor did."

David filed that away in the back of his mind as something to ask Carew's brother when next he saw him.

Meanwhile, Fitztosny studied David, his hands clasped before his lips in an attitude of contemplation. He spoke over them. "It's seventy-five miles to London."

"Then we must change horse seven times," David said.

Fitzstosny gave a snort and dropped his hands. "We are blessed with a clear night and the moon is only a few days from full. I must caution you, however, that I cannot send men with you. Our stations house only four horses at one time."

"We are only two." David gestured to Henri.

"Three." Thomas turned to Fitztosny. "With your permission, master."

Fitztosny bowed to David. "You have the full support of the Templars, my lord—and our prayers—this night."

29

Near Kingston

17 June 1293

Lili

"Riders are coming, Lili," Nicholas said. "We need to get off the road."

Lili sighed and directed her horse towards the margins of the track, following Nicholas on his horse. Then they both dismounted to hold their horses' heads, because they didn't want them to spook and because it was custom in England for those of lower rank to move aside and bow their heads when noblemen passed by. She'd witnessed it hundreds of times since becoming queen—never quite getting used to it—and it was odd now to see it from the other side. It was probably good for her too. Regardless, they followed the custom because the last thing they wanted was to behave in any way that would call attention to themselves.

This close to the solstice, dawn came so early that her initial idea to rise with it hadn't happened. Lili had slept right through the ringing of the bells for dawn prayers, and it was only the crying of Alexander that had woken her. She'd nursed him and then risen to find Nicholas saddling the horses and Huw packing the saddle bags with food for their journey.

"Clare will be crowned at noon," Nicholas said by way of greeting when she walked into the stable, Alexander on her hip.

"He went to Parliament and actually asked for the crown?" Lili said, aghast. It was the worst-case scenario.

"No, he didn't. He asked for authority to wage war on France, but several representatives spoke eloquently about the need for consistent rule and that Clare had proved himself worthy of the throne time and again. The Archbishop of Canterbury was there, and he supported the idea. They voted, and Clare will be king."

"An election is what David has always wanted, except that I can't help but think that those representatives were bought." Lili shook her head. There was irony in the archbishop opposing Dafydd's reforms at every turn, but then using them for his own ends when it suited him.

"Clare is the wealthiest man in England," Nicholas agreed. "Once he is crowned, he will be seen as anointed by God and the Archbishop of Canterbury. Whether or not he was crowned under false pretenses, he will still be king."

"And if Dafydd turns out to be alive?" Huw asked, though as he did so, he bit his lip. The question had come from the heart, which he hadn't intended to expose so plainly.

"At the very least, the throne will be in dispute. Will Clare truly step aside once that crown has settled on his head? And will David be willing to fight for it if it means civil war?"

Lili put both hands to her cheeks, her head spinning and her thoughts muddled. "Then the farther we are from London by noon the better. Clare will have what he wanted, and he will have no further cause to bother with us."

"I wouldn't be so sure of that, my lady," Nicholas said, "but we will do what we can to remain inconspicuous."

Nicholas often acted as Dafydd's purser, and he carried gold with him as a matter of course. Because Clare had been pretending he was on the side of the angels when he'd sent them to the King's Tower, he hadn't taken either Carew's sword or his gold. Consequently, Carew had fled the castle with enough money in his purse to buy two horses from the monastery. Having transportation wouldn't necessarily make their journey faster, since Huw and Raff would still have to walk, but riding would relieve Lili of the weight of carrying Alexander, and Nicholas could better look the part of a knight.

Last night, travelers on the road had been too overcome by the news of David's death, which was being broadcast from every village green from here to Chester, to worry about why a knight was walking. The monks had assumed without Nicholas having to lie that his horse had been stolen, and since his gold was as good as the next man's, they hadn't objected to selling him replacements.

"Templars," Nicholas said in disgust as soon as he recognized the characteristic white mantles with the red cross. "Three of them." As the riders pounded along the road towards them, they scattered the mid-morning travelers and merchants, who were heading into London to sell their wares.

"They put the Order of the Pendragon to shame," Huw said. "I see now that we were too closed and secretive, and that allowed Clare to manipulate us."

"The Templars are equally secretive, so I don't think that's it," Lili said. "It was what we focused on. We thought loyalty to Dafydd was enough to unite us, but it wasn't. Templars serve God and crusade to the Holy Land. There's nothing to gain personally for any individual except acclaim. Clare joined the Order of the Pendragon to undermine us. He wouldn't have joined the Templars because all he's interested in is earthly power."

The Templars drew closer, riding as hard as ever, but then the foremost rider, who had seemed intent on barreling past them, suddenly slowed his horse. He still passed their party, because the horse had been galloping too quickly to stop on the spot, but then he turned the horse's head and came back.

His two companions slowed too, and one said, "What is it, my lord?"

The lead rider didn't answer, just trotted up and dismounted. Nicholas, Huw, and Raff bowed their heads, since Templars were not to be trifled with, but Lili wasn't feeling conciliatory, and she didn't look away.

And then she couldn't look away. All she could see of the man's face were his eyes, shining through the slit in the visor of his helmet, but she would know those blue eyes anywhere. She gave a little cry and put the back of her hand to her mouth, unable to speak, think, or even weep.

Dafydd pulled his helmet from his head and tossed it aside. He reached her in two strides and picked her off her feet in an all-encompassing embrace. Squashed between them, Alexander let out a muffled cry. Dafydd set Lili down again, but he didn't let her go, and they stood together with their arms around each other.

Still too overcome to say anything, Lili held on. She had prayed that he wasn't dead, and the only thing in her head was the fact that he was alive and standing in front of her.

"My lord—" Nicholas choked on the words.

Dafydd laughed out loud, and with a kiss for Lili and then Alexander, he overrode whatever Nicholas was trying to say by wrapping him up in a bear hug too. Huw stood next to Nicholas, tears streaming down his cheeks and not making any effort to stop them. Dafydd's hug for him was just as enthusiastic. "I can't tell you how good it is to see you!"

"You gave us a mighty scare, my lord," Nicholas said.

"I know. I know."

Lili touched Dafydd's arm, needing to know that this wasn't a dream and that he really was standing before her. "What—" But then there were too many questions to articulate, and none were important.

Dafydd understood without her having to speak. "Philip took an arrow in the shoulder first, and then I stepped in front of him before he could be mortally wounded. The Kevlar vest saved me, *cariad*. We fell from the battlements at Chateau Niort and ended up in the river below."

She nodded. It was just as she had dreamed.

He tipped his head. "You aren't surprised by my story."

"I *saw* it, my love."

Dafydd held her by her shoulders. "When?"

"Before midnight, four nights ago."

"That's when it happened." His eyes narrowed. "Is it because of you that the Templars at Le Havre and Portsmouth knew to look for me?"

"Nicholas spoke to his brother, Godfrid de Windsor of Temple Church."

Dafydd turned instantly to Nicholas. "Thank you. If not for you and your password, I wouldn't be standing before you today."

"You used it?" Nicholas's expression lightened.

"At La Rochelle. It probably saved the life of Philip of France as well."

Nicholas swallowed hard. "It was nothing, my lord."

"Believe me, it was far more than nothing."

Lili put her hand on Dafydd's arm again. "My love, you did not travel to Avalon when you fell. Why?"

"I don't know. I wasn't in enough danger, perhaps, though I find that hard to believe. Maybe it was simply that I needed to stay." Dafydd suddenly looked around. "Lili, where's Arthur?"

Lili took in a breath. "He is in Avalon—with Gwenllian."

Dafydd gaped at her. "What?"

"Gwenllian jumped with him from the window in the King's Tower at Westminster."

Dafydd was left momentarily speechless, and he scrubbed at his hair with one hand while he thought.

"These two helped us escape the castle," Lili gestured to Huw and Raff, "along with Geoffrey de Geneville, at great risk to himself."

"I assume you have a plan for stopping Clare, my lord?" Nicholas was recovering from the shock of seeing Dafydd and from the grief of the last four days.

"Oh, I have one." Dafydd gave a laugh. "Whether it's any good or not remains to be seen. Where have you come from and where are you going?"

"We spent the night at the monastery at Kingston," Nicholas said. "We've come perhaps three miles today."

"We were heading for Wales," Huw said, speaking for the first time.

Dafydd shot a longing look west, and then he turned to look in the opposite direction, to the northeast, though he couldn't see London from where they stood. "It is my plan to confront Clare and Parliament *before* they crown him. I ride in haste for Westminster."

"The whole country believes you dead, my lord," Nicholas said.

"The radio stations were the first thing Clare took over," Huw said.

"Don't I know it! These damnable newsmen! When I built the radio, I had no idea what a weapon it would become, or how it could be used against me, by Clare of all people. Even if I oust Clare today, it will take six months to convince everyone I'm actually alive." He laughed. "I suppose it will be a nice problem to have under the circumstances."

"I'm more concerned that Clare has spread the story that France had you murdered and that he himself is innocent in your death," Nicholas said. "You can't simply challenge him at Westminster and expect the people to accept that he is the villain of the piece. They don't love Clare as they love you, but they have grown used to your brand of justice, in which every man is allowed his day in court. Clare has charm, and if he denies any culpability, then it is your word against his, and many will feel you are hanging an innocent man. Do you have proof that he arranged for the assassination?"

Dafydd gave a mocking laugh. "Not enough. I have a Welsh arrow that I pulled from my chest. That's it."

"Nicholas is right," Lili said. "The people have always been on your side, Dafydd, but we need a pre-emptive strike to keep them there. Even if you succeed in stopping Clare's coronation, he isn't going to admit fault or give way. You can't have him stabbing you in the back later if you are forced to let him go for lack of evidence. And you don't want to mar your triumphant return with imprisoning him out of hand. It will look petty. Better to win the war of words before he has a chance to counter you or even knows that we are fighting back."

"How?" Dafydd said.

"We need to take Lambeth station," Huw said.

Lili hadn't thought about the station when they'd passed near it yesterday afternoon. For reasons she didn't understand, the main station for London—and the country—was located in a marsh. The station's towering antenna broadcast line-of-sight to antennas located on the highest ground all around London, which then broadcast to the rest of England. Lambeth station's electricity came from a waterwheel in the Thames, while the antennas on the hills were powered by wind.

"Preferably sooner rather than later," Nicholas said. "Once we take it, we can tell the whole country that you are alive."

There were nods all around from the others too—all except Dafydd, who remained skeptical. "And how are you going to do that? Three men, a woman, and a baby—against how many of Clare's men?"

Huw patted the axe on his hip. "We are not without resources, my lord." Raff lovingly stroked the hilt of the long knife in his belt.

For Lili, it was decided. "I don't have my bow, and now I really wish I'd brought it, but we will take it for you, Dafydd. It won't be so guarded now that Clare believes he has won. Even if he does fear that you are alive, he won't think it possible for you to have reached London by now. If I didn't see you standing in front of me, I wouldn't have believed it either! It hasn't even been five days!"

Nicholas put a hand on Dafydd's shoulder like a benevolent uncle. "I have seen you perform many miracles, my lord. We are all prepared to witness one more. You see to Clare in person, and let us do our job."

"Rupert runs the Lambeth station," Raff said.

"Is that a good thing?" Dafydd said. "I wouldn't have called him an admirer."

"He is not a soldier," Lili said, "but he will do the right thing." *She hoped.*

By way of an answer, Dafydd put his arm around her again and bent to kiss Alexander's forehead. The baby reached for his father, and Dafydd took him, bouncing him on his hip once before giving him back. "I stink of horse."

"I will never chastise you for that—or maybe anything else—again," Lili said.

"You shouldn't stop, *cariad.* You made me promise to wear the Kevlar vest night and day, and that I obeyed saved my life."

Dafydd's two companions had dismounted and approached several minutes ago, but neither had spoken, in large part because the conversation had taken place in Welsh, which they didn't understand. Dafydd finally remembered them too, and he turned to introduce them. "This is Henri, who has been at my side since La Rochelle, and Thomas Hartley, formerly of Carlisle. He saved my life once."

Lili remembered and nodded a greeting at the two newcomers, who bowed before her.

Dafydd plucked at his lower lip, looking from one to the other. "I hate to let you out of my sight again."

"If Rupert is still alive, he will be manning the Lambeth station because Clare's crowning is a story he would not miss, even for a second," Lili said. "He knows Carew and me. We'll be fine."

Dafydd was still looking concerned, but he nodded. "Templar dress will get us into Westminster without question."

Lili put her arms around her husband, unable to bear parting from him again, knowing that they were both going into danger—he more than she—but seeing no way around it.

"Just tell them that the rumors of my demise have been grossly exaggerated," Dafydd said with a laugh.

Lili wanted to shake him for his flippancy, and Dafydd knew it because he gave her a rueful look. "Time and again, we have paid for my decision to take the throne. Don't think I don't know what you've sacrificed. But I can't let Clare win—not this way."

"No." She bent to retrieve his helmet from where he'd dropped it on the ground and handed it to him. "None of us can."

Disguised again as a Templar, Dafydd mounted his horse and, with Henri and Thomas, raced away. The four companions who remained looked at each other.

Huw cleared his throat. "I am ashamed that I lost faith."

"No," Lili said. "Even if Dafydd appears to be the return of Arthur, he is not holy. He is a mortal man, though maybe blessed with more luck and goodness than the average man. He would not begrudge us our grief, because he does not see himself as someone in whom we should have faith."

"In fact," Nicholas said, "he is angry at himself—far more than we could be at him—for making the mistake of trusting Clare."

Raff took Alexander from Lili so she could mount her horse, and then handed the baby up to her. Alexander was tired of his wrappings, so he stood in front of her, held close to her body by the sling in which she normally carried him. She cinched it tighter so that he wobbled less. She had known, back before she'd married Dafydd, that having small children to care for would be inconvenient at times. She just hadn't thought it would be this difficult—or that her heart would hurt so much to be parted from Arthur.

"How far have we come?" she asked Nicholas, trying to distract herself from the fate of her firstborn son.

"Three miles back to Kingston, then another ten to Lambeth." He checked the sky. "It will be close to noon by the time we reach the radio station. We should hurry."

"We should ride double." Lili lifted her chin to Huw and Raff. "Take the other horse. Nicholas, you ride with Alexander and me. This heavily laden, the horses won't be able to gallop, but they can canter thirteen miles if we need them to."

"And we do," Nicholas said.

Two hours later, both horses were dragging with exhaustion. Alexander was no longer enjoying the ride but was clutching Lili around the neck on the verge of what Dafydd called *a meltdown*. But they had finally reached the narrow road that would take them towards the Lambeth radio station. Lambeth Palace, the seat of the Archbishop of Canterbury, was built on the same marsh. Mostly the archbishops came and went by boat rather than navigate the wetland that surrounded them.

The radio station lay to the south of the palace, for here the Thames ran north to south. Once again, they were a stone's throw from Westminster, and Lili felt that if she stretched out her arm, she could reach out and touch Dafydd, who should surely be there by now, waiting for her to speak. While getting inside the station was itself terrifying, she was suddenly feeling inadequate because she had no idea what she was going to say. She'd never given a public speech before.

Nicholas started frowning as the antenna came into view. "Where are the guards?"

"Maybe they're all at Westminster," Lili said.

Truthfully, there was no reason for Clare to station more than a handful of men here. Dafydd was dead. He was about to be crowned king. Who was there to threaten him?

They dismounted and moved with the horses to the edge of the road. Lili's dress became instantly soaked to the knees by the long grass.

"Leave the horses." Without waiting to see if Huw and Raff obeyed him, Nicholas crept forward, as if scouting out an enemy location was something he did every day.

When they were still forty yards from the station, two men, one red-haired and burly and the other thin and dark, came around the side of the building. They looked to be on patrol.

Lili, who was crouched behind Nicholas, froze. "What do we do?"

"Do you recognize either man, Huw?" Nicholas said. It didn't appear that they'd been spotted yet, though that would change in a heartbeat if Lili couldn't keep Alexander quiet. He was nursing while wrapped in the sling, but he was so easily distractible at this age that he might rear up at any moment and demand a different kind of attention.

"No," Huw said, "which means they might not recognize me."

"I'll go first," Raff said. "I've just come to London. They'll know from my accent I'm not from here. While I distract them, you work your way around to the rear of the station, and the three of us can jump them at the same time from different directions."

Nicholas jerked a nod, indicating that he agreed. Raff headed back the way they'd come, so as to approach the station openly and as if he'd just arrived. Nicholas put a quelling hand on Lili's shoulder. "You stay here, my queen."

For perhaps the thousandth time, Lili wished for her bow, because she could have removed both men from the equation with two arrows. Nicholas and Huw headed into deeper woods to the right, and Raff set out towards the station along the road, whistling, with his hands thrust deep in his pockets. He was whistling a ballad about King Arthur, sung in taverns from Hythe to Bangor and believed to reference Dafydd. Probably not the best choice of music today.

The two guards didn't notice or care, nor did they immediately move to arms. As Raff approached, the red-headed man said, "Who are you?"

"Lost." Raff laughed and shrugged elaborately, his hands upturned. "How do I cross the Thames?" Raff had started to roll a bit as he walked, implying that he'd drunk a great deal.

"Not here." The guard rolled his eyes in the direction of his partner. Both men looked on with amusement as Raff got to within two feet of them, and it was only in the instant that Raff moved that Lili realized—a half-second before the guards—what he planned to do.

Since his hands were up already, he needed hardly any motion to pop his right fist into the red-haired guard's throat. Then, at somehow nearly the same instant, a knife appeared in Raff's left hand, which he drove into the chest of the thin guard. They both dropped, at which point Nicholas and Huw bounded out of the woods.

"You didn't wait for us!" Huw said, offended.

Nicholas approached the red-haired guard, who had his hands to his throat and was gasping and choking, trying to get his breath. "Sorry about this." And he stamped hard on the man's neck, breaking it.

Lili shuddered and looked away, her nostrils flaring at the scent of violence in the air. She was glad that Alexander hadn't seen it. She came out from behind her tree and approached the five men: three living allies and two dead enemies. "Is there anybody else here?"

"I guess we'll find out," Carew said.

30

17 June 2021

Christopher

J on had come at six in the morning, fed the animals, and left with a wave. "Stay here. Everything's good. I'll be back in a few hours, and we'll figure out what to do next."

But he hadn't come back in a few hours, and by eleven, Christopher had been pacing for quite some time, trying not to show his anxiety to Gwenllian and Arthur. He'd spoken with his father again, but neither of them had any better ideas about where to go or what to do. Christopher felt humiliated by his indecisiveness and was sure that David would have done way better.

His father had parted with the FBI agents on good terms last night. He hadn't been able to find a flight to the east coast until this morning, and it had left California three hours ago heading east. But it would be hours still before he would land in Philadelphia. Christopher had never felt so alone, which had to be only a fraction of what Gwenllian and Arthur had been feeling since they arrived in the twenty-first century.

Since both Christopher and his father assumed that the only reason the FBI had let him go so easily was because they figured he'd lead them to Christopher, it wasn't as if he could meet his dad at the airport either. His dad didn't believe the FBI wanted to do more than question Christopher about the fake Jim Jensen, and Christopher could totally understand why they wanted to do that. But, impossible as it sounded, Christopher had bigger concerns than the impersonation of an FBI agent.

"What are we going to do?" Gwenllian finally asked the question that she'd probably wanted to ask hours ago, but hadn't out of politeness.

Before Christopher could answer, Jon slipped through the back door, a finger to his lips and a gun in his other hand. Christopher opened his mouth to ask what the hell he was doing, but Jon motioned for them to get down below the level of the counters.

Christopher obeyed, knowing that Jon wouldn't be here with a gun unless it was serious. Bent double, he hustled over to him. "What's going on? And why the gun?"

"I thought we might need it, you know, in case the bad guys showed up again."

"Whose gun is it?" Christopher felt his voice rising, and he tried to calm himself down.

"My dad's."

"Who are we hiding from?"

Jon lifted his chin to look out the front windows. "Everyone."

"That is not helpful."

"Mark Jones called me, looking for you. He's been talking to the FBI on and off all night. Mark's number was the last one Jim Jenson called, and they want to know why."

"Yeah, I know. They've been talking to my dad too. What did Mark tell them?"

"That he'd arranged for you to speak to Jenson because of what happened in Wales last year. He had a few more questions to wind things up, and Jim agreed to liaison between you and MI-5."

"That really makes no sense," Christopher said.

"Apparently the FBI men didn't think so either. Mark is actually way less worried about the FBI than whoever is after you. He's really worried that whoever this is was able to connect you to Jim Jenson so quickly."

"So am I! Why do you think we've been hiding here all night? Who does Mark think the fake agent works for?"

Jon's eyes were flicking around the kitchen as if a man in black was going to pop out of one of the cupboards at any moment. "One of those private security corporations that has been hunting David for years. Back when he and Anna went to Wales in 2010, things were different, but now everybody and his mother has a satellite. Anyone could have seen the flash when Gwenllian and Arthur arrived." He talked matter-of-factly, like he'd been in on the secret for years, even though it had to still feel weird to him. "They must have hooked into your phone the moment Mark called you, which may even mean that he has a mole in MI-5."

"Not just anyone would attack an FBI agent to get to us," Christopher said.

Jon shrugged. "And then there's the fact that I saw a black SUV go by our house, heading for here."

Christopher gaped at his friend. "You could have said that first thing when you came in!" He was glad he'd moved his car onto a dirt road that went through the woods on its way to the main road. The track wasn't wide enough for any car bigger than his. If he had to go down it fast he might bottom out the undercarriage, but it would allow them a quicker getaway if they needed it.

"Someone's here." Gwenllian had been peering through a front window of the guesthouse. Christopher and Jon ran over to look with her in time to see a black SUV pull into the driveway and park in front of the house.

"How did they know where we were?" Christopher turned to Jon. "Did your dad call them?"

"No. I swear it," he said. "Last night when I got home, I told him you'd calmed down after a while. He wasn't mad or anything. He's worried about you."

"You tried to tell him about us, but he didn't believe you," Gwenllian said, still peering out the window. "People are getting out."

"What do we do?" Jon said.

Christopher put his hand on the top of the gun, which Jon had been waving around to emphasize his sentences. "We put that away right now." Without waiting for Jon's consent, he took it from him, walked into the bathroom, and hid the gun inside a stack of towels under the sink. By the time he came out, two agents—one male and one female, both in suits—had exited the SUV. Neither of them was the fake Jim Jenson.

"Hide!" Christopher waited for Arthur and Gwenllian to run down the hallway to their room, and then he walked to the door and opened it. His hands in the air, he called as loudly as he could. "I'm Christopher Shepherd. I'm coming out!"

Walking out of the house to face two possibly fake FBI agents was probably the most terrifying thing he had ever done. In fact, his heart was pounding so fast he seriously wondered if it would gallop right out of his chest.

The man in the suit dropped his hand from where it had been resting on his gun in its holster, the universal position for cops when they were wary, and beckoned to Christopher. "Come on out, son."

Christopher walked down the path towards the driveway, and then Jon appeared behind him. Having his friend with him gave Christopher a bit more courage, though maybe they were both being totally stupid because if these two agents were fake, they might shovel them into their SUV and drive away, which would leave Arthur and Gwenllian on their own.

Too late now.

"We just want to ask you some questions. I'm Agent Hightower and this is Agent O'Conner." The man showed his FBI badge, which he would have done even if he wasn't a real agent. Christopher knew from the TV shows he watched that real FBI seals were made of solid metal, not aluminum. How much effort they put into the badges depended on how far these guys were willing to go to deceive him. Then again, the fake Jim had gone pretty far.

"How about you come with us." That was the female agent, O'Conner, who'd brought out her badge too, and her question wasn't a question.

"Can you just talk to me here?" Christopher said.

"Downtown would be better," Agent O'Conner said.

"I'm not under arrest, though, am I? I don't have to go." Christopher had a sudden thought. "And hey, I'm not eighteen, so ... I don't think you have a right to question me at all."

Some kind of unspoken conversation went on between the two agents, because O'Conner shook her head. "Why don't we go inside the house." Again, it wasn't a question.

Arthur and Gwenllian were inside, but since the woman was already walking to the open door of the guesthouse, Christopher hustled after her. When they entered the living room, Arthur and Gwenllian weren't to be seen.

"Why don't we all sit down," Agent O'Conner said.

Jon and Christopher perched on the edge of the yellow and white sectional sofa. Hightower sat in a chair opposite, and O'Conner remained standing. Christopher would have expected one of them to search the house, but neither did. Of course, they didn't have a warrant.

"Please talk us through what happened yesterday," Agent Hightower said. "Why were you to meet with Jim Jenson?"

"It has to do with stuff that happened over Christmas in the UK," Christopher said, going with the story Jon had said Mark was telling. "The MI-5 agent, Mark Jones, just wanted to talk to me about it again, and since he couldn't fly here himself, he sent Agent Jenson."

"Why wasn't that a conversation you could have had over the phone?" Agent Hightower said.

"Mark said it wasn't the same as seeing someone's face when they talked." Christopher had made up that excuse on the spot, but from agents' reactions, he was right on. Too much television watching was clearly paying off.

"Why don't you tell us what happened in the UK that Mark Jones was so worried about," Agent O'Conner said from her place by the window. She'd paced around the whole room already in a manner that reminded Christopher of David.

He was impatient with her questions that were really orders, but answered anyway. "I don't know if I should. It has to do with MI-5."

Agent O'Conner scoffed. "We have clearance."

"Yeah, but I don't know that, do I?" Christopher said. "It was six months ago."

"Have you heard by now that the man who met you at Bryn Mawr was not our agent?" Hightower said.

Christopher nodded. "I'm sorry. I really don't know why anyone would want to impersonate him just to talk to me." That was a total lie, of course, but it was dawning on Christopher that the FBI didn't know about the flash or about Arthur and Gwenllian at all. They really didn't know what Jim Jenson had been meeting them about. Either Jenson really didn't remember, or he wasn't talking.

Agent O'Conner had been looking through the lacy curtain, and now she turned to her partner, frowning. "Did you request backup?"

Hightower leapt to his feet and went out the door, which they'd left open. Christopher got up too and looked out the window. Another black SUV had pulled into the driveway. While he watched, three men in suits got out. They formed a triangle around Hightower as if he was a threat.

O'Conner motioned that Christopher should move away from the window. She pulled a card from an inner pocket and handed it to him. "If something happens, call this number. They'll see you safe."

"Who are those men?" Jon said.

"I don't know," O'Conner said. "CIA maybe."

"I thought they couldn't operate on U.S. soil?" Jon said.

"They don't. Usually." She pulled out her phone and dialed. "Get in the kitchen." Her eyes never left the window and what was happening outside, which at the moment was just talking.

Christopher obeyed, but when he reached the island in the center, Jon wasn't with him. "Come on!" He jerked his head to the back door. "We should get out of here!"

"Better if I don't. I can cover for you." Jon rolled his eyes. "Man, I can't believe I'm offering to dupe the CIA."

"Jon—" Christopher left his sentence hanging, unsure of what to say.

"Dude, let me do this. You're not the only one who can be a hero."

Then Gwenllian peered out of one of the cupboards in the island. "What's happening?"

"I don't know. Nobody seems to know." He could hear O'Conner talking urgently into her phone, requesting backup. "We have to get out of here."

Arthur and Gwenllian spilled out onto the floor, and Christopher scooped up Arthur. He then pushed through the screen door at the back of the kitchen, Gwenllian on his heels. Maybe the CIA was just following up on intelligence and would be as benign as the FBI. He'd heard the whole story about David's abduction in Cardiff, and how in the end the CIA and MI-5 had worked together with Callum, when he'd been named head of The Project.

But that was years ago now, and who was to say that the same people were in charge? Probably they weren't. That thought, more than anything else, had Christopher stumbling down the back steps of the guesthouse and racing for his car, just visible through the trees. He was so wound up, he hardly noticed the extra weight of Arthur in his arms. He shifted him so he could get his keys out of his pocket. If the car had been newer, Christopher could have started it remotely, but his car didn't have that kind of technology.

He and Gwenllian reached it at the same time, and they wrenched open their doors. As he sat, he plopped Arthur into her lap. Then he jammed the key into the ignition, swearing because the wheel had locked, and he had to wiggle it while turning the key to start the car. Finally, after two seconds, though it felt like ten years, the engine roared to life with a *vroom*. He shifted into first gear and hit the gas.

Shouts came from the back of the house and sirens from the front, though he didn't know what either might mean. Fifty yards down the track, the main road appeared ahead of him, somewhat downhill from his current position. He accelerated towards it, thinking only of where he was going to go and if he could get to his dad before anyone else did. Though, if fake Jim was the only one the private security company had sent to Bryn Mawr, its U.S. wing was a low-budget affair.

The woods thinned out ten yards before the road, and Christopher looked to his left, hoping no car was coming so he could turn onto the road without stopping. Unfortunately, he had underestimated his speed. If he'd been driving on pavement, he might have had a chance to stop. But as it was, the road through the woods was muddy from yesterday's rain and gave him no traction.

Christopher tried. He slammed on the brake, but the car skidded the last few feet—right into the path of a fire truck barreling down the highway towards him.

31

17 June 1293

David

David did not have a terrific plan for stopping Clare. His plan began and ended with entering Westminster Abbey before Clare's crowning and revealing himself in such a way that nobody could deny that he was alive.

Unfortunately for David, Archbishop Winchelsey and Pope Boniface seemed to have had a mind-meld at some point and talking to one was like talking to the other. He wasn't surprised to learn that Winchelsey was all for a Clare dynasty. Under Clare's rule, he certainly wasn't going to be hearing about the rights of Jews and heretics. It was irksome, to say the least.

"We should go first to Temple Church. Godfrid de Windsor can get you inside Westminster without Clare knowing who you are," Thomas said. "The last thing we need is a Clare supporter recognizing you and putting a knife into your gut."

"Godfrid will already be at Westminster, preparing to witness the crowning of Clare," David said. "I can't take the chance that we will be delayed. I need to get inside before Lili broadcasts. Remember, we have no real proof of Clare's wrongdoing—not in our possession anyway."

Thomas didn't argue further, though his expression remained skeptical—and for good reason as it turned out.

Though Westminster Castle was on the western edge of London, the streets surrounding it were full, and the mood of the people was ugly. If David hadn't been trying to push through the crowd, it would have been gratifying to see how much the people missed him. David, Henri, and Thomas managed to navigate along side streets until they were within a hundred yards of the gates of Westminster Abbey, but then they had to push through those crowds too, which were even more densely packed. Some people were even hanging out of second-story windows while others stood atop carts to get a better view.

The Westminster Abbey that lay before them now appeared much the same as it did in Avalon, but Westminster Castle in this world was totally different. In Avalon, the castle had burned (twice) before being replaced with a massive monument to the British Empire that was the seat of Parliament in the twenty-first century. The only similarity to this structure was that it lay in the same place, between the abbey and the Thames River.

All during David's journey from La Rochelle, people had respected and feared him as a Templar. Typically, Londoners turned out to be the exception. Perhaps it was the anonymity of living among so many people, but even when people moved grudgingly aside to let David pass, they did so slowly and jostled his horse. The gate to the abbey slowly grew closer. Oddly, it was open, and the abbey grounds were as packed with people as the streets.

David leaned down to a man who was pressed up against his horse's withers and had distinguished himself from the other spectators by offering a muttered apology for his closeness. "What's happening?"

"We thought we'd let Clare know that he can't become king without us," the man said with clear satisfaction and without looking at David. "The crowning's moved from the abbey to the castle because Clare fears us. We got too close." He pointed towards the gatehouse of Westminster Castle fifty yards away.

What the man said was true. Just visible through the dropped portcullis was a fine red carpet, which had been laid across the cobbles in preparation for Clare's open air crowning. Clare must really have been afraid that the people of London would stop the ceremony to have moved it from the abbey. They'd denied Empress Maud the crown. They could do it to Clare if they chose. He was still allowing a portion of them—

those who could get close enough—to watch by leaving the wooden gates to the castle open.

Henri shouted over the hubbub to David. "No guard is going to raise the portcullis to let us in, not with this crowd pressing against it."

"I'll scale the wall if I have to," David said, "but we might be able to enter through the rear gate."

He was running out of time. Once Lili infiltrated the Lambeth radio station, her voice would broadcast from the speaker located high up on the gatehouse wall. This was one of the best places to hear news in London because the speaker had come out of the Cardiff bus and always worked.

Just as at La Rochelle, every castle had some kind of narrow side entrance, a sally port or a postern gate, which was easily reinforced from the inside and was a waste of time to try to batter down, since any men who made it through would be killed one at a time. Westminster Castle was no exception. David led Henri and Thomas off the street, around to the north side of the castle, and a hundred yards along the wall to the square north tower.

It was quiet here. The wall was thirty feet high and as solid as they come, so there was nothing to see. David approached the gate, which was recessed into the wall under the shelter of the gatehouse. Since the portcullis was down and the great wooden gate behind it was closed, he didn't bother asking for admittance through there. Instead, he looked to his right where a narrow wooden door, reinforced in metal, faced him. Once it was opened, men could enter single file in order to navigate the narrow, U-shaped passage, which led to an identical door on the other side of the portcullis. As at the commanderie of La Rochelle, a little iron-barred window was located in the door at eye height.

David knocked.

After a moment, the shutter for the window opened, but it was impossible to see who was behind the door, as it was pitch black on the other side. David was glad again of his Templar garb because the chances were very high that the guard would know him on sight. It was one thing to assume nobody would know him at Portsmouth, a place David had never been before. It was quite another to expect any kind of anonymity at Westminster Palace, his seat in London.

"Our orders are to let nobody in," the man said.

Thomas put his face to the little window. "I am Sir Thomas Hartley, Templar knight. I must speak to Godfrid de Windsor, the Templar master, who is within, on an urgent matter!"

"I'm sorry. My orders are clear."

David knew why that was true. Clare didn't want to give anyone a chance to stop the ceremony. Thomas stepped back and looked at David, who shrugged. It seemed he had no choice. He removed his helmet, swept his hand through his sweat-soaked hair, and bent to the window so the guard could see his face clearly. "Let me in."

The man gasped, stuttered several my lords, sweet Marys, and a few curses, for which he immediately apologized. Two seconds later, the door swung open. "You're alive!"

David stepped into the doorway and put a hand on the man's shoulder. "Not a word."

The man's eyes were as big as serving platters.

"What's your name?" David said to him.

"W-W-Walter Vaughan, sir."

David canted his head, recalling the face. "Were you at Windsor when we defeated William de Valence?"

"Yes, my lord! I was! And a great day that was, if I may be so bold as to say, my lord."

"It was a great day. Hopefully, this will be another, but I need cooperation from you." David looked at him intently. "As soon as I head into the courtyard, I need you to gather four or five men and stand guard over the radio speaker. Queen Lili is going to speak, and once she does, you need to turn the volume up all the way."

"Y-y-yes, my lord. Of course, my lord. It's up on the battlement."

David knew that. "Will getting there be a problem?"

"No, I don't think so." Walter was starting to recover, now that he had a specific task before him.

David moved down the passage, Henri and Thomas following, but leaving the horses behind, since they wouldn't fit. David had a moment's pang, thinking of the horse he'd left outside the commanderie at La Rochelle under not too dissimilar conditions. The horse had belonged to the man he'd killed. He wished he could leave the memory of driving that arrow through the man's neck as easily as he'd shed the man's possessions.

Then Thomas stopped and turned back to Walter, who'd shut the door. "Get someone to take care of our horses too, if you will. They belong to the Templars."

"Yes, my lord!" He looked past Thomas to David. "May I just say, thanks be to God that you're alive."

David mustered up a grin and saluted him. Then he clapped his helmet back on his head so his features would be hidden when he came out the second narrow door and into the castle, having bypassed the portcullis and the gate completely. He didn't want anyone else to recognize him before he was ready.

Walter came hustling after them, last of all. But then he hesitated as he looked past David to the activity in the courtyard near the main gate. Music was being played on a flute. It had the rhythm of a processional, presumably for the

Archbishop and Clare, though David couldn't see them from where he stood. As the music rose in volume, the audience in the courtyard and the crowd outside the castle fell silent.

"Oh no," Thomas said, his voice rising in concern. "The ceremony is starting."

32

17 June 1293

Rupert

"And that's the news."

Rupert leaned back in his chair, pleased by his writing but not by what he was going to have to broadcast in a few minutes. The story was about Clare's crowning at Westminster, which Clare viewed as such a foregone conclusion that he hadn't released Rupert from his responsibilities at the station to witness it. Clare didn't want a real report of what happened at the ceremony. The story would read as Clare wanted it to read, even if the Archbishop bobbled the crown and dropped it before he put it on Clare's head.

It was a travesty of journalism, but after only a few days under Clare's authority, Rupert knew with certainty that this would be par for the course for news as long as Clare was in charge.

Here Rupert was, the premier newsman in England, for God's sake, in the world even, muffled by a jumped-up dictator.

Rupert mouthed the words to himself: *the world's premier newsman*. He would have put it on his office door at Westminster Castle if he could have done so without David mocking him mercilessly for it, or more likely, giving him the raised eyebrow look he had that meant he didn't have to say anything.

But now David was dead, murdered in France, and Rupert was being forced to be a mouthpiece for Gilbert de Clare. Back at home, his colleagues would have been drooling to have the kind of access he had to power, but he'd learned something in the last six months. For all that he'd been appalled to find himself in the Middle Ages, it had been the story of a lifetime, and David had allowed him to tell it—as long as he called the modern world *Avalon*.

Heavy feet outside the door had him turning in his chair, frowning as Tom Dale, one of Gilbert de Clare's soldiers, entered. The man closed the door behind him and took his chair in the corner behind the door as he always did. He put his feet up on an adjacent table, scattering some of Rupert's notes to the floor. Clare's soldiers had no respect for their captive, not that Rupert was officially a captive. Gilbert de Clare had been entirely sincere in his desire to maintain order in England.

But Rupert's request to speak to Lili had been denied, and from that moment on, he hadn't trusted a single word Clare had said.

"I should be at the ceremony."

"My lord Clare felt England would be better served if you remained here. You should be getting ready to broadcast."

Rupert didn't bother to hide his irritation. He should have hidden it better three days ago when Clare's men had stumped into his office at Westminster Castle and asked him—or rather, demanded—that he come with them. He'd met Clare in the castle's receiving room. Lili hadn't been on her throne, and when Clare had told him why, Rupert had almost cried himself. David might have been a young American kid, but there was something about him that never ceased to surprise Rupert and that he'd learned to respect.

Clare, however, had straight out told him that he'd taken over the Lambeth Station—and all the stations in England—and that every broadcast from that moment on had to be vetted by him before it went out. In addition, all communication by two-way radio was cut off, except for what Clare authorized.

Which is why Rupert had been forced to write his story according to Clare's version of events, rather than what might really be happening in the next minute or two.

Someone knocked on the door. Clare's soldier didn't move. It was petty of Tom to make Rupert get up to answer it, but it was only one of many indignities Rupert had suffered the last few days.

Rupert stood, taking his time as he sauntered to the door, and opened it. Nicholas de Carew, buttressed by Huw and a man Rupert didn't know, stood on the doorstep. At the sight of Rupert, Carew didn't shove the knife he held in his hand through Rupert's gut, but put a finger to his lips and raised his eyebrows.

"Who is it?" Tom had deigned to rise to his feet and was moving towards the door.

Rupert gave a nearly imperceptible tip of his head and stepped back, leaving the field to Carew, who knew exactly what to do. He gripped the edge of the door and, with enormous force, flung it wide.

It caught Tom square on the nose. By then, Huw, axe in hand, had rounded the door. Carew caught the door as it rebounded off Tom's head, and Huw grasped the stunned Tom, whose nose was streaming blood, and threw him to the ground.

Then Queen Lili, of all people, entered through the door, holding baby Alexander. Carew closed the door behind her, and the third man picked up the knife Tom had dropped.

"Roll him onto his belly, Raff, and tie his hands," Carew said.

"He's Clare's man," Huw said. "Why don't we kill him?"

"Too many are going to die in the next few days in the aftermath of Clare's treason," Carew said. "Following orders is not a hanging offense."

"I don't know about that," Rupert said, "though I suppose I followed plenty I didn't like in the last few days because I didn't feel like I had a choice."

Huw glanced at Rupert, but he did as Carew had asked.

Lili moved swiftly to Rupert's side. "I need to send a broadcast right now. We must tell everyone that Dafydd is alive."

Rupert grimaced, searching for a way to gently break the news to Lili that he wasn't. "He isn't."

"He is. I met him on the road to London not two hours ago."

Rupert looked at Carew, who nodded. "He's alive. Clare's man shot him just before midnight on the 12th. He raced here from Chateau Niort to stop Clare from being crowned."

Lili put a hand on Rupert's arm. "Dafydd has gone to Westminster, but the crowning is due to happen at any moment. With Clare's men filling London, Dafydd needs the people on his side, but unless I tell them that he's alive, it will take too long for the word to spread."

That Rupert understood. He was a newsman, after all. He'd spent his life chasing down leads and searching for a story that would make him famous. Well, this was *the* story of the year, and she wasn't wrong to think that Rupert would want to tell it.

Dismay, irritation, and fear had given way to excitement, and Rupert turned to his equipment. "I don't know how far this will go out, because Clare has captured the other stations. They'll be waiting for me to start broadcasting Clare's version of events, but when it turns out to be you, they might shut down. Once Clare told everyone that David was dead, he wouldn't let me say anything but what he prescribed."

"As long as the people around Westminster can hear me," she said, "it will be enough for now."

"Westminster is easy." Rupert tipped his head to indicate the castle, which lay to the west just across the Thames.

Carew came up behind them. "Thanks for the warning, Rupert."

The newsman glanced at Carew. "Our would-be-king doesn't exactly favor freedom of speech." Rupert stepped back and gestured to Lili.

Lili's eyes widened. "Already?"

Rupert grinned. "You're on."

33

17 June 1293

David

"*M*y *people, I pray that you open your ears to me. This is Lili, King David's wife, Prince Arthur's mother, and the woman who has been your queen. Five years ago, you bestowed the honor of ruling you on my husband. At the time, you didn't know me at all. You didn't know King David well either—*"

Henri, Thomas, and David had just reached the tail end of the audience that had gathered in the courtyard to witness Clare's crowning. The person playing the flute hesitated at the initial blare of the loudspeaker. As Lili continued to speak, he stopped playing entirely.

David found his throat thickening to hear his wife's sweet voice and the beautiful words she was saying, but it turned David's stomach to realize how close he and Lili had cut it.

As Lili said David's name again in the English way, he began edging his way towards the central stage, where Clare was on his knees before the Archbishop. In the sunlight, Clare's hair was looking particularly red, though when seen up close David knew it was shot with significant amounts of gray. Both he and the archbishop were dressed in the full regalia of their stations—the Archbishop in robe and headpiece, with his golden staff in his hand, and Clare in a rich green robe, under which he wore unrelieved black, which David thought was an interesting choice.

Thomas and Henri were invaluable in clearing the way for him, wedging themselves through the crowd as a buffer between the people and him, and the space around him widened with every step.

"—but you took us into your hearts anyway. I am speaking to you today because you need to know that we were lied to by the man you even now are preparing to crown as your king. Clare told us that King David was dead and that he'd been killed by agents of France. These were lies. Let me say that again and more clearly. David. Is. Alive. And the men who tried to kill him were not from France but servants of Clare himself—"

The silence was as near to total as one could expect from a thousand people as the entirety of the crowd—inside and outside the castle gate—listened to what Lili had to say. After she claimed that David was alive, several people did shout the news to those in the street, many of whom might not be able to hear the loudspeaker as well. Then the men and women in the courtyard began talking animatedly to one another too. Earlier, people had been pressed against the portcullis, but now they were openly banging on it. David didn't think they could actually tear it down, but they looked like they were going to try.

"—The assassin failed to kill either David or King Philip of France. David has returned to London, intending to enter Westminster Abbey. Even now he might be standing among you."

—In Shrewsbury, as Lili had started speaking, Cassie had been crossing the courtyard, having just had a shower. David had promised Bridget that he'd arrange for one to be built, along with a flushing toilet, and he'd been as good as his word. Callum had kept the radio manned around the clock, if only to hear whatever propaganda Clare was broadcasting. When Lili's voice came tinnily through the speaker, Cassie shouted for Callum, who'd been conferring with Jeffries and Peter on the final arrangements for their army's departure from Shrewsbury. He came running to find his wife standing before the radio, her hands clasped before her lips and tears streaming down her cheeks.

—In Caerphilly, Meg had been up all night—first with Llywelyn's counselors putting the finishing touches on their strike on Gloucester tomorrow, and then, just when she thought she might get some sleep, with Elisa, who'd spent the hours from three to six in the morning throwing up. Meg didn't know if Elisa had a bug, or if her sickness was from a tension and grief that Elisa herself was too young to express in any other way.

Grief and fear had brought low all the adults in Elisa's life. Meg had been sitting at the table in the hall with a cup of coffee before her, desperate to think about anything besides the fate of David, Gwenllian, and Arthur—and wishing she'd put something stronger in her drink. She'd lost and recovered David enough times by now that she refused to believe outright that he was dead. Now, as she listened, she cried, her forehead to the table.

Llywelyn came up behind her and put his hands on her shoulders. "That's my girl."

Meg managed a smile through her tears when she realized he wasn't speaking of Meg herself, but of Lili.

David had been steadily moving through the crowd. His pace had been slow at first, but once people recognized his Templar garb, they made way for him.

Lili continued to speak: *"The Normans conquered England two hundred years ago. Since then, except for King David himself, only a Norman has worn the English crown. But you, as a people, have a long history of choosing your kings. I'm asking you now to have faith that what I'm saying is true, to question what you've been told, and to give your king time to show himself—"*

It was the moment David had been waiting for. He pulled off his helmet, then his white cloak, and then the tunic with the red cross, leaving him dressed just in his mail armor. Having lost its shine several hundred miles ago, it looked gray in the noon sun in comparison to the grandeur of Clare and the onlookers, all of whom were dressed in their absolute best.

David managed the last thirty yards in long strides, which took him to where Clare knelt. Just before the dais, Godfrid de Windsor stepped into David's path. "It is good to see you in one piece, sire." Then he bowed and gave way.

As David passed by, he put a hand on Godfrid's shoulder but didn't say anything. He had no words to express his thanks. He owed the Templars, and no matter the cost in the end, he couldn't regret asking them for help.

At the sight of him stepping onto the dais, gasps came from all around as the people finally realized that Lili's words were true. The entire crowd fell to its knees.

Clare rose to his feet, but David ignored him. The Archbishop of Canterbury had the nerve to give David a small smile, and David allowed himself a brief narrowing of the eyes in return. Then he opened his arms wide and turned in a circle on the spot, allowing his people to behold him.

He might have been king for only five years, but he hadn't kept himself locked away in a tower. He'd walked the streets; he'd given speeches; he'd stood before Parliament and pledged to serve England. These were Londoners—and whether of Norman or Saxon origin, they *knew* him.

Silence fell in the courtyard with a rippling effect, spreading throughout the onlookers, hundreds of them, most gaping, all staring, some even crying. Thus, Lili's final words rang out into near total silence:

David has said many times that he would not be king if you—the people of England—had not chosen him. He still believes you have that right, and he offers you that choice again. You have only to raise your voices and ask.

Before, the people at the portcullis had wanted to batter it down. Now, the iron bars rattled in time to their words. "King David! King David! Long live the king! Long live the king!"

The chant spread within seconds to the men on the battlements. Walter was among them, and he was literally jumping up and down with excitement. The nobility in the courtyard were perhaps least happy to see David in their midst, but even they got on board quickly. Geoffrey de Geneville, who held the chest in which the king's crown was kept, was beaming.

Clare, however, though he'd initially risen to his feet, now knelt before David with the rest. "Please know, sire, that I had nothing to do with the attempt on your life. It was France." It was what Lili had told him Clare would say and what he'd been telling Parliament.

David had a bone-aching need to be horizontal right now, but instead had to muster up the intellect to counter Clare. He stepped closer, since his words were for Clare and the Archbishop alone, and he didn't want to argue with Clare in front of everyone. "Your men attacked mine, killed mine. It seems they also sent you the news that I was dead."

Clare pushed to his feet and grasped David by the shoulders, a huge grin on his face. "I am so glad to see you alive!" He pulled him into a hug.

David winced in pain and tried to pull away, but Clare held him for another second before releasing him. "This is a great day!" He held up a hand to the crowd and spun on one heel, as David had done a moment ago. "Our king has returned. Let us begin the celebrations!" He got the people cheering, and then he began moving through the crowd, heading for the rear gate through which David had entered the castle.

David would have cursed if he hadn't been in public. This was ridiculous, and he felt tongue-tied. It was exactly what Lili had feared Clare would say, and all David could do was stammer. Proof of Clare's misdeeds remained in Aquitaine. David could arrest Clare and refuse to play this game, but Lili was right that his people would have niggling questions as a result. Clare couldn't be crowned king now, but he could walk out of here as if he had committed no crime.

His expression grave, Archbishop Winchelsey approached David. "What proof do you have of your accusation against Gilbert de Clare? He has done nothing to deserve your ire, sire. He stepped in to aid England in your absence."

David could hardly bear to look at him. "I have proof enough."

"I am so pleased to see you alive, sire," Geoffrey de Geneville said.

David held out his hand to him. "I know what you did. Thank you."

Geoffrey grasped David's forearm. "I feared for your family."

Archbishop Winchelsey wasn't done. "You're exhausted, sire. We can all see it." He leaned in. "You are wise to let Clare go for now."

Clare had reached a point perhaps a hundred feet from David.

"Am I?" David drew in a breath. "Gilbert de Clare!"

Clare stopped, hesitated, and then turned around.

"Come here." David motioned with a hand.

Not daring to disobey, but with stiff legs and spine, Clare began walking back towards him.

The people around both men scurried to get out of the way, drawing back until they had formed a large circle around Clare and David and reminding David horribly of the lead up to a middle school fight.

When Clare had crossed half the distance and was approximately fifty feet away, he stopped. His chin was up, and his eyes blazed. He had the look of a man who'd already won the day. As David stared at Clare's mask of innocence, anger rose in him of such intensity that his hands shook with it. This man had tried to kill him. He would have killed David's wife and sons in time. He didn't deserve to walk away. He didn't deserve to live.

Clare bowed. "I have always been a faithful servant, and I am hurt that you would think otherwise, even for a moment. I have done nothing wrong."

David pulled his sword from his sheath. "Five days ago, your men tried to murder me and King Philip at Chateau Niort in Aquitaine." He took a step forward, and his expression must have been menacing enough to give even Clare pause, because he swallowed hard and some of the surety left him.

"No, my lord. Those weren't my men."

"My new Templar friend Henri and I journeyed three hundred miles from La Rochelle in two days, crossed the Channel overnight, and rode here from Portsmouth this morning to prevent the grave mistake that almost took place a moment ago in this courtyard."

Even the Archbishop's jaw dropped. Geoffrey managed in French, *"C'est impossible!"*

David laughed, though his laughter was entirely mocking and without a trace of humor. "Yeah. That's me. Always doing the impossible."

"Again, I say, you have the wrong man," Clare said. "It was Charles of France who sought your death. He wants Philip's throne."

"Even as you want mine."

Clare shook his head. "I did not ask for the throne yesterday. It was offered to me, and I accepted it because England must remain strong and united to counter the French threat."

"There is no French threat except of your own making. Together Philip and I escaped the Chateau by falling from the battlement into the river. But when we sought refuge in a nearby village, your men were searching for us. They told the villagers that Philip and I were dead and to be on the lookout for two assassins. Your men put the whole countryside on alert so nobody would aid us."

As Clare had been talking, the circle around him had widened even more. People were afraid to get too close to someone accused of treason, so now the closest person was over ten yards away. A chant of "kill him, kill him," had started among some of the onlookers. David looked down at his sword, the baring of which had given them the idea that Clare's death was imminent, and he threw out a hand to silence the chant. The people did as he bid.

Clare put his hand to his heart. "That was not my doing, sire. My captain must have been bought by Charles." He went down on one knee again. This time he raised his hand to the sky, and his voice rang out so everyone in the courtyard and at the portcullis could hear him. "I swear to you I am telling the truth. If I speak falsely, I beg that God strike me down right here and now!"

David was still vibrating with hatred, but he couldn't ignore the voice of reason at the back of his mind. "That isn't the way the world works, Clare. That isn't the way I work."

Henri stepped to David's side. "You should kill him now, my lord."

"No." David had spoken louder than he intended, and the *no* reverberated around the courtyard, echoing off the stones. Even he could hear the iron in his voice.

Henri bowed, more deeply than anyone had so far. "I ask your pardon, my lord. I mistook your intent."

A shiver went through David. Killing Clare would be fair retribution for the loss of Justin and all David's men. But then the face of the man David had killed rose before his eyes for the second time since his arrival at Westminster—or maybe it had been coloring his vision this whole time. When he'd stabbed the man, blood had sprayed from his throat, covering not only the man's gear but David too. David's hands had dripped with blood because of Clare.

Henri was right. He *should* kill Clare now. Clare deserved death for what he'd done, and nobody would begrudge David taking his life once they knew the whole truth. But he couldn't do it. He couldn't violate everything he believed in, everything he'd worked so hard to achieve as King of England, because he was angry. His barons needed to fear the consequences of betraying David, not fear him as a capricious king who changed the rules when he was angry enough or when it pleased him. Even as he gazed down at Clare's upturned face, he knew that taking Clare's life wouldn't remove the stain of blood on his own hands.

With a silent curse, David thrust his sword back into its sheath. "Understand, Henri, that it isn't resolve I lack, or the courage to do what is necessary. I choose not to sully my soul again as he has tarnished his. As he has tarnished mine."

David addressed Clare again. "Your fate isn't going to be decided in this courtyard by a lightning strike from heaven. It will be decided in a court of law, by a jury of your peers, and I will bring all the evidence necessary to prove your guilt."

Clare hesitated for a second, at first disbelieving that David really was going to let him live. Then he rose to his feet. As he turned away, David saw the glint of triumph in his eye and the momentary sneer that crossed his lips. Like many others, Philip included, he saw David's refusal to act as a sign of weakness.

David and Philip had discussed power and its uses at length. David had the power to kill Clare here and now. But how much more powerful did it make him *not* to kill Clare in cold blood? To unsheathe his sword but not use it? To refuse to mar his legacy in an act of justifiable revenge. David found genuine laughter—almost joy—rising to his lips.

Clare's prison was of his own making.

David himself was free.

And with that, suddenly, all the air was sucked from the atmosphere, and a blue car fell out of the sky and hurtled into the middle of the courtyard. Spinning, it skidded across the paving stones. If Clare had been prepared for it or moving to get out of the way, the car might have struck him only a glancing blow. But he was standing as immobile as everyone else. The car's front end hit him on the shins, and the force of the blow flipped him over the hood. He landed on the roof with a sickening thud, and then slid off the back end as the car came to a halt a few feet from the curtain wall.

The silence in the courtyard was absolute.

David limped forward and pulled open the passenger door of the car. Gwenllian and Arthur gaped at him from the front seat. Christopher was looking at him too from the driver's seat, open-mouthed.

"Thank God you're all safe." David scooped up Arthur from Gwenllian's lap and straightened, wincing again at the ache in his chest. No hug had ever felt as good as this, especially when his small son put his arms around his father's neck and held on.

The courtyard had been plunged into shocked silence by the arrival of Christopher's car, an event that the people couldn't possibly understand. But an embrace between a father and son was as familiar as the sun rising in the east. A few people applauded. Then David reached down to help Gwenllian out of the car and pulled her into a hug too. "I am so proud of you, sis."

"I was so scared." She hugged him tightly, her arms half around him and half around Arthur.

"But you acted anyway, didn't you?"

She nodded into chest.

Christopher had climbed out by then too, and David met his eyes over the top of the car. "Thanks for bringing them home, Christopher."

Christopher's shocked look turned into a grin, and then a laugh. David found himself snorting laughter, and the noise level around them rose as the crowd in the courtyard and the street outside began to stomp and cheer.

David spared a glance towards the back of the car where Clare lay on the ground, unmoving. David didn't need to look more closely to know that Clare was dead, since his neck was bent at a disconcerting angle from his body.

Only the people in the courtyard and those pressed up against the portcullis could have had any kind of view of what had happened, but everyone had heard Lili's broadcast. Now Walter climbed into the crenel between two merlons on the curtain wall, somehow having gotten himself the flag of the King of England on a pole, and began to call in an amazingly loud voice. "Long live King David! Long live the king!"

The people in the courtyard and the street took up the call. With Arthur's arms around his neck and Gwenllian's hand gripped tightly in his own, David headed to the gatehouse.

Reaching it, he motioned with two fingers to indicate that the guard should wind up the portcullis. The man shook his head, not in disobedience but in what looked more like terror. Thomas took over the portcullis mechanism and began to crank up the iron bars.

Geoffrey de Geneville fell into step beside David. "If you don't mind my saying so, sire, opening this gate is completely mad."

"That may be," David said. "But it's been a mad kind of day."

Geoffrey actually laughed—and then walked with David outside the gatehouse and into the jubilant embrace of his people.

34

Calais, France
Christopher

Christopher paced behind David and Humphrey de Bohun towards the practice arena at the Templar commanderie. He'd met a handful of Templars that first day after he'd driven the car into the courtyard at Westminster and killed Clare, but a Templar commanderie was a new experience for him. Pretty much like everything else had been during the last two months.

When David had left Philip at La Rochelle in June, the French king had been at death's door. Two months on, he was capable of winning a mock battle with the newly knighted William de Bohun, David's former squire. Both kings and their retinues were guests of the Templars this week, since their commanderie was neutral ground for all parties. In a few minutes, the kings would be on their way to the hearing that would decide the fate of Philip's brother, Charles, who'd been part of the conspiracy with Clare.

David had turned out to have a cracked rib, and it had taken seven weeks for both David and Philip to be healed, which was one reason David hadn't come to France again until now. The other reason was that he'd spent that time sorting out the mess Clare had made of his country. Clare had been David's richest baron, with extensive lands in England, Ireland, and Aquitaine, all of which had now fallen to David. All of the barons—Bohun among them—were clamoring for pieces of it. While David had occupied Clare's lands with the men Bohun, Mortimer, and Callum had mobilized, he was determined not to make the mistake he'd made with Clare: no one man should be entrusted with that much power. He was drafting a new policy on land reform that would give the people of England the opportunity to own land in a way they never had before.

And that was already way more politics than Christopher had *ever* thought he'd have to know.

"Psst! Christopher!"

Christopher looked to his left. Rupert was signaling to him from a little alcove off the corridor. Christopher glanced at David and Bohun, who were now several paces ahead of him and entering the arena. "What do you want?"

Rupert looked affronted. "Is that any way to talk to the foremost newsman in the world?"

Christopher grinned. He and Rupert had developed an understanding over the last two months. Though thirty years apart in age, they were both fish out of water here. Much like Gwenllian had said back in Radnor about the twenty-first century, the Middle Ages was exactly like and nothing like Christopher thought it would be. For starters, he'd killed a guy on his first day—his first minute—in the Middle Ages, and he really wished he could talk to his dad about it. David had understood the weird mix of emotions he'd felt as a result—like really nobody else could—but he was Christopher's cousin, not his dad.

At one point Christopher had taken Rupert aside and asked if it was theoretically possible to communicate with Avalon by radio if the frequencies were just right.

"I've tried it," Rupert told him flatly. "At the moment, the answer is an unequivocal *no*."

Christopher wasn't ready to give up on the idea, but in the meantime, he was doing his best to acclimate to the Middle Ages and make the most of the time he did have here. Though he missed his parents and sister, Christopher was treating the whole experience like the first year of college—moving away, making his own decisions—except for the fact that he couldn't even call his parents.

Just because David hadn't time traveled when he'd fallen from the balcony in Aquitaine didn't mean he never would again—and Christopher figured there was no reason he couldn't go back and forth with him, just like everyone else had at one time or another.

"I need an interview with King Philip when this is over," Rupert said.

"And you think because I'm David's squire that I can get you one?" Christopher said incredulously. "I've been learning French for only two months! Why don't you ask Dr. Abraham?" David had sent three doctors to Philip immediately after the events at Westminster, Abraham among them. To nobody's surprise, Abraham spoke fluent French. Christopher had learned Spanish in school, which might prove useful if he ever met a Spaniard, provided the man understood Christopher's American accent.

"I tried. He refused."

"You'll just have to make something up, then," Christopher said. "I'm sure there will be no shortage of material."

Rupert had set up France's first radio station on a bluff above the town of Calais. Though fifty miles from Dover, the antenna had line-of-sight across the English Channel and plenty of wattage from the windmill that powered it.

"What about Queen Lili?" Rupert said. "She and Philip's queen get along well."

Christopher rolled his eyes. "I'm not going to ask her for you either." Lili and the boys had come with David to France this time, since she swore that David got into far too much trouble when they were apart. She'd arrived at Westminster Castle, having crossed the water from Lambeth station, only a few minutes after Christopher had appeared in his car. She'd kissed his cheek, thanked him for taking care of Gwenllian and Arthur, and immediately taken him under her wing.

"You are no help at all." Rupert made a shooing motion with his hands. "Run along and be the stroppy teenager you're so good at."

Christopher saluted, again with a grin, and hastened back to the arena where William and Humphrey de Bohun were having an animated conversation about fighting techniques while David was talking to King Philip. Christopher hesitated before approaching either group. He was definitely interested in fighting techniques but Bohun's points looked more like criticism of his son than an actual discussion. David was Christopher's cousin so it would be easy to walk right up and start talking, but he'd been warned that Philip was arrogant and wanted to be treated like a king all the time. Christopher must have made some kind of motion, however, because David glanced over at him, signaled that he should come closer, and introduced him to Philip.

Trying to remember all he'd been taught about protocol, Christopher bowed to the French king.

Philip studied the pair of them and spoke very slowly, apparently aware of the limitations of Christopher's French. For now, he understood a lot more than he spoke.

"God truly favors you, David."

"I was lucky," David said.

"Nobody believes that anymore, not even you." Now Philip openly looked Christopher up and down. "And what about you? How does it feel to be heralded as the hero of Westminster?"

"Uh ..." Christopher had no idea what to say, and probably couldn't have figured out how to say it in French even if he knew.

David laughed. "He saved you a trip across the Channel. I would have had to call you to testify against Clare."

Philip still had his eye on Christopher. "So you're one to watch too, are you? If David is the return of King Arthur, who does that make you?"

Christopher looked blank, and as Philip turned away in response to a question from one of his underlings, David leaned in and said, "Who do you think? Gawain? Geraint?"

Christopher played along. "They were way too good at sword fighting compared to me."

"Hey." David put a hand on Christopher's shoulder and shook him a little. "You're doing great. Just ask Darren or Peter—or even Callum—when you see them next. These things take time." He eyed Christopher assessingly and then said gently, "No, I think Sir Galahad is the one for you."

Then he patted Christopher's shoulder one more time and walked to where Philip was waiting for him in the entrance to the arena. As Christopher followed him, he remembered something David had talked to him about last Christmas but which he hadn't understood until now: back in Avalon, Christopher was just a kid whose mom didn't want him to while away the days playing computer games. Here, he was the *hero of Westminster*, and his cousin, who happened to be the King of England, had compared him to Sir Galahad.

At home, Christopher had been casting around for a way to make a difference in the world. Being a cop had seemed way better and more immediate than going to school for another four years. His dad, on the other hand, claimed making a difference was easy: all Christopher had to try to do was be of service to other people. He was right, but it felt like there was a big difference between slinging hamburgers at the diner with a smile as a service to humanity and returning the King of England's son to him.

Or maybe not. There was nothing like grilling a quality hamburger to make a lot of people happy in a short amount of time. Still, acting as David's squire was a good start.

Maybe this medieval gig was going to turn out okay after all.

The End

Acknowledgments

First and foremost, I'd like to thank my lovely readers for encouraging me to continue the *After Cilmeri* Series. I have always been passionate about these books, and it's wonderful to be able to share my stories with readers who love them too.

Thank you to my husband, without whose love and support I would never have tried to make a living as a writer. Thank to my family who has been nothing but encouraging of my writing, despite the fact that I spend half my life in medieval Wales. And thank you to my posse of readers: Lily, Anna, Jolie, Melissa, Cassandra, Brynne, Carew. Gareth, Taran, Dan, and Venkata. I couldn't do this without you.

About the Author

With two historian parents, Sarah couldn't help but develop an interest in the past. She went on to get more than enough education herself (in anthropology) and began writing fiction when the stories in her head overflowed and demanded she let them out. While her ancestry is Welsh, she only visited Wales for the first time while in college. She has been in love with the country, language, and people ever since. She even convinced her husband to give all four of their children Welsh names.

She makes her home in Oregon.

www.sarahwoodbury.com

92311448R00202

Made in the USA
Columbia, SC
25 March 2018